PRINCESS
Ever After

Books by Connie Glynn

The Rosewood Chronicles

UNDERCOVER PRINCESS

PRINCESS IN PRACTICE

THE LOST PRINCESS

PRINCESS AT HEART

PRINCESS EVER AFTER

The ROSEWOOD CHRONICLES

PRINCESS
Ever After

CONNIE GLYNN

PENGUIN BOOKS

PENGUIN BOOKS

UK | USA | Canada | Ireland | Australia
India | New Zealand | South Africa

Penguin Books is part of the Penguin Random House group of companies
whose addresses can be found at global.penguinrandomhouse.com.

www.penguin.co.uk
www.puffin.co.uk
www.ladybird.co.uk

First published 2022
This paperback edition published 2022

001

Set in 13/16pt Goudy Old Style
Typeset by Jouve (UK), Milton Keynes
Printed and bound in Great Britain by Clays Ltd, Elcograf S.p.A.

The authorized representative in the EEA is Penguin Random House Ireland,
Morrison Chambers, 32 Nassau Street, Dublin D02 YH68

A CIP catalogue record for this book is available from the British Library

PAPERBACK
ISBN: 978-0-241-45841-9

All correspondence to:
Penguin Books
Penguin Random House Children's
One Embassy Gardens, 8 Viaduct Gardens, London SW11 7BW

Penguin Random House is committed to a
sustainable future for our business, our readers
and our planet. This book is made from Forest
Stewardship Council® certified paper.

Dedicated to homework radio for being the soundtrack to my late-night writing sessions. 'That 2 a.m. Fresh Air' truly hits different.

Prologue

There are magical places in this world where a person can always get lost. Jamie knew that more than anyone.

Some of these places welcome you, like a daydream on a rainy day, or a sweet song that reminds you of home. Others can be frightening – like dense fog in an unfamiliar wood; while some are so vast and deep that a person feels sure they could never find their way out. It is the type of lost reserved for the sky, for space, for the endless reflection of a starlit lake at midnight, much like the one Jamie Volk found himself staring into as a distant church bell echoed through the mountains, a bell that tolled to announce his birthday.

Growing up with no parents and no idea who he really was, Jamie had never had much cause to celebrate the occasion. All that had changed now was that he'd found his father. What a difference it made to have a father waiting to rejoice in the day you had been born.

Gentle as summer rain, a hand pressed down on Jamie's arm, pulling him back into his own body. He glanced over his shoulder, to see his most loyal friend and guard smiling down at him.

'Won't you come inside?' Haru asked.

Jamie returned his gaze to the expanse of night sky. 'Just give me a few more minutes.'

'I'll wait until you're ready.'

Of course he would. Haru would wait as long as it took.

The two boys' reflections were cast adrift among the mirrored stars. Jamie supposed it was better than being alone.

'Would you let me say it?' Haru's voice came out in a whisper, his words as soft as spider silk, and they caught Jamie off guard.

He hesitated. 'I don't usually let people celebrate this day.'

His Partizan grinned, a mischievous glint in his eye. 'Tell that to Ingrid,' he warned. 'She's baked a cake for you.'

Jamie turned to Haru in disbelief, the absurdity of the image threatening to pull a smile from his lips.

Violet clouds moved across the sky. Haru did not move. He continued to wait, just as he'd promised.

'You can say it, you know,' Jamie said eventually, and he felt the other Partizan light up beside him.

Haru beamed at the person he'd do everything in his power to protect. 'Happy nineteenth birthday, Jamie.'

There are magical places in this world that feel lonely. Sometimes these places are filled with people or rambling chatter, and sometimes they're desolate, like a lone boat in the ocean. Sometimes they are lurking in your own home. It's an upturned house after a party, or a dining room with a birthday cake and a princess who sits on her own to blow out the candles. Much like the one in Maradova.

The room was littered with discarded wrapping paper from expensive gifts, each one showy and impersonal and marked with the names of unfamiliar foreign politicians and royalty. An unwanted perk of revealing her royalty to the world after years of secrecy.

What always amazed the princess was how she could be showered with all of life's luxuries – yet with no one to share in it, it was worthless. Almost as worthless as she felt.

With a sigh, she held up her spoon and grumbled at her warped expression in the curved silver.

Nothing made her feel lonelier than the thoughts that preoccupied her. That she deserved to be alone, that she was a monster who brought nothing but trouble to everyone she was close to, especially the people she loved.

'Happy eighteenth birthday, Ellie,' she muttered to herself with a sneer. 'You've really made a mess of things now.'

There are magical places in this world that feel like home. Christmas mornings, when the tearing of wrapping paper finds a rhythm with the crackling fire, or under the covers of your bed after a long day, or safe in the arms of the person you most cherish. Sometimes home is in a scent or a sound, in a shared laugh with a best friend who grins as wide as you, or the smell of a freshly baked cake made by doting parents.

Lottie Pumpkin knew this feeling well, and she knew how much it hurt to have it ripped away from you. The ache was still there. There was a missing part of her heart in the shape of her princess and Partizan, and a pain that remained ever since Jamie and Ellie had left.

What she didn't know, as she sat down with Binah Fae's family to enjoy the birthday meal they'd prepared for her, was that on very rare occasions magic could live inside a person. Lottie Pumpkin was one of those people – the ones for whom magic remained.

'Happy eighteenth birthday, Lottie.' Binah grinned at her from across the table and, despite the ache in her heart, Lottie found herself smiling back.

There was hope, and, as long as it remained, there'd always be a home to return to.

She was unstoppable.

PART ONE

KIND

(adjective)
Being generous, friendly,
helpful and considerate

1

Over the past three years Lottie Pumpkin had managed to outrun a deadly trained killer, evade kidnapping – and have her heart broken. Not bad. Yet for all this, nothing – no deadly assassin, no monstrous royal secret – could hold a candle to the discomfort she felt now, sitting in the stuffy office of Anderson's Personal Accounting.

Mr Anderson was the most plain-looking person Lottie had ever seen. So plain, in fact, that she was sure she wouldn't have been able to point him out in a line-up of precisely one.

In contrast, his office had a unique rhythm to it, with the ticking of an old cuckoo clock on the wall and the silver balls of a Newton's cradle clacking. Everything in the room fell in time with the nib of Mr Anderson's fountain pen as it scribbled signatures and numbers across piles and piles of complex-looking documents. Lottie was sure that if she didn't break the tension soon, the whole room would pop from the pressure.

'Excuse me –'

Mr Anderson held up a finger, immediately cutting her off. 'One moment, please.'

Lottie bit her tongue at Mr Anderson's curtness, and his scribbling continued until at last he looked up and pushed his reading glasses up his nose.

'Now, Miss . . . Pumpkin?'

'Yes.'

He double-checked her name. 'I must say,' Mr Anderson began, 'I've been an accountant for quite a long time, and I can safely say I've never dealt with a case as peculiar as this.' He cracked his knuckles, looking as if he were about to bite into a particularly juicy steak. 'Not just the complicated legal proceedings with the foreign account, but the walls upon walls of security.'

If Lottie didn't know any better, she'd think this man was actually excited.

'Whoever set you up with this bank account certainly did their homework. There's no way that anyone could easily discover who it belonged to or where the payments are coming from.'

Lottie blinked at him from the opposite side of the desk. 'Is that a good thing?'

Ignoring her question, Mr Anderson went on. 'That said, once I could prove your identity via the information in the severance letter you received last month from the supreme court of Maradova, it was simple enough.'

'So?'

'So –' he quickly slid one of the papers across his desk – 'if you sign this, the money is yours to spend as you choose. No limitations.'

'Oh!'

In normal circumstances this would have been wonderful news, and yet all Lottie felt was dread. She wasn't here for the money. Lottie had really been hoping for a chance to speak to the Wolfsons and warn them. Somewhere out there Claude Wolfson, the disgraced would-be king of Maradova, had a terrible plan for revenge against the family that had deprived him of his crown. Lottie might not know what form his bitter vengeance would take, but she did know when he planned to enact it: the Golden Flower Festival. It was not long ago that Lottie would have been guaranteed an invitation; now she could only wait around like an abandoned dog, hoping pathetically that she might still be offered entry.

Lottie had to warn Ellie and her family before then, which would have been simple if every line of communication hadn't been blocked. Letters were returned, emails bounced, calls never went through. Lottie had been well and truly cut off.

The worry must have been visible on her face, because Mr Anderson narrowed his eyes. 'Is something wrong, Miss Pumpkin?'

Lottie hesitated, fiddling with the edge of her dress. 'It's just . . . Is that really it?' Her voice noticeably hitched. 'There's no one I should talk to? No communication needed at all?'

'Nope, nothing to worry about at all.' Mr Anderson smiled. 'With you reaching the age of majority in Maradova, and the legal proceedings finalized, the money is all yours.'

Lottie's hand wandered up to the wolf pendant round her neck, the last link she had to Ellie and Jamie. 'I see. I just thought I'd have to speak to someone.'

The Newton's cradle slowly came to a stop, and a frown settled over Mr Anderson's face. 'I don't think you understand, Miss Pumpkin,' he said. 'This is going to change your life.'

Unable to explain her reasons for wanting to get in touch with the Wolfsons, Lottie continued to fidget.

Mr Anderson tried again. 'Look, let me break this down for you. Counting my fee and all relative tax, with all your monthly payments while being employed as Princess Eleanor Wolfson's Portman, and the bonuses added in the life-endangerment clause, plus the lump sum included in your severance negotiations, you're now in possession of 697,790 Maravish alexi, which equals 711,452 Great British pounds.'

'I understand. It's only . . .' She paused. 'Wait, excuse me?'

Mr Anderson grinned. 'Put simply, Miss Pumpkin, you find yourself rich.'

Lottie's mouth fell open.

'I see that's finally woken you up.' Mr Anderson held out his initialled fountain pen. 'Could you sign, please?'

Eyes growing wide, Lottie took the pen. She was vaguely aware of the scratching sound, as she signed her way into a new life, but she knew that if she were given the chance, she'd trade all the money to speak to Ellie and Jamie again.

'Spend it wisely, Miss Pumpkin,' the accountant said.

'You don't have to worry about that, Mr Anderson,' Lottie replied. 'No amount of money in the world could get me what I want.'

Binah looked up from a black leather sofa in the waiting room, a bag of chocolate raisins in her hand. But when she saw Lottie's despondent face she said, 'Oh dear.'

Lottie shook her head. 'No. It's good news. Sort of . . . Er, I seem to have suddenly acquired quite lot of money.'

'I should hope so after you risked your life as Ellie's Portman for three years,' Binah said bluntly, tossing a raisin into her mouth. 'But you didn't get to speak to anyone connected to the Maravish royal family.'

It wasn't a question; the answer was clear from Lottie's expression.

Leading them out into the posh streets of Knightsbridge, Binah fanned her face with her hand, trying to stave off some of the intense city heat. 'We still have nearly a whole year to warn them,' Binah said with a sigh. 'Although it would be easier if we actually knew what the plan was.'

Lottie had become stockier after staying with Binah's family over the summer in their London town house, thanks to the endless access to delicious home-cooked meals and an idyllic jogging route through St James's Park. Lottie had used the opportunity every morning to clear her head and pick up coffees and treats from a nearby patisserie as a thank you to Binah's parents. A burden was the very last thing she wanted to be. But, for all the comforts of a pretend home, she couldn't escape the shadows that lurked in the corners of her mind, shadows that took the shape of a certain Jamie Volk. They whispered the words he'd written in a letter before leaving to join his father and Leviathan, the malicious group that had vowed to end the Wolfson family's rule. He had promised that he would come back for Lottie, and Jamie never said anything he didn't mean.

When Claude had revealed himself as Jamie's father, he'd stolen the boy Lottie had called a friend. She feared that he was twisting Jamie into something she wouldn't recognize. One day Jamie would come back for her, and she had no idea what she'd do. Who he'd be. What if Claude had turned him into a monster?

'What are you thinking about?' Binah asked, her eyes narrowing behind her glasses.

'Honestly?' Lottie let out a shuddering sigh. 'I was thinking about the Hamelin Formula.'

Pursing her lips, Binah hummed thoughtfully. 'I don't think Claude would use it on his own son,' she offered. 'He doesn't seem to use it on any members of Leviathan.'

Lottie hoped she was right.

Claude had so many cards stacked in his favour, and worst of all was the Hamelin Formula, a mind-controlling substance. Lottie had seen its effects first-hand in their friend Percy. It ripped away everything that made a person unique and turned them into a mindless zombie.

'But we have to remember that Claude is ruthless,' Lottie asserted, shaking away the horrible images. 'He tried to kill Hirana – the mother of his own child – just because he thought a son out of wedlock would endanger his claim to the throne.'

'And he lies,' Binah added. 'He'll have Jamie believing it was Ellie's parents that were responsible for her death.'

Lottie swallowed down a hard lump in her throat because Claude's limited use of his mind-controlling concoction suddenly made sense. 'Who needs the Hamelin Formula when stories are just as good for brainwashing?'

If Claude got his way, he could have the whole world wrapped round his finger with his mind games alone.

'Let's get coffee,' Binah gently suggested, trying to pull Lottie out of her thoughts of doom.

Slipping into the nearest cafe, the two took a spot by the window next to a magazine rack, while Lottie explained about the money.

'So, yeah, it's a lot more than I was expecting,' Lottie said, stirring her iced white mocha.

'But –' Binah dragged the word out – 'you feel guilty because you should be happy. However, all you feel is deflated because yet another attempt to speak to the Wolfsons and warn them that Ellie's evil uncle Claude is coming for them has failed.'

Lottie froze. 'How do you do that?'

Binah laughed, sipping her tea. 'It's a gift. I'm great at explaining things that people can't see. But in this instance it's just obvious.'

Binah was right, of course. In the end it had been two members of Leviathan who had given Lottie the information she needed. Ingrid, with her senseless ramblings about Alexis, the very first Wolfson to take the throne in Maradova. And then Haru, whose diary contained dates that corresponded with every Golden Flower Festival. It only took a little research to learn that the Golden Flower Festival was celebrated every ten years in honour of when Alexis took the throne. The whole thing had just slotted into place. With Claude's penchant for theatrics, it made sense that he'd enact Leviathan's mysterious plan on such an important anniversary.

'Who would have thought the hardest part would be speaking to them?' Lottie grumbled, leaning back in her chair.

'We should make a toast,' Binah suddenly announced, holding up her steaming mug. 'To your new riches, and to our last year at Rosewood . . . even if it isn't how we imagined.'

Lottie slowly lifted her cup. 'And,' she added, 'to whatever plan we come up with next definitely working.'

With forced optimism, their cups clinked together and both took a deep sip, as though the answer to all their problems might miraculously appear at the bottom of their mugs.

Lottie sat back, pondering. Six months. Ellie and Jamie had been gone from her life for six months.

Despite that, she kept the wolf pendant round her throat, and she still had the velvet box in which she kept her family's tiara, plus the star ring meant for Jamie that she kept on her finger. So many mementoes. So many memories. But there was also the ache in her chest from having her heart broken and the fear in the pit of her stomach that Leviathan might be coming for her, that Jamie might be coming for her, that she might never get through to him, that –

Her panicked thoughts were cut off when her gaze snagged on one of the magazines to her side. 'Oh my God.'

Plastered on the front cover of *Toffee* magazine was Ellie's face. Or, at least, it was a version of Ellie's face. But this was a pretend plastic-princess version of the girl Lottie knew. Her hair was styled into a sleek chin-length bob, which made her look almost cute – a word that could never normally be applied to Eleanor Wolfson.

The stylists had fashioned Ellie into a classic regal look, with a fancy velvet dress and accessories. Where there used to be bold colours and a devilish smirk, there was now subtle make-up over a serene expression. The colours appeared to be chosen specifically to match her newly dyed blonde hair.

Lottie grabbed the magazine off the rack.

Binah pushed up her glasses to peer closer. 'Oh my God!'

First-ever exclusive interview with
the enigmatic princess of Maradova!

Binah's eyes darted quickly from left to right as she read. 'Very peculiar.' With an amused smile, she glanced up at Lottie. 'They've made her look like you!'

'Give me that.' Lottie snatched the magazine and Binah giggled as she read, hiding her face with a coy sip of tea.

Once again Binah was right. There was no denying it. This version of Ellie was some strange Freaky Friday twist. It was a miraculous transformation, and Lottie wondered which misguided godmother was responsible.

'Now the question is,' Binah said, 'whose fairy tale is this?'

Lottie's shoulders dropped, as bitterness flooded her, the same bitterness she'd endured ever since Ellie had gone. 'Fairy tales aren't real.'

It burned her throat to say such a thing, yet she couldn't take it back. All this fanciful thinking . . . all it had done was cause trouble. She couldn't afford to be naive any more.

Binah narrowed her eyes and Lottie quickly put her best smile back in place so as not to concern her friend. 'The point is,' she continued quickly, 'Ellie's trying her best. This is probably her attempt at a misguided message to Jamie to show she's taking responsibility for her family's wrongdoing.

15

But it's also a message for me – to say she's fine, that I don't need to worry. I can feel it.'

Binah raised her eyebrows. 'Do we believe her?'

Gulping down the last of her drink, Lottie shoved the magazine back on the rack, the phony image of Ellie crumpling at the edges.

'No.'

2

When Ellie had enrolled at Rosewood three years ago, the first thing she'd noticed was the hundreds of flowers. They flooded the grounds with the thick sweet smell of roses and lavender. The second thing was a girl with pink cheeks, who was equally lovely, who Ellie had nearly destroyed.

'This is the right thing to do,' she told herself.

For all the trouble her family had caused her friends, and Lottie, and Jamie, she had to finally do something to make amends, and if that meant walking into the jaws of a school ready to eat her alive, then so be it.

St Agnus's, her new and decidedly less floral school, was not lovely, and it was most certainly not peaceful. It was cold and industrial, and, like almost everywhere else in Maradova, nothing could grow in its grounds.

'Would you like me to accompany you inside?' Samuel, her guard, asked as he held the car door open for her.

Ellie fidgeted with the sleeves of her blouse, trying to remember what her father's advisor Simien had told her about leaving a vehicle while wearing a skirt. 'No, thank you. Just . . . give me a second.'

She stared up at St Agnus's, which loomed above her. The triangular point of its black clock tower pulled everything into its shadow. There was no going back.

Jamie's been through worse, she told herself.

Her family had essentially kept him prisoner his whole life without his knowledge, all because of who his father was. This was nothing compared to what he'd been through.

This would be an important moment, the first time the real Maravish princess would greet her fellow students, and all she had to do was not mess up getting out of a car.

She took a deep breath, closed her eyes and whispered, 'What would Lottie do?'

Like casting a spell, everything melted away.

It ached to think of Lottie – a deep wrenching pain that cut from chest to guts. Guilt and awe spiralled inside her like petals in a storm. The image she conjured was when she'd first seen Lottie at Rosewood: graceful, pink-cheeked and smiling. Always smiling.

Ellie missed that smile. Kindness was second nature to Lottie, and she shared it with the rest of the world like a rose shares its blossoms. That was a real princess, and that's what Ellie needed to be.

'You're doing the right thing,' she whispered to herself.

She slipped across the seat, exiting the car with a discreet sweep of her legs. Then she turned, eyes cast down in the way she'd seen pretty girls do a million times before. 'Thank you, Samuel. That will be all.'

Samuel nodded and climbed back behind the wheel. Before she even had a chance to say goodbye, he was driving off.

It was one of the main benefits of attending a school in the Maravish capital city of St Krystina: inconspicuous security. A whole squadron of royal guards could protect the school, while also keeping her under constant surveillance as though she were no more than a child. Was that what she'd become?

Unlike the previous year at Rosewood, Ellie's family drama wouldn't cause unpleasant restrictions for the other students. Her friendships there had been shattered because she was from a royal family of liars and deceivers; Jamie had disappeared and she'd pushed Lottie away to keep her safe. At St Agnus's only Ellie was being monitored.

The iron doors at the top of the steps let out a furious groan as Ellie let them slam shut behind her. Inside she learned exactly to what extent she was being monitored; only it wasn't by the guards. Every single St Agnus's student – a mass of navy and grey uniforms with bobbled hats and scarves – seemed to be staring at her, extending their necks to get a better look.

The room filled with hushed whispers and pointed fingers as Ellie cautiously made her way through.

'That's her definitely.'

'It's cute how she's trying so hard to look the part.'

'I bet she's a brat in real life.'

'That's probably why they had to lock her away.'

It was infuriating to feel so exposed. Ellie's fists began to clench, freshly manicured nails digging crescent moons into her palms.

It was just as she was getting ready to turn round that it hit her. This is exactly what Lottie must have had to put up with when she first attended Rosewood: whispers and rumours she couldn't control. Ellie had put the only girl she'd ever loved through so much, all because she'd forced her to take on the role of Portman. While Lottie had pretended to be the princess of Maradova, Ellie could flounce about with no worries. All the responsibility had been on her dearest friend. Lottie was the best thing that had ever happened to her, while Ellie was quite sure that she was the worst thing that had ever happened to Lottie. How could she have been so selfish?

Ellie's hands slowly unclenched while she took another deep breath, holding her head high. She couldn't fail. Not now.

Look, Lottie, she told herself. *Can you see me? I'm going to be the perfect princess so you never have to worry about me again.*

Pulling her blouse tighter over her chest in an unconscious attempt to protect herself, Ellie wandered down an artificially lit corridor in the tomb of a building to find her classroom.

At Rosewood every building and room had a unique feel, a rich personality blossoming from hundreds of years of passion and nurturing. It could not have been more different to St Agnus's. Ellie soon learned that the rooms were identical, each a concrete box with three windows opposite the door, the windows looking out over the stone steps if you were on one side of the building or an artificial grass pitch on the other. Worst of all were the archaic blackboards and erasers that made the air feel musty and stifling.

The bell rang shortly after Ellie located her classroom; the only way to tell them apart was the bold black numbers outside each door.

Each identical seat at each identical desk became immediately filled with students, while Ellie stood at the side, watching, waiting to be told where she belonged.

These were the people she'd rule one day. But it was obvious from their narrowed eyes that they felt just as cold towards her as the Maravish weather.

Maravish people tended to have thick dark hair, high cheekbones and strong brows. Looking around the room, it was clear why so many models were of Maravish heritage. Ellie was painfully aware of her own body, unable to stop herself comparing it to the most confident girls in the class. They wore their femininity so easily, hair sleek and bouncy, lips pouty, posture effortless, legs crossed comfortably.

Ellie wasn't like that. She felt most comfortable in her armour of black hair and loose-fitting clothes that hid her. But that didn't matter now. She'd had to retrain herself to be the perfect princess. For Lottie and for Jamie – she could do it.

One chestnut-haired girl leaned forward to the girl at the desk in front of her and whispered loud enough for Ellie to hear. 'Why is she staring at us like that?'

Both girls giggled as Ellie furiously turned away.

On the tip of her tongue Ellie could taste the strawberry lip gloss she'd been forced to wear, the smell as disgusting as its pink colour. Deciding it was part of his job as king's advisor, Simien had helped dress her up as prettily as possible, which was not an easy feat when you were working with a prissy grey uniform and a model whose legs and torso were too long.

No wonder the other students were laughing at her. To make matters worse, that chestnut-haired girl was right – she *had* been staring. Princesses didn't stare; they were stared at.

With her subtle make-up, starched uniform and hair pushed back neatly with a headband, Ellie felt like she was cosplaying the type of girl she'd usually fall for. The irony wasn't lost on her that after years of running away from being a princess, it turned out 'princess' was exactly her type. Exactly like Lottie.

'You look lost?'

Ellie jumped like she'd been caught doing something she shouldn't have, namely fantasizing about Lottie when she'd sworn to let her go. She turned to find a tall broad-shouldered boy with coiffed hair and the kind of winning smile that made girls swoon. He was handsome, with the classic thick eyebrows of the Maravish people, and lashes so heavy it almost looked like he was wearing make-up. It occurred to her suddenly that, with her new princess look, this was exactly the kind of pampered boy she might accidentally attract.

She chose to err on the side of caution. 'Is that so?'

He chuckled, and she found herself believing that he really wanted to be helpful.

'I'm Leo. Leo Gusev Jr.'

'Gusev, as in the Golden Goose Gusevs?'

'The very same.'

Having been prepped by Simien that she would be attending St Agnus's alongside many of the country's powerful noble families, it wasn't that much of a shock to find that the first person she spoke to was heir to the world's biggest poultry-farming business. One that wasn't known for animal welfare.

Ellie's first thought was how much Lottie as a card-carrying vegetarian and lover of all things cute and helpless would hate that.

'Might I make a suggestion?' Before Ellie could even respond he went on. 'If you want to make a good impression, Miss Belsky usually asks someone to beat the erasers before class. I'm sure she'd appreciate it if you did that.'

Ellie weighed up the pros and cons. Not usually the trusting type, she was tempted to ignore his advice, but once again she thought of Lottie, wondering what she would do, and decided she needed to have a little more faith in the people she'd be sharing a class with.

'Noted. Thank you,' she said with a forced smile, watching Leo take a seat behind the only empty desk left.

Sucking in a big breath, Ellie approached the blackboard, ignoring the way the whispers and giggling started up again. The erasers were bigger than she'd expected, and she must have banged them together with a little too much force because a huge cloud of white chalk immediately flew up into her face, causing the whole class to burst out laughing.

'Miss Wolfson.' A shrill voice screeched from behind her, and Ellie turned in time to see her new teacher drop her papers in shock. 'Is this your idea of a joke? Trying to impress your new classmates?'

'I-I was j-just . . .' Ellie stuttered. Wasn't this what she'd been told to do? 'I thought –'

'You thought you wouldn't get caught trying to mess up my classroom?'

Realization slowly dawned on Ellie. She'd been naive to trust anyone at this school.

'I don't know what kind of childish pranks you were able to get away with when you had that unfortunate girl taking on your responsibilities, but you are here now to be moulded into perfection. We will not tolerate this kind of behaviour.'

Miss Belsky's voice managed to get higher with each sentence, until her wiry grey eyebrows started to remind Ellie of steam shooting out of a kettle and the words stung like the scald of boiling water.

People had not been happy to learn of the Portman arrangement. Articles had piled up, calling it everything from irresponsible to archaic, and everyone had truly started to love Lottie – and Princess Ellie was nothing like her.

'Now please go and open a window, then take your seat in front of Mr Gusev.' Ellie flinched at this, knowing exactly where this was going. 'Hopefully some of his good behaviour will rub off on you.'

Ellie felt fire under her skin from the fury and humiliation. She'd been set up and, worst of all, the boy who'd tricked her was grinning with smug satisfaction. And now she had to sit with him.

Ellie gritted her teeth. 'I'm sorry, ma'am. I promise I'll do better next time.'

She sat in front of Leo, as instructed. With determination, she conjured up images of Lottie and Jamie, remembering why she was doing this, knowing that if she lost it now, then it would all be for nothing.

However, to add insult to injury, the second Miss Belsky turned her back, the desk behind her creaked, and she felt Leo's breath against her neck.

'I know all about your little plan.' His voice spat into the air like venom. 'I'm the prince of this school, and I'm not going to sit back and let anyone mess that up for me.' He kicked the back of her seat to make sure she was really listening, and his next words were more painful than any physical blow. 'Especially a princess as fake and pathetic as you.'

It was only day one, and Ellie already knew in her bones that she was the worst princess ever.

3

Something was wrong at Rosewood Hall. The golden gates yawned open in welcome, yet a strange scent wafted over every student as they entered the grounds.

'The flowers are depressed,' Binah said, sniffing the air.

Lottie took in a deep breath. 'It certainly seems that way.'

They dragged their suitcases up to the main building, resisting the temptation to cover their noses. It wasn't just the smell of decay. Even in the lingering light, the roses were noticeably drooping.

With the sun low behind the silhouette of the school, its inky shadow reached their toes. Before Lottie stepped into the gloom, she paused, turning her gaze up to the stone towers and arches. She'd learned quickly last term that Rosewood was simply not the same without Ellie or Jamie. What used to feel like the warm embrace of home was now like the artificial embrace of a waxwork. This was the advent of her very last year, and it already felt like a mess.

Both girls dropped their suitcases and phones with an attendant, and Lottie tried to ignore the attention from other students. Every year at Rosewood had somehow resulted in all eyes being on her. The only difference this time was they were staring because of who she *actually* was, not who she was pretending to be.

The voice of a particularly enthusiastic Year One pupil echoed through the courtyard. 'Oh my God! That's her! That's the princess's pauper girl.'

Lottie groaned internally, sure her cheeks must be bright pink. She knew her fellow students didn't mean anything cruel, but every careless remark twisted the knife in deeper.

Is Ellie dealing with stuff like this? How will she handle it? What would Jamie do if he heard people talking about me like that?

'It's not the school, you know,' Binah said.

Lottie blinked in confusion, pausing outside the arched doors of Stratus Side. 'Pardon?'

Binah looked like a little yellow canary in her uniform. No one in the whole school quite suited their uniform as much as Binah did. 'It's not the school making you feel so peculiar,' she said. 'It's the other way round.' Before Lottie could reply, she checked her watch, her eyes suddenly widening. 'Sorry, Lottie.' She began backing up towards the door. 'We'll grab you during the opening fireworks, 'K?'

Lottie barely had time to nod before Binah vanished into the Stratus tower. She had no choice but to face her own dorm.

Blank squares of wall that once held posters, photographs and scraps of Ellie's life sat like wounds on the ivory plaster. Now the room was dressed only with prettiness, soft pinks and pastels, sugary and sweet. The edges that Ellie had added to Lottie's frills had been completely smoothed out, making what used to feel so natural, cold and anaemic.

Lottie sighed. 'I know. I miss her too.'

She reached into her bag and pulled out one of the last remnants of Ellie she possessed. She placed a velvet box on her bedside table, flipping open the top to reveal the crescent-moon opal nestled in a tiara of woven silver. At this point she'd usually repeat her mantra – *be kind, be brave, be unstoppable* – but the words felt hollow. It was a mantra built around fairy-tale princesses, but now, thinking about Ellie, it all felt wrong. The crescent moon glinted as Lottie rolled her eyes. 'I'm conflicted, OK?'

Her thoughts were cut off by a sound at the balcony window, and Lottie looked up to see two glowing yellow suns in the darkness.

'Vampy!' Lottie could have collapsed in relief.

She rushed over to pull open her balcony doors. The black cat broke out into thunderous purring as he leaped inside, immediately beginning to weave between her legs. She picked him up, groaning at how heavy he'd become, and the two of them collapsed on to the bed beside her stuffed pig Mr Truffles.

'You must be lonely,' she cooed.

'*Mreow!*' The howling sound Vampy made was distinctly unhappy, and Lottie wondered why Percy wasn't looking after him. Why hadn't Raphael or Saskia come to see her, let alone Anastacia and the twins?

'Where is everyone?' she said aloud.

Lottie stared at the ring on her index finger, a gold band woven with stars. Hidden inside were words in another language. It had been given to her secretly by the maids in Wolfson's Palace; this ring was meant for Jamie. It was a memento from his late mother Hirana, and it was Lottie's responsibility to give it to him, to relay whatever message Hirana had left for him before she died. Jamie was one of her dearest friends, so why did the thought of seeing him again make her blood run cold? She knew the answer. She was scared he would have turned into his father, Claude Wolfson.

The fairy tales she'd read as a child told her that even the most desolate of people could change the world, but now it all felt like cruel lies. She was just one girl on her own – what could she possibly do?

An unseasonable draught blew in from the balcony, bringing a chill with it, and in the distance she heard a student screeching with laughter like a crow cackling. It hit her so abruptly it nearly took her breath away, fear curling in her belly and squeezing at her heart. She was entirely alone for the first time since she'd started at Rosewood. Once again she felt like a sad lonely little girl with only her fairy tales and a cat for company. Forgotten, discarded, vulnerable . . .

Suddenly Lottie's ears pricked up as a far more sinister sound came from outside her room. Barely audible above the heaving of her chest was a methodical scraping from the other side of the door. Sensing her fear, Vampy sprang up and hissed, while Lottie watched, stuck to the bed, as the doorknob slowly turned.

Blood turning hot in her veins, the years of being Ellie's Portman kicked in and Lottie flung herself forward as the door flew open. Hurtling towards it, fists raised, everything was a blur of panic.

Only – with a flash of understanding – she saw that there was no evil foe, no covert member of Leviathan come to do her harm or take her to Jamie. Instead she found before her the dainty Lola Tompkins.

'Lola!' Lottie spluttered. 'I'm so sorry. I thought you were –'

'*Mon dieu*, Lottie.' Anastacia's distinctive accent echoed from behind Lola. 'You look like you've seen a ghost.'

Lottie let go of Lola's wrist and flung herself over the poor girl in a tight embrace, trying her best to cover up how scared she'd actually been. The last thing she wanted to do right now was worry everyone.

Lola laughed, rubbing Lottie's back as though it were nothing. 'It's no biggie. Sorry for startling you, but we need to hurry while everyone's still distracted by the fireworks.'

Anastacia eyed her warily, but Lola quickly led them away and Lottie found herself being dragged through Ivy Wood.

'Wait! Where are we going?' she puffed, as the three of them flew out through the front doors and into the balmy night, still trying to get her heart to calm down.

'Just wait and see.' Anastacia couldn't hide her mischievous glee. 'And be thankful. They wanted me to blindfold you, but I insisted it was way too tacky.'

There was a great boom above them and the sky lit up bright yellow, the colour of joy.

'Perfect timing,' Lola said, as another hiss and fizz sent tendrils of green and red into the night. 'Everyone will be too distracted to notice us.'

Squeezing Lola's hand, Lottie was grounded, the colours from the opening ceremony a reminder that she was safe at

Rosewood. Even if the school didn't feel like home without Ellie or Jamie, there were still people here for her.

Lola kept a lookout all the way to Stratus Side, peeping round every corner and shushing when they were too loud, until they reached the empty stairwell at the base of the Elwin statue.

Carved with painstaking detail, the wise falcon Elwin, the mascot of Stratus, towered over them, his outstretched wings casting a shadow of protection over every student that entered the building.

Lottie had stood in this exact spot many times before and knew exactly what lay underneath his talons. 'You're taking me to Liliana's secret study?' Lottie's voice wavered and she hoped they didn't notice.

Anastacia's answer was to flip the W on Elwin's name, turning it into an M – the key to unlocking the ancient room.

Elwin lifted from the ground, hidden cogs creaking like the stretch of an old stiff body to reveal the stairs down to the dormant room. The ceremony of it was still as grand as the very first time Lottie had seen it. But, despite having been down there what felt like a million times, Lottie hesitated.

'You coming?' Lola asked, her fingers slipping from Lottie's grip as she descended into the darkness.

Lottie stood at the threshold like a rock on a mountainside. This was the last thing Lottie had kept to herself: the room at the heart of the school that held an ancient secret about its founder William Tufty. Down in the tunnels of the school lay Lottie's legacy, a lost truth that connected her to the school by blood.

'Hey!' Anastacia whispered, appearing next to her. 'I thought you'd want to come here; it's your ancestor's after all.'

Lottie gulped. It was true – usually the space held great comfort for her. The dusty old study contained evidence that William Tufty's real identity was that of the lost princess of legend Liliana Mayfutt. Paintings and diary entries showed that she had married Lottie's ancestor Henry Pitkin and gifted him the tiara that now belonged to Lottie. So if Liliana shared her blood, why did she feel so unworthy of it?

'I know,' Lottie said, trying to downplay the strange dread that had formed in her belly. 'I just . . . sometimes I find it hard to believe that everything down there belonged to someone related to *me*.'

It felt like a mean joke that Lottie Pumpkin, the lonely naive girl who'd pretended to be a princess, would turn out to be the only known ancestor of the notorious wild and ferocious lost princess Liliana. How could someone who'd achieved so much and lived so boldly be related to Lottie?

'I promise that what's down there will make you feel much better,' Anastacia assured her, unusually earnest.

Lottie nodded and took a deep breath, hoping Anastacia was right. And once more she found herself stepping into the dark.

'OK, seriously,' Lottie whispered into the eerie quiet as they tiptoed down the echoing spiral staircase, 'this is starting to feel a little sinister.'

At the bottom Lottie was swallowed by the gaping black of the cavernous room and fumbled for one of the switches she'd installed. 'What's going –'

The room lit up before she could finish the question. Amid the warm amber glow from the sea of star lamps floating above her were her friends. Her family.

'SURPRISE!'

Raphael, the twins, Binah, Percy, Anastacia and Saskia – the Rosewood crew, minus Ellie and Jamie, were all smiling beneath the shimmering fairy lights. On the wall behind them, where they usually kept a blackboard, was her real surprise, something they must have been working on secretly. A large screen had been set up and grinning at Lottie from the other side of the world was her best friend from Rosewood's sister school in Japan.

Lottie choked, trying to hold back joyful tears. 'Sayuri? How? What . . .?'

'It was Binah's idea,' Sayuri said simply.

Binah shrugged. 'It seemed sensible that we should work together.'

In a flash Miko's blue-topped head popped into the left side of the frame, followed by Rio on the right side, and Wei was behind them among a tangle of wires, managing the computer signal. All of Banshee were there!

Sayuri cleared her throat. 'OK, listen, everyone. Now that Ellie has gone back to Maradova and Jamie has joined his father, it's up to us to make sure Leviathan, and more importantly Claude, don't get what they want.'

It was so good to hear her voice again. Even on the other side of the world she had allies. She wasn't alone at all; she had the greatest friends she could hope for and that was stronger than any fairy tale. This was real.

34

I don't need those stories any more, Lottie told herself, ignoring the dread that squeezed her stomach again. Instinctively she moved away from one of Liliana's paintings and closer to the screen.

'They've taken something from all of us,' Sayuri continued, pulling Lottie out of her thoughts. 'We have a year to take them down and we can only do it together.' Everyone in the room nodded, and Lottie felt herself light up as Sayuri went on. 'From now on you're all honorary members of Banshee.'

'We can do this,' Lottie said with matching conviction. 'They might have the Hamelin Formula, but by working together we can figure out Leviathan's plan, save our friends and make Claude pay.'

The room broke out into booming cheers, everyone raising their drinks in celebration of the triumph they could practically taste.

Sayuri nodded at her through the screen, and Lottie smiled back.

'Man,' Raphael said after everyone had calmed down, 'wouldn't it be convenient if we could talk to Jamie and Ellie as easily as this?' He laughed in the charming way only he was capable of.

'Or if any of us could have any communication with them at all.' Lottie had meant it as a joke, but her voice emerged flat – until Percy signed the very last thing any of them had expected anyone to say.

'I've spoken to Jamie.'

Raphael spat out his drink. 'WHAT?'

'What did he say?' Sayuri asked through the video, the other members of Banshee leaning in.

Saskia's hand flew to her mouth. 'He says he's spoken to Jamie.'

'Percy –' it was taking all Lottie's willpower to stay calm – 'how is that possible?'

Percy shrugged and, as he rapidly signed, Lottie was glad they'd all learned BSL. *'Ever since he left . . . Jamie's been sending me letters.'*

4

Jamie had always loved music. It made sense and followed patterns.

When the royal Wolfson family had taken him in, they'd allowed him to start piano lessons. At the time it had felt like a privilege beyond worth. On special occasions Jamie would even play for them, taking solace in their kindness. Yet it had all been a lie. There'd been no kindness in the gesture. He'd been raised as Ellie's Partizan, a loyal protector, told that the royal family had taken him in as an orphan out of the goodness of their hearts and given him a role in the household. In reality he'd been no more than a prisoner. An equerry, a playmate, a servant under their close watch. But he did have a place in the Wolfson household. He was the true prince.

Nevertheless, Jamie still loved music, and, right then, no sour memory could spoil the crisp, bright sound of his brand-new gift, an inky-black grand piano.

'Let's see,' Jamie muttered to himself, flitting through the pages of one of the many books of sheet music that Claude had gifted him upon their arrival at the new Leviathan safe house. He settled on 'Dance of the

Sugar Plum Fairy', thinking the atmosphere matched the permanent winter of Maradova. His fingertips came to settle over the ivories, the music beginning, and with it his thoughts began to swirl.

Claude Wolfson had been in his life for barely half a year, though the lies surrounding him had stared down at Jamie from the palace walls for much longer. Claude was the black sheep of the Wolfsons: the king-to-be who ran away from the throne, turning his back on the people of Maradova and leaving the responsibility to his younger brother,.

Lies, lies – everything twisted and fake.

Claude was Jamie's father; Jamie simply hadn't known it. Claude had been forced to leave the kingdom for falling in love with the wrong woman. This man who'd been framed as selfish and cruel had, with no question or expectation, surprised Jamie with his very own grand piano. Although Jamie wondered if perhaps selfishness was in the Wolfson blood. Because music meant nothing to him now. Not if he couldn't play for the person he cared for most.

He'd escaped from the clutches of the wolves and found where he belonged, yet every note he played carried the sombre tone of guilt. Deep down he knew he couldn't rest until he was sure the one thing that was most precious to him would be safe from the Wolfsons forever. *I have to keep Lottie safe*.

A soft knock at the door pulled him from his trance. Immediately he recognized the familiar pattern of the *tap, tap, tap*.

'Come in, Haru.'

As he entered, the rogue Partizan shut the door behind him, leaning back against the grey-painted wood until the bolt clicked shut. 'I just want to make sure you're happy in your new accommodation, my prince – I mean, Jamie,' Haru quickly corrected himself, spotting how Jamie winced at the title. Nothing ever seemed to get past him.

'This room is very generous.' It was all Jamie could think to say and he turned back to the piano.

Haru took in Jamie's wistful look, and his dark eyes widened under his brown glasses. 'I hope you didn't stop on my account.'

'Oh no, I was only testing –'

Without asking, Haru strolled over and sat on the stool beside Jamie, placing his fingers on the ivories. With an immediate and effortless grace, he picked up the accompaniment to the melody. Haru had, of course, been listening before he came in.

Haru beamed at him. 'Play with me.'

Jamie placed his hands back on the keys. With both of them playing, the melody sounded unsettling and impish, exactly as it was meant to, and, despite himself, Jamie liked having someone to play with.

'Is it strange being back in Maradova?' Haru asked, not missing a beat.

Jamie didn't hesitate. 'I'd guessed that we'd be coming to a safe house here for the last part of Claude's plan.' He paused to do a particularly quick trill. 'Although it's somehow colder than I remembered.'

'I love it,' Haru replied honestly. 'It's melancholy yet resilient, and I love it because it's yours.'

Jamie nearly missed a note. He'd forgotten this was the first time Haru had been to Maradova.

What an odd thing it was to think of this land as belonging to him. Whenever Jamie thought of the Maravish landscape, of the tundra and icy air and golden cities that smelled of snow and cinnamon, he pondered what it meant to have a kingdom. Surely it should feel like home – so why, then, did it not feel that way? What was missing? *Who was missing?*

With immaculate precision, Haru's fingers danced over the keys and Jamie hummed in approval.

'There is something I've been meaning to ask you,' Haru announced. 'What will you do when you see the Portman again?'

The melody became tangled and Jamie stood up from the piano.

Haru smiled apologetically. 'I seem to have made an error.'

Jamie shook his head. 'No, I think it was me. I need to . . .' He exhaled sharply, walking to the door. 'I need to get some air.'

To his relief, Haru didn't follow; he was smart enough to know when he'd crossed a line.

With slick black furniture and built-in technology, everything in the house was so modern it bordered on sterile. Laid out in interconnecting cubes and rectangles like a monochrome game of *Tetris*, the entire concrete building was built around an open-plan living space, with a floating staircase leading to three platforms that all looked down into its core.

Jamie would be lying if he said he didn't miss the cabin by the lake. The new house felt too exposed; only the bedrooms and Claude's office offered any privacy.

As he reached the second storey, he took a turn, hoping to grab a drink from the kitchen without bumping into Phi, Julius or either of the housekeepers. No such luck. Instead a tiny figure hurtled into him and crashed to the floor.

Ingrid looked as terrified as a kitten cornered by dogs. 'I'm so sorry, my prince. Er, Jamie. Damn it!' She took a breath to calm herself. 'Please forgive me.'

No matter how many times Jamie had insisted the rest of Leviathan not refer to him by his title, it seemed an impossible habit for them to break. 'It's fine.'

'I could have hurt you.'

'No, I mean, it's fine that you called me that here.' Jamie leaned down and pulled her up in one swift motion, ignoring the way she yelped in surprise. 'Are you OK? That sounded like a pretty hard thud.'

When Ingrid finally looked up at him, he glimpsed the chestnut freckles that spattered across her nose. He was starting to become convinced she was avoiding him, which, considering their awful past, wouldn't surprise him. He'd have to fix that.

'You're worried about *me*?' The words came out in a hiss, as if she were mad at Jamie. 'I'm the one who –' She cut herself off, her eyes drifting to Jamie's shoulder where he had blocked the trajectory of her knife, the knife that had been meant for Lottie.

'Just try to be more careful,' Jamie said. 'I know that you're surprisingly delicate.'

It was the wrong thing to say. All he'd done was remind her of the times they'd fought and how badly they'd hurt each other. He could see by the way her fingers twitched that she was remembering the damage he'd done to the bones there. Something he deeply regretted.

Ingrid's face twisted. It seemed today was not for building bridges.

Jamie made to walk round her, not wanting to upset her more. 'Never mind.'

'Wait! I was coming to tell you that the Master wants to see you. He's in his office.'

Jamie headed up to the top floor to find Claude's office. He'd learned that his father valued timeliness.

The office was located at the back of the building behind a large iron door. Jamie knocked twice and was immediately called in.

As soon as he stepped inside, the wash of bright grey from the skylights that flooded the rest of the house blinked out, and Jamie was swept into a shadowy world of deep plum and spiced wine. A Persian rug led to a dark oak desk that was almost empty save for a laptop and a tumbler of amber liquid. But directly above it, high on the wall, was something Jamie could never bring himself to look at – the sacralized head of a doe.

Claude turned away from the window where he'd been gazing out at the spruce trees.

This is my father, Jamie reminded himself. *This is what I'm made of*.

'Ah, hello, my son.' His voice was as smooth as the silk robes that he wore. 'Thank you for coming.'

There was a wildness to Claude that Jamie recognized in himself, and, just like Jamie, he kept it under lock and key. The burning hunger for life broke free in other ways – loose strands of hair, twitching lips and the fire in their eyes as all-consuming as an exploding star, but where Jamie's were gold, Claude's were green, with a spark that warned of a forest fire.

'Good afternoon.' Jamie stood rigid. Not because his father scared him, but because he was curious. He saw himself as a hunter, watching the leader of his pack and learning every move he made.

'I trust you're settling in well?'

Jamie nodded.

'Your room is warm enough? The piano in tune?'

Jamie nodded again.

'And how about the view? It's not too depressing having a panorama of all that awful grey slush, is it?'

'I don't imagine any of the other bedrooms have anything better. Besides –' Jamie shrugged – 'I'm accustomed to it; one might even say I like it.'

The corner of Claude's mouth twisted upward ever so slightly, the expression familiar enough to Jamie that it almost felt like looking in a mirror. 'Quite.' He chuckled softly. 'Your mother liked the weather here too.'

Hirana.

Jamie's mother was the whole reason he was here; she was the deer the wolves had eaten because a member of their pack had fallen in love with her. The tale was simple. Hirana had been the palace gardener, cultivating what she could from the barren land, and his father had fallen for her.

43

They'd had a child, the result of which saw him exiled for going against the family's wishes and choosing love over duty. Claude had suffered years of penance, watching Jamie grow up oblivious to who he was, serving the family that had betrayed him, protecting their princess, all while Claude had been banished.

'I'm glad to hear it.' It was all Jamie could muster; the anger and betrayal were too fresh.

Claude picked up his glass and took a long sip of the amber liquid. Sighing, he said, 'There is something I've been meaning to ask you.'

Jamie noticed the similarities to his conversation with Haru. 'Yes?'

Claude smiled. 'I want to know about those letters you've been sending.'

Jamie relaxed, but he didn't miss the way Claude's eyes narrowed. 'I should have told you sooner, but it's such a ludicrous thing.'

His father tilted his head, a lock of black hair falling to the side. 'I'm listening.'

The last thing Jamie wanted to do was tell this story. He prided himself on being logical and reliable, and he'd hoped to avoid having to explain the letters.

'You see,' he began. 'I have – well, *had*, this cat, or, rather, the cat chose me, and I was stuck with it.' He was rambling.

'A cat?'

'Yes. A greedy brute. I should be glad to be rid of him, only . . .' He reminded himself it was better than having to talk about Lottie with his father. 'I couldn't leave the cat without making sure he was being taken care of. I've been sending letters to my old room-mate Percy, partly to apologize for lumping the cat on him and partly to make sure he has all the information he needs.' Jamie ran a hand through his hair. 'I assure you I am not usually this ridiculous.'

There was a moment of suspended silence, which was abruptly broken when Claude threw his head back and laughed. 'Of course Hirana's child would concern himself with something so small and insignificant.' His father swirled his drink and took another sip. 'Jamie, I assure you Percival – and all the others who have been harmed by my brother's family – will be compensated when we put you in your rightful place.'

'Thank you. I –'

'The Portman too.'

Jamie swallowed. 'What about her?'

If Claude noticed the stiffness of his reply, he didn't comment on it.

'I know you want her taken care of.' Claude's voice dropped an octave. 'You need only say the word.'

There it was. All he had to do was ask and Claude would bring Lottie to him, where he could keep her safe, far away from anything that might hurt her. However, although this was his deepest desire, he knew that bringing her here was wrong.

'She'll be fine,' Jamie blurted. 'So long as we keep her apart from Ellie – Eleanor – until we put things right.'

The silence was so loud Jamie felt it ringing in his ears, but Claude appeared as calm as ever. His father smiled in a way that made Jamie feel uneasy. 'Very well.' Claude's voice sounded rich with satisfaction. 'I'll let you get back to your piano practice.'

Then Jamie did something he couldn't quite explain. He ducked his head and gave a deep bow – the type of obsequious bow he would normally have only ever given to King Alexander or the queen mother.

When he dared to glance up again, his father's smile had grown wider, more sinister . . . more satisfied.

5

Sleeping alone at Rosewood was something Lottie was still getting used to. The night seemed so much darker, the moon twice as lonely and the stars half as bright. But, worst of all, where there had once been the gentle lullaby of Ellie's breathing was now an inescapable quiet. All she could hear was her own heartbeat, and night after night she willed herself not to panic at the inevitable loneliness that stretched out until morning.

So it came as a shock, three weeks into term, as the weather started to turn, when Lottie heard the slow rhythmic breathing of someone in her room. The sound was so real and familiar that Lottie had Ellie's name on the tip of her tongue – but it couldn't be. Ellie had left her.

She was lying curled up, but then she felt it. The dip in her mattress and the tell-tale chill of a breeze from her balcony. Whoever was in her room had come in through the open door. Someone was sitting on her bed.

She balled her hands in the sheets, pulse pounding. But, before she could turn round, something caught in her nostrils, a smell she recognized – cinnamon and spice, warm and sharp.

With a gasp, she turned over. *Jamie!*

He was sitting at the bottom of her bed, his eyes shining in the dark with flecks of starlight. He was just as she remembered, but something was wrong. With his face in the shadows, the wild strands of his hair looked like horns.

Lottie tried to stay calm. 'What are you doing here?'

The shadowy silhouette chuckled. 'I told you I'd come back for you.' The words were warped, like both a scream and a whisper, and Lottie covered her ears. 'I'll always keep you safe.'

Although she couldn't see him clearly, she knew he was smiling, and it sent a chill through her that had nothing to do with the open window.

'Jamie, I'm sorry, but I won't come with you to Leviathan.'

The silhouette laughed again.

With reflexes too fast to be human, Jamie's hands reached out from the shadows and pulled her hands away from her ears, forcing her to listen.

Lottie's face stretched in horror, because these were not Jamie's hands; they were pale and hardened, and it only got worse when he finally came out of the shadow.

She'd been wrong. It wasn't hair – he had two velvet antlers.

'Can you really do it, Lottie?' the monster version of Jamie asked, eyes glowing. 'Can you fight me if it means saving Ellie?'

There was no time to answer – not even time to shout – before her eyes flew open, a furious ringing bringing her back to reality.

She was awake. It had just been a dream.

A horrible dream.

When Lottie finally wandered down to the Ivy dining hall, she found Percy waiting for her at their usual table by the window with a pond view, a still-warm bowl of porridge and fresh strawberries laid out before him. He gave a sideways glance at her exhausted appearance, but she shook her head, not wanting to talk about her strange dream or what it might mean.

Besides figuring out and thwarting Claude's plan, with the pressure of their final year, everyone had enough to worry about. They didn't need to know about her weird nightmares and fears too.

One small blessing was that the near-constant gossip about her Portman job had calmed down, and Lottie could eat her breakfast in relative peace. Three weeks had already passed since their return, enough time for everyone to have got entirely bored of Lottie's situation, and the whispers had been replaced by the occasional sympathetic smile.

'*You're not upset with me about the letters, are you?*'

Lottie blinked. 'Should I be?'

Percy watched Lottie for an uncomfortably long time.

Whenever Lottie was close to him like this, she always thought he was like a long piece of liquorice with his glossy black hair, sunken heavy-lashed eyes and the faint aniseed scent of his cologne. It was funny to think that his boyfriend was the total opposite, a sweet little blond candy cane.

'*Because I didn't tell you about them sooner,*' Percy signed, guilt on his face. '*You must be worried.*'

'I'm not upset with you,' she said sincerely.

Percy nodded. *'If you're feeling down, you could always do your little mantra.'*

Heat thrummed in Lottie's cheeks. 'How did you –'

'Lottie, come on! I can read lips.' It was taking some effort for Percy not to laugh. *'I see you mouth it to yourself all the time. I think it's nice, and it obviously helps you.'*

Lottie stared down at her bowl, trying to imagine herself putting on her family's tiara. *Be kind, be brave, be unstoppable.* That was the mantra. But the words now carried a reminder of Ellie on the glossy magazine cover, and how it must feel for her to be forced into that role.

'It's complicated,' Lottie said quietly. 'Being a princess doesn't work for everyone.'

To Lottie's surprise, Percy chuckled. *'People contain multitudes.'*

Pondering this, Lottie gulped down a spoonful of porridge. All she'd ever known was a desire to be like the princesses from her mother's fairy tales, and now the thought made her feel naive. If she wasn't that girl any more, who was she?

'So, Banshee,' Percy signed, sensing Lottie's discomfort and changing the subject, *'they seem . . . intense.'*

Now it was Lottie's turn to chuckle, thinking of how intimidated she'd been by Sayuri when she'd first met her but how close they were now. 'Wait until you see them on their motorbikes.' Percy scoffed at this, not realizing Banshee was very much a biker gang. 'But they're harmless really. Miko and Rio can take a joke too far sometimes, but Wei always keeps them in check. And more importantly they have the same goal as us. Claude brainwashed Sayuri's

Partizan, Haru, and now Banshee are going to make him pay.'

Percy nodded, chewing over Lottie's words, before looking up again. *'I remember Emelia, you know.'*

Spoon almost at her mouth, Lottie froze at the mention of the one member of Banshee she hadn't met. It was rare Percy talked about his time under Leviathan's control, when they'd kidnapped him and Emelia to test their mind-control drug. Claude had treated them as nothing but pawns, using their family connection in the confectionery business to infiltrate Tompkins and get his hands on the Hamelin Formula.

'She wasn't like me,' Percy said. *'They couldn't completely control her. She was too angry, too sure of herself.'*

Lottie thought of Emelia, who had wriggled her way out of Claude's grasp.

'I think if we're going to beat Claude, we need to know exactly who we are. There's no room for doubt with him or he'll latch on to it and make you question everything about yourself.'

Lottie nodded, not saying a word. *Who am I?*

Lottie's last lesson of the day was English, a subject that would distract her from her Jamie nightmare until the meeting with Banshee after school. They'd scheduled the meetings fortnightly, giving them enough time to come up with independent ideas and avoiding the need for too many calls with the awkward time difference.

Lottie knew for sure that if Binah found out about her nightmare, she'd have to go through hours of dream analysis, and currently she didn't want to relive the experience. *I'll tell her later in the week.* But even to herself this sounded like a lie.

'And for you, Miss Pumpkin.'

A heavy document was slapped down on the desk in front of her, and she looked up to find Ms Kuma beaming in all her colourful jewel-adorned glory, her floral scent as invigorating as her cheerful attitude.

None of the teachers had commented on the fact that she'd been Ellie's Portman. That Lottie had been pretending to be the princess of Maradova as part of an ancient and archaic job to keep the real princess safe seemed too bizarre for them to address. Not even Lottie's own house mother Professor Devine had brought it up, and it was likely she was still processing that the rebellious Ellie Wolf was the real princess.

Lottie wondered if the staff had been told not to bring it up for the sake of Lottie's 'comfort' or something equally embarrassing.

'These papers contain the texts and topics you can choose to write about for your final essay,' Ms Kuma continued, moving between desks. 'I hope you all find something that inspires you.' The bell rang as Ms Kuma handed out the last batch of papers.

Lottie flicked through the heavy booklet on her way out, her glance instantly snagging on the only fairy tale – 'Little Briar Rose' or, as most people knew it, 'Sleeping Beauty'.

She felt oddly annoyed. Why she was still attracted to whimsy when it hadn't helped her? Shaking off that thought, she told herself she was simply curious and flipped through

52

the pages, mostly finding what she expected – feminist perspectives and retellings. It wasn't until she reached the end of the document that she paused, causing a Conch girl in a red ribbon to stumble directly into her.

'Hey!'

'Sorry,' Lottie mumbled, not even looking up from the page.

It was rare for something in a fairy tale to surprise her – especially one so well known. But at the bottom of the page one question made her skin tingle.

In most versions of the story the kingdom is put to sleep alongside the princess. How does the description of the lifeless castle and gardens aid in the mythologizing of royalty in fairy tales?

Something awakened at the back of her mind. It made Jamie's ring on her finger burn.

Lottie was still absent-mindedly rubbing her finger as she made her way up the spiral staircase in Stratus Side towards Binah's room. What on earth did the ring Jamie's mother had left him have to do with Sleeping Beauty? Why was it burning now? What was she not remembering?

'Oh, thank God you're here, Lottie!' Binah appeared and pulled her into her room, a worryingly excited look on her face. 'You're missing quite a show. Have you been sleeping OK?'

'Yes, fine. What's going on?' Lottie avoided Binah's question about her sleep. The answer to her own question wasn't immediately clear – Anastacia and Saskia were currently locked in a showdown with a laptop in Binah's room.

'So, if I am to understand correctly, in the two weeks since we last spoke none of you have come up with any plan to contact the Wolfsons?' Even through the computer speaker, Sayuri's disappointment was soul-crushing.

'Useless . . .' Miko muttered from somewhere behind Sayuri, tailing off with a string of Japanese expletives that Lottie was glad she couldn't understand.

'Hey, that's completely unfair.' Saskia marched towards the screen as if she expected to fight them through the monitor, only stopping when her girlfriend grabbed her arm.

'Now, now, Saskia,' Anastacia said gently. 'Our friends in Banshee are projecting their own insecurities, having not made any progress themselves.' Putting on a deeply condescending tone, Anastacia went on. 'It must be hard for them knowing that we were the ones who figured out that it'll take place at the Golden Flower Festival when they haven't done anything at all.'

There was an awkward pause and Binah's eyes darted back and forth. Just when the silence was almost too much to handle, a harsh cackle came from the speakers.

'She's got us there!' Rio hooted, nudging Wei, who seemed entirely unamused.

It was only then that anyone seemed to notice Lottie.

'Well,' Lottie said, placing her hands on her hips, 'it's great to see you all so enthusiastic about saving Ellie and Jamie.'

A faint smile spread over Sayuri's lips and the tension in the room instantly dissipated.

'In the meantime, we can keep trying to figure out their plan, and I can check Oddwood's diary again.' Lottie hoped she sounded more confident than she felt, because right now they all needed her to be strong. 'We still have until the Golden Flower Festival. We can't get discouraged this quickly. And –' Lottie gazed round at the gathered faces – 'it's nobody's fault progress is slow. We just have to keep focused and hope something comes up.'

For a split second Saskia looked riddled with guilt, but then Anastacia gave her a sharp look.

'Shall we continue the meeting? Argh!' Lottie cried out, rammed by Binah's door as someone hurtled through it.

'Oh my God, Lottie! I'm so sorry! Here . . .' Raphael leaned down, his smile bright and charming even as Lottie clutched her arm.

'Raphael! For goodness' sake!' Anastacia scolded while Saskia tried not to laugh. 'Where on earth have you been?'

Before Raphael could answer, the sweet trill of the twins' voices could be heard from the hallway. 'Don't tell them without us!'

This time Lottie was smart enough to move out of the way when Lola, Micky and Percy barged through.

'*Are we all here?*' Percy signed.

'What's going on?' Lottie asked, still rubbing her arm.

A mischievous grin spread across Raphael's face. 'I'll show you.' He marched over to the desk and slammed something down.

Saskia's mouth dropped open. 'No way!'

Rubbing her chin thoughtfully, Binah examined the object. 'Why didn't I think of this?' she said.

'Isn't it great?' The twins were giddy, practically dancing on the spot.

While everyone else beamed, Lottie remained silent.

It wasn't just a letter; it was a taunt. A gorgeous, intricately scribed, sweet-scented last resort that Lottie had prayed they wouldn't have to use.

> *The royal house of Wolfson cordially invites you*
> *to Wolfson Palace in honour of our decennial*
> *Golden Flower Festival in which we celebrate*
> *the anniversary of our claim to the throne.*
>
> *Your presence is requested:*
> *15 June*
> *Reception from 5 p.m.*
> *Festivities to begin from 6 p.m.*
> *Dress code: white tie*

Every inch of the creamy paper, from its glossy wax seal to the exquisitely fragile pressed primroses that clung to the card like a vision of summer, was a painful reminder of what Lottie had lost. The world she had been barred from when Ellie had left.

Sayuri cleared her throat. 'What is that?' she asked.

'Oh, this?' Raphael grinned, picking it up again to fan his face dramatically. 'This is our plan B.'

6

To say Ellie had had the day from hell would be a severe understatement, and she had the marks on her body and uniform to prove it.

No one was hurting her in an obvious way, not physically at least. The students of St Agnus's preferred a perfectly refined concoction of underhanded remarks and well-practised snubbing. The gash on her thigh had come from a violent swipe of a stray ice hockey puck that no one had warned her was coming.

In another universe Ellie would have snatched up the puck and called out the room for failing to warn her, but princesses didn't do that. In contrast, Lottie would have smiled, quickly patched up her scraped leg in the infirmary and thrown out her ruined tights – exactly what Ellie was doing now, trying her best to channel her inner princess. Grace at all times – wasn't that the way?

'What are you doing in the laundry room?'

Ellie froze at the unmistakable sound of Midori's voice. She turned to see her with Hanna, the two of them blocking the doorway in their immaculate white aprons.

'Do you even know how to use a washing machine?' Hanna added.

There was no escape, and the maids' eyes widened as they spotted Ellie's bloodied skirt.

'No one did this to me,' she said quickly. 'Please don't tell my parents.'

The maids shared an anxious glance.

Ellie knew they felt sorry for her because they thought she was trapped by her new image. She needed to prove to them – to everyone – that she could be the princess she was born to be.

Ellie let out a slow exhale. *What would Lottie do?*

A memory blossomed, as sweet and soft as the scent of a rose. It was a rainy day in November. Rosewood students were dotted around the school grounds, and Ellie couldn't find Lottie anywhere. She'd discovered her friend in the Ivy kitchen covered in flour, a tray of freshly baked cookies on the table that smelled like a childhood Ellie had never had. When Ellie had reached for one, Lottie had batted her hand away, explaining that a girl in her royal history class had recently learned that her beloved golden retriever had passed away. Lottie was baking to cheer her up. Effortlessly charming, merciful, kind, brave and unstoppable. Just like a princess.

'I need your help,' Ellie blurted out.

Hanna crossed her chubby freckled arms. But Midori smiled cautiously. 'What can we do for you?'

Ellie huffed out the last of her pride. 'I need to make friends. Can you . . .? Would you take me to the kitchen? I'd like to bake some cookies.'

When Ellie arrived at the iron doors of St Agnus's the next day, there was a secret weapon at her side in a pretty pink box. The plan was simple. Hand out the cookies at lunch, show everyone what a talented and generous person she was and – if Lottie was anything to go by – they would all love her for it.

What hadn't been part of her plan, was the mousy boy and girl waiting for her by the dining-hall entrance.

'Psst, Princess!'

It took Ellie a moment to realize they were talking to her. Without further warning, they grabbed Ellie and made her sit down at a corner table with them.

'Hey, what's your prob –' Ellie coughed, trying to cover up the slip in her patient demeanour. 'I mean, sorry, can I help you?'

The boy and girl were small, probably in the year below, and, apart from the set of pink braces the girl was sporting, they were almost identical, with tawny freckles spattered across their skin, and buck teeth. It was as though they'd been stamped by the same printing press. Twins, Ellie realized, like Lola and Micky – although these two looked more like fuzzy rats.

Ellie loved rats. She immediately decided she liked their style.

'We're saving you,' the girl said, her voice squeakier than Ellie expected.

'Excuse me?'

As they'd been talking, the boy had snatched her box of cookies and eased open the lid, releasing their delicious scent. Ellie and the maids had spent all evening baking.

He looked up. 'Please tell me you weren't seriously planning on handing these out?'

Heat flooded Ellie's cheeks. 'So what if I was?' The words tumbled out before she could stop them, an entirely unprincessy thing to say.

The Rat Twins snorted in unison, giving each other a knowing look that only infuriated Ellie more, and to her absolute horror the boy grabbed one of her precious cookies and nibbled on it.

It was taking every ounce of Ellie's self-control not to break face and whack the cookie out of his hand.

'Listen, sweetie, we've been watching you,' Rat Girl said, fluffing up her already fluffy hair. 'We're a month into term and you haven't made a single friend.'

Ouch.

Ellie forgot she was angry for a second.

'If it makes you feel better,' Rat Boy said through a mouthful of cookie, 'it's not entirely your fault. Good cookies by the way.' He waved the one he was eating in Ellie's face. 'But they wouldn't have helped.'

Ellie snatched back the box. 'You don't know that.'

'Please.' Rat Girl rolled her eyes. 'It's embarrassing that you would think of something as trite as handing out cookies. Look around you – this isn't some cutesy Hallmark movie.'

Double ouch.

Ellie looked at the anything-but-cutesy dining hall. Students huddled together in their utilitarian uniforms, the concrete walls and barred windows as lifeless and bland as the food. No better were the students' expressions, which were cold and uninterested, and whenever Ellie made eye contact they'd quickly look away. The twins were right. She was pathetic.

Ellie breathed out slowly, willing herself to stay calm. 'What did you mean, it wasn't my fault?'

The twins' eyes lit up.

'Someone was spreading rumours about you before school started.' The delight in Rat Girl's voice was nauseating. 'Stuff about how you're only putting on this image to trick people – that you're trying to butter up the nobles to get info from them so you can blackmail their families for future favours.'

Suddenly Leo's comment about 'knowing her plan' made perfect sense.

'What? That's not true!'

Rat Boy shrugged. 'Nothing to be done about it now. You just need to prove them all wrong.'

'And how am I meant to do that?' There was desperation in Ellie's voice now, and it only made the twins' eyes shine even brighter.

'You need to show your vulnerability,' Rat Girl advised. 'Let them see the real girl behind the smooth exterior. If they feel as though you're giving them a peek into your life, then they might just trust you.' Her argument rolled easily off the tongue, as though she'd been practising it for weeks.

Her brother continued. 'Obviously it won't be the real you. I don't think people would be keen on that. But you just need to make them *believe* it's the real you. People are less scared of being blackmailed if they feel like you're also exposed.'

Ellie hesitated, hurt that they wouldn't like the real her, but knowing it was true. 'I don't know if I can . . .'

They both burst out laughing – a mischievous sound that was so over the top that a few students glanced their way, eyebrows raised. At least they weren't ignoring her.

'We're not expecting you to run naked through the school halls or anything,' said Rat Girl.

'It's simple,' Rat Boy explained. 'You need to invite them into your world, create the illusion of trust and make them feel like they know you. And the best way to do that is to host a party at the palace.'

Ellie shook her head. Now it was her turn to laugh, because that was easily the most ridiculous idea she'd ever heard. 'There's no way –'

Rat Girl cut her off. 'We'll tell you who to invite and they'll definitely say yes if we say so. We'll make you popular yet.'

'And if you're worried about your parents, don't be.' Rat Boy leaned forward as though he were letting Ellie in on a secret. 'What's better than bringing home a select few peers to show how well you're adjusting?' He sat back, pleased with himself. 'You get to make friends and prove yourself to your family.'

Ellie sighed. 'They'll still need persuading.'

Rat Girl beamed. 'We can help you with that if you're happy to introduce us as your friends.'

An ember buried deep under the ash in Ellie's heart glowed. She could show her parents and grandmother that she'd done it, that she'd made friends, that she was worthy of the title of princess.

Ellie thought of Hanna and Midori. If she could prove she was able to fit in and be the princess they needed her to be, they would stop pitying her and her new classmates would all stop looking at her suspiciously. *And Lottie will see that you're fine.*

'OK, but I have a question.' Ellie spoke carefully, needing to know one more thing before she agreed to this plan. 'Why are you guys helping me?'

'Isn't it obvious?' the girl asked, twirling a lock of her wiry brown hair. 'You're going to be queen one day, and, unlike the rest of the idiots in this school, we know it's better to be on your good side.'

In any other circumstances Ellie might have taken offence to this, but right there in the dining hall filled with students she was meant to rule one day, all of them refusing to look at her, it was a relief to have someone – anyone – on her side.

'Thank you for your honesty, I guess.' Oddly enough the twins suddenly felt like the most trustworthy people in the whole school.

'You're welcome,' they said in unison.

When Ellie looked up, the wall clock informed her that she only had ten minutes until the bell rang. 'I'd better grab some food quickly.'

Rat Girl nodded. 'Sit with us tomorrow?'

'Yeah, great.' The twins beamed at her as she made to leave, and she turned back again. 'Sorry, what are your names?' She couldn't exactly keep calling them Rat Boy and Rat Girl forever.

Their smiles grew even wider, showcasing pearly rodent teeth.

'Sam,' said the girl, indicating her brother.

Sam placed an arm round his sister's shoulders. 'And this is Stella.'

7

Night in the new safe house was always as cold as metal. The silver light of the moon from the skylight drowned everything in a misty glow, turning the furniture monochrome. Ingrid wanted nothing more than to curl up in her bed and squeeze her eyes shut until she fell asleep, but she had been called in to see Claude.

You should be happy, she told herself. *You have everything you wanted.*

The rest of the household was tucked away in their respective quarters, and she gritted her teeth as she walked past the prince's room, casting his closed door a filthy glance. She still felt furious about their exchange a few weeks ago.

Jamie's words had been eating away at her. The audacity, the sheer nerve he had to look her in the eye and tell her to be more careful because she was *delicate*. No one had ever referred to her in such a way, and the very idea would usually make her gag. Only when Jamie had said that with complete sincerity it hadn't made her feel weak; it had made her feel precious. And that terrified her.

Suddenly she was something to be cherished, someone worth more than what she could offer in return, and that put a cruel hard fracture right down the middle of everything she thought she knew. Even with Julius, who she'd known since childhood, she'd always maintained a level of indifference around him; they both did. They both understood the other could be taken away at any moment. Attachment was weakness. All one needed was loyalty, nothing more. Or at least that's what she'd always thought. Now everything was confusing and it made her want to break something.

Outside Claude's door Ingrid took a deep breath before gently knocking.

'Come in, Ingrid,' the Master called.

Perched at his mirrored dressing table, Claude was already in his silk night clothes, combing his wet hair, a clear sign he did not intend for this conversation to last long as he would likely be asleep soon.

His eyes never left his own face even as she entered the room, and Ingrid supposed she might be as fascinated by mirrors if she were as beautiful as the Master.

'What can I do for you?' she asked.

He still didn't look at her. 'I want to make sure none of you have mentioned Sam and Stella's mission to my son.' He waved a hand towards his bed. 'Pass me that towel.'

Ingrid grabbed it. 'No, sir, of course not – you told us not to.'

His emerald eyes instantly snapped on to hers in the reflection. 'Of course not?' he repeated.

'We would never disobey you.'

Claude hummed to himself. 'Good,' he said at last. 'Because I've received word from them. They've made contact with the little pest and apparently she's so desperate for friends that she'll believe anything they say. Sad really.'

Images of Eleanor Wolfson flashed through Ingrid's mind. All this time she'd been focused on the rosy-cheeked blonde girl who had constantly got in Leviathan's way. She'd never realized that the real princess was the girl with the sword skills – the one with the rogue smile and a storm in her eyes. To think that she was now diminished, dressed up pretty and trying to please, it felt back to front.

'That is sad.' The words escaped Ingrid before she could stop them, and she blinked in confusion, not even sure where the sentiment had come from. She quickly passed it off. 'Pathetic even.'

Thankfully Claude was too focused on his hair. 'I'm sure you've noticed how magnificent my son is.' His mouth curled almost teasingly, making Ingrid nearly blush. 'But he cares too much about every small, insignificant thing.' Ingrid flinched, suddenly seeing herself in those words, and she prayed the Master didn't notice how uncomfortable this conversation was making her. 'I fear he will not be able to see the bigger picture, and it's important none of you upset him.' Then Claude sighed, a deep melancholy sound that instantly pulled Ingrid back.

She took a hesitant step further into the room.

Claude turned, giving her a perfect view of his soft features. With the lights on either side of the mirror behind him, the glow reflected off the black silk covering his shoulders like wings, and she remembered why she had sworn to follow him anywhere.

'Ingrid –' she basked in the sweet sound of her name in his voice – 'he needs to be able to rely on you to handle the nastier parts of our plan.' Claude tilted his head slightly. 'Can you do that for me?'

Ingrid nodded. There were a million things she wanted to say to assure him of her loyalty, but she swallowed them down. Leviathan's loyalty to Claude was silent, and shown in actions, not words. 'Yes, of course. You can always count on Leviathan, Master.'

Claude chuckled, as if at a private joke, and turned back to the mirror. 'Wonderful. I can always rely on you, Ingrid. You're the most resilient of them.'

The compliment, like a hook, reeled her right back in. She beamed. 'Thank you, Master.'

'You're welcome, Ingrid. Goodnight.'

Ingrid quickly left the room, but wandering back down the silvery corridor to her room her knees trembled and it had nothing to do with the cold. The Master had praised her. Normally she'd have run to Haru's room to wake him up and shout the news in his face. Only tonight she didn't want to. The word played over and over again in her head. *Resilient.* Every syllable pressed on something inside her that ached at the touch.

She should have been happy, but instead she felt unsure of herself. It wasn't true. Another person had called her something else entirely. Jamie had said she was delicate – and she had no idea whether the Master or her prince was right.

8

When Lottie had first stepped inside Professor Devine's quarters in her initial term at Rosewood Hall, the circumstances hadn't exactly been positive. It was almost laughable now to think that her biggest fear back then had been expulsion for sneaking into the kitchen in the middle of the night. So much had happened since.

Now she was ahead in all her classes, and even had a detailed chart of the universities and courses she was applying to. With an approved request for early examinations, it was safe to say Lottie knew what she was doing. So it was hard to find any reason for her to be in a careers meeting at all. Especially when she had more important things to worry about – such as how on earth she was going to get her hands on an invitation to the Golden Flower Festival.

Oblivious, the professor smiled. 'Just a moment.'

Lottie had never considered herself impatient; she was usually the exact opposite. There was, however, no possible way that Professor Devine could pour a cup of tea any slower.

'Here you are, Miss Pumpkin.' The professor held out a brimming teacup with a manicured hand, the nails painted lilac to match her house colours.

With a purple rose brooch placed proudly on her lapel, Professor Devine looked immaculate in a tailored red skirt suit. She had the poise of a ballet dancer, with short hair dyed a red as bright as the intelligent glint in her eyes. The professor was practically perfect to Lottie – other than her slowness with a teapot. Lottie told herself not to tap her foot as Professor Devine began painstakingly preparing another cup.

There was a languid elegance to the professor's quarters, with its plum-velvet sofa, the crackle of burning apple wood in the marble fireplace, and the rhythmic tinkle of a spoon swirling Darjeeling in a Ginori teacup. Lottie had learned enough in her princess training to recognize the understated expense of every item.

At last the meeting began.

'You've decided on King's College as your first-choice university – wonderful. But it appears from your teacher's midterm reports that you're currently months ahead of schedule.'

Lottie wasn't sure how to explain that she was trying to get all her work done as early as possible so she had more time to focus on saving the most important people in her life from Leviathan's royal conspiracy – a conspiracy that she had yet to figure out. Instead she took a sip of tea and meekly said, 'University applications are competitive.'

The teacup paused in front of the professor's mouth, leaving Lottie unable to read her expression. 'Indeed.'

Lottie waited another minute while the professor took up a pair of silver tongs and eased a sugar cube out of an antique pot to place in her tea. 'Ms Kuma says you've chosen

"Little Briar Rose" as your main coursework text – a perfect choice for you. And how is your research going?'

Lottie had told herself not to believe in fairy tales any more, and never to rely on them, so she was unable to explain why she'd chosen this particular text. She could say it was a tactical choice, because she knew it would be the easiest way for her to get a good grade, but that would be a lie. The truth was she'd given in to that tingling fascination, even though she knew it made her as foolish as a donkey following a carrot on a string. Old habits truly did die hard.

'I already have the texts I need,' Lottie replied, trying to mirror some of the professor's enthusiasm so as not to alarm her. She knew from experience that Professor Devine picked up on every small detail.

Leaning forward for a slice of Battenberg cake, Lottie caught a glimpse of a wayang golek puppet on the wall behind the professor; it was a refined character with a white face and golden headpiece, its long thin arms rigid at its side. It was another thing Lottie recognized from her knowledge of folklore and storytelling, and the puppet looked down on her. In the world of puppets and stories, this was the equivalent of royalty, and Lottie felt at once small and humble under its gaze.

'Now I understand your circumstances have recently changed,' the professor said, abruptly changing the subject, 'and it appears your new emergency contact has been updated to Mrs Fae . . .' The professor cleared her throat. 'I'm sorry, Miss Pumpkin, I have to ask, are you covered financially for any future endeavours you may pursue?

University housing, living expenses – there's a lot to consider, but we can help you with –'

'I'm covered financially.' The last thing Lottie wanted was for her teachers to worry about her unnecessarily.

The professor was obviously taken aback. 'Oh, of course you are, after – Yes, of course.'

Lottie sank back into the sofa. It was suddenly abundantly clear that every teacher at Rosewood had been avoiding the topic of Lottie's Portman arrangement – and, more specifically, what had happened to Ellie and Jamie.

Professor Devine placed her teacup and saucer down on the table with an expensive rattle of china. 'Lottie . . .' Lottie was surprised to hear her first name; teachers never addressed pupils in this way. 'Let me be frank. We are all impressed with how focused you've managed to stay, considering what you've been burdened with. Your strength and dedication are remarkable – a true example of the pillars our school is built on.'

Lottie opened her mouth to speak but was halted by the professor holding a finger in the air.

'What I'm trying to say, Lottie, is that you are meant to be at this school. You belong here. No matter the circumstances; don't forget that.'

Sure her face must have gone as red as an apple, Lottie found her voice. 'Thank you. I am very lucky to have had such amazing opportunities. I promise I won't waste them.'

The professor batted away her thanks. 'No, no, my dear, you misunderstand. I'm not asking for gratitude.' She almost sounded exasperated. 'There is something compelling about you and this school. I've worked here nearly thirty years and I can say with confidence I've never seen anything like it.'

Lottie lowered her eyes. Fairy tales, lost princesses, Rosewood – they were all part of her.

'It would take a fool not to notice the connection,' the professor went on. 'I'm sure you know more about it than you will admit. But what does confound me is how you seem to ignore it.' She gave Lottie a pointed look, and Lottie wondered if she was seeing William Tufty in her image.

There was a painting of the school founder in the headmaster's office, but no one appeared to know he was really Princess Liliana, Lottie's distant relative. If the professor had recognized the same noble profile in each of them, she didn't elaborate.

'You know, I can tell exactly what type of mood you're going to be in, simply by looking at the flowers in the grounds – it is most peculiar. If the roses flourish, I know you're happy. If the hyacinth bow their heads, I know you're sad. You're connected.'

Lottie nearly choked on her tea. It was her instinct for fairy tales again. It was even in the question she'd chosen for her essay: how the royalty is linked to the grounds they inhabit. As Liliana's only known relative, Rosewood was Lottie's by blood. Could these myths be more than superstition?

Jamie's ring suddenly seemed to burn, and the pain sparked another memory, something Hanna and Midori had said when they had entrusted it to her.

After he was born, the gardens grew wild. The queen mother stopped bringing people in to tend them.

'Is something the matter?' said the professor, peering at her.

'No, it's just something you've said,' Lottie mumbled, trying to keep face. 'It reminded me of a book I wanted to get for my English research.'

This seemed to please the professor. 'Well, then, I won't keep you; it seems you're on top of everything.'

Lottie jumped up, already halfway to the door when Professor Devine called her back. 'And, Miss Pumpkin.'

They were back to formalities, it seemed.

'Yes, professor?' With her hand on the doorknob, Lottie turned, and was immediately frozen in place by Professor Devine's serious expression.

'Don't forget what brought you to Rosewood.' The professor spoke with measured tones, as though every word counted. She kept Lottie fixed in her level stare. 'Don't ever forget who you are.'

Then she broke the spell with a dazzling smile. 'That is all.'

Wandering through the horseshoe curve of Ivy House's halls, Lottie pondered what Professor Devine had said. *Don't ever forget who you are.*

But Lottie was starting to wonder if she'd ever known. All she knew was that without Ellie, and without Jamie, nothing was the same.

It was mid-evening, after dinner, with most students in their rooms. The professor's words seemed to linger in the air like the smell of damp lavender, as Lottie turned into the common room to find it dark and empty. Sunset was coming earlier and earlier with the approaching winter. As she headed for the door, her vision snagged on what looked like a ghost in the window – a white flash in the glass that made her jump. She froze and took a tentative step back before giving a sigh of relief. It was nothing more than her own reflection.

The two figures stared at one another. All of it was familiar – the wheat-coloured curls that hung around her shoulders, the summer-sky blue of her eyes, round pink cheeks, sturdy legs, her purple tartan pinafore that showed she belonged at Rosewood Hall and in Ivy House. Yet something was wrong; an important part was missing. No, not something, someone.

Ellie.

A voice from somewhere deep in her mind whispered her princess's name, but it didn't click, as if her own reflection were telling her she'd got it wrong.

Leaning forward, she came so close to the glass that her breath made angel wings of condensation. The reflected image flickered and Lottie felt certain that *Liliana* had been there – just for a split second – before she had blinked and the vision had flown away. It had been her ancestor – and she'd looked furious. The fiery fury of a rogue princess.

Lottie rubbed her eyes and let out a cry when she looked back. There was a new face pressed up against the other side of the cold glass. Not a vision or a reflection, but an actual person watching Lottie peering at herself. Staring at Lottie with her tongue playfully stuck out was Binah. Then Anastacia and Saskia appeared beside her, all three of them gesturing for her to go outside.

'It's so cold,' Saskia moaned, hiding her face inside her puffy coat the moment Lottie stepped out into the Ivy House garden.

'Unseasonably so, particularly in correlation with the recent annual weather patterns,' Binah added, rubbing her mittened hands together. 'How was your meeting?'

The four girls headed towards the benches overlooking the pond where the Ivy mascot Ryley stood proudly in bronze, his antlers glistening with an icy sheen that sparkled in the lantern light.

'It was fine,' Lottie said distractedly, as they sat down.

There was a strange intensity between Lottie's friends, and if they'd come to her dorm this close to curfew, there had to be a reason – a bad reason. She turned to the only one she knew wouldn't beat around the bush. 'Ani, give me the bad news.'

Anastacia flipped a lock of chestnut hair over her shoulder, her long red nails expertly avoiding her fluffy earmuffs.

'Well,' she began, and Lottie immediately knew her suspicions were right, 'the twins got their GFF invites, with plus-ones, so they're covered, as well as Percy.' It took Lottie a second to realize 'GFF' was an abbreviation for the Golden Flower Festival, but she quickly caught up. Anastacia talked in a rush, as though she just wanted to get everything out. 'And so did I, so that's me and Saskia, and, even though they haven't accepted an invite before, we assume Binah's parents will have invites again, seeing as they're, like, you know, the most important medical professionals of all time.'

Binah leaned forward with a grin, oblivious to the cloud of dread forming over Lottie. 'Muma already said I can have hers!'

Swallowing hard, Lottie had the crushing realization that the Wolfsons had invited everyone to the Golden Flower Festival. Every single person . . . except her.

Lottie glanced out over the pond and willed herself not to cry, but the scene only reminded her of the huge frozen pond in the gardens of Wolfson Palace, where Ellie had once promised to teach her to ice skate.

'But there's also good news,' Binah chirped, pulling Lottie out of her daze.

When Lottie turned back to the others, an uncomfortable look had settled over Saskia's face. It gave Lottie the strangest sense of déjà vu. Then it hit her – it was the look she'd shared with Anastacia a few weeks ago. They were hiding something.

Anastacia nodded, and Lottie realized she was about to be let in on a secret.

Saskia let out a great sigh. 'Speaking of mums,' Saskia began, then she abruptly stopped and turned to her girlfriend. 'Do I have to?' she moaned.

'Yes,' Anastacia said flatly.

Saskia let off a string of fiery words in Portuguese then in French, which Anastacia rolled her eyes at.

'Fine, OK. The truth is, I actually have another plan for getting in touch with the Wolfsons.'

Lottie's eyes widened, a spark of hope reigniting inside her. 'Saskia, that's amazing.' She was almost giddy. 'What is it?'

With another great huff, Saskia turned to Lottie, her face screwed up like she'd just eaten a lemon. 'I can ask for you to have an official meeting with the Partizan council and they can warn them for you.'

Lottie didn't see what was so bad about that, until Saskia added, 'But it means I'll have to speak to someone high up in the Partizan rankings – someone I haven't spoken to in nearly five years.' She took a deep breath. 'My mother.'

9

Growing up in an ancient palace, you become immune to the haunted atmosphere left by generations of royalty: the way the wind moans through the hallways and the dust settles on your skin like ghostly fingerprints. The only time Ellie really became aware of how cold and creepy Wolfson Palace could be was on the rare occasion someone new was invited inside the usually private areas. The family dining room in particular had a collection of antique Sèvres porcelain, which rattled like a haggard cough whenever the doors were opened or closed.

It wasn't something Ellie would usually notice, but tonight she wasn't dining alone in her room, avoiding her parents like she usually did. Tonight she was lodged in the middle of the table between her mother and father, and they had guests.

Sam looked admiringly down at his plate, his teeth sticking out from under his top lip. 'This looks impeccable. You must send our regards to your chef.'

'Thank you again for inviting us into your home, Your Majesty,' Stella said in a sing-song voice, expertly picking up the correct fork to begin tucking into her Wagyu tartare.

Home. Ellie could have laughed. There was nothing homely about the palace. She couldn't remember the last time she'd sat for dinner with her family. Too much had been left unspoken since learning Claude was Jamie's father and that they'd kept him as her Partizan as a sick sort of punishment. Her resentment and frustration clung to them like a bad smell.

Ellie took a bite of her food, eyes locking on to Stella who gave her a reassuring grin, her braces glinting in the gloomy atmosphere.

From where he sat at the head of the table, trapped in dim mauve light and still as death itself, Ellie's father looked more like one of the cloistered ornaments they had on display. Situated at his side like a guard dog stood his Partizan Nikolay, whose great size only further highlighted the king's delicate appearance.

'It's our pleasure,' King Alexander intoned. 'We're glad to see Eleanor making the right kind of friends.' His thin lips pulled up into a half-smile that made Ellie's chest lurch.

In reality there was very little that Jamie and King Alexander had in common appearance-wise, but ever since she'd found out Jamie was her cousin she'd see it sometimes. It was in the way her father's tawny hair would kink at the edges, never quite tameable, or the way he left behind the faint trace of cinnamon wherever he went. Worst of all, she could see it in that smile – the inescapable Wolfson half-smile.

At the other end of the table, dressed entirely in white silk like a ghost bride, Ellie's mother took a large sip of her Muscadet. 'Eleanor tells us you two have really been helping her fit in.'

Ellie's dishwater-blonde mane that was so uncharacteristic of the Wolfson lineage was incomparable to her mother's, whose hair was soft and yellow like butter. The only thing they really had in common was their skinny, board-flat bodies. While Ellie owned hers with boyish conviction, her mother was slight in an elven way, as if someone had taken the very essence of femininity and bottled it up in the form of Matilde Wolfson. She was everything Ellie needed to be and, like her father, it made her hard to look at. Her feminine grace sent a pang through Ellie – an aching pain that was unmistakably shaped like Lottie.

Just as Ellie felt that being this close to her parents would cause her to explode, Stella piped up again.

'She's being modest. If anything we should be thanking Ellie.' The pre-prepared lie rolled so easily off Stella's tongue that even Ellie forgot that what she was saying was a complete fabrication. 'Before she came to St Agnus's there was a lot of childish squabbling between the children of the noble families and she's really brought everyone together.'

'Really?'

Ellie tried not to take offence at the disbelief in her father's voice.

'Oh yes. Ellie's an incredible mediator,' Sam said, chiming in.

Ellie nearly choked on a large chunk of tartare as her parents turned to her in unison. 'Uhh . . .' This was it. She just had to say something, anything to persuade her parents she was thriving at school, that she was responsible enough to have a party – a party to help her prove that she really did belong at St Agnus's.

Stella's eyebrow twitched and her eyes widened, urging Ellie on.

'You know me,' Ellie chuckled unconvincingly. 'I love to mediate. Mediating? Love it. It's the best. Just call me Miss Mediator.'

Sam stared at her in disbelief, shocked by how entirely useless her response had been.

Stella interjected with a perfectly timed fake laugh, covering her mouth with her hand as she giggled. 'See? She's such a tonic, and always making these little jokes. We adore her.'

Across the table, Alexander and Matilde gave each other an uneasy look before Matilde put on one of her neutral smiles. 'Well, I'm glad people are seeing your charm, Ellie.' Her voice was like warm honey.

Ellie was confused for a moment and then she realized why. Her mother had called her Ellie. 'Thank you,' she replied, turning away from her mother. 'I'm really glad we made the decision for me to go to St Agnus's. You were right, and I'm really enjoying getting to know my people better.'

When Ellie looked up again, Sam nodded approvingly.

Stella sighed, making sure she had the king and queen's attention before she went on. 'It's a real shame Leo Gusev had to cancel his soirée because of his father's skiing injury,' she said. 'It would have been the perfect opportunity for us to cement our new-found friendship.'

The effect was instantaneous. Ellie could practically see the lightbulb turn on in her father's brain. He was a king after all. He knew how to win people over.

'Why don't you host some of your friends here, Eleanor?'

Stella's face was so smug that for a split second she looked conniving. But the impish grin was quickly dropped to be replaced with puppy-like excitement. 'Oh, Ellie! Everyone would love that so much.'

'A splendid idea, darling,' Matilde joined in. But Ellie could feel her icy-blue eyes on her, like she was waiting for her daughter to let something slip. Ellie had no idea what she was hoping to catch.

Ellie put on her best Lottie impression, rounding her cheeks as she looked at both her parents individually. 'Would you really let me?' she asked, trying to look demure.

'I think you've shown us you're responsible enough to host some of your school friends,' Alexander announced, and by the way the wrinkles around his eyes became deeper it seemed he was genuinely smiling. 'Perhaps you can visit your grandmother after our guests depart and tell her the good news.'

Ellie froze, her fork hovering in front of her mouth, and despite the lack of movement from anyone in the room the dishes on the mantel shook, the clinking sending a shiver through Ellie's bones.

'How is the queen mother?' Sam's voice was distant as Ellie sank deeper in her seat. 'We would love to pay our respects before we leave.'

Matilde gave her husband a look as gentle as a lullaby, and a million words were exchanged between them in the silence while Ellie continued to fall into panic. 'That will not be possible.'

'My mother is very sick,' Alexander explained, tilting back the last of his wine. 'She is not fit to receive external visitors, I'm afraid.'

Only Stella seemed to notice the change in Ellie, whose usually round eyes had narrowed into slits. 'Please send our best wishes.' Then she looked at Ellie, the subtle purse of her lips a wordless question.

Ellie only shook her head. This was not a conversation she was ready to have with anyone; she was hardly able to have it with herself.

To say Ellie's grandmother was sick was an understatement. The reality was far worse, and even though Ellie knew she'd have to confront it sooner or later it still made her breath catch when she thought of how such a scary, imposing woman could become so frail and confused. It was awful to see someone stripped of everything they were.

'This beef really is delicious,' Sam said emphatically, pulling Ellie from her thoughts and effortlessly turning the conversation. 'Where do you source it from?'

Alexander nodded his approval at the well-executed pivot in topic. 'The Wagyu is imported from Tokyo.'

'Ah yes, the meat trade deal your family orchestrated in 1988 continues to be beneficial for everyone.'

The king and queen made a pleased sound and the conversation continued. But with every bite of her food Ellie swallowed down the fears she had about facing her grandmother again.

By the time the twins left, Ellie hoped it would be too late to visit her grandmother.

She had no such luck. With little time to prepare herself, she found herself outside Willemena's quarters. Even through the thin gap under the door, Ellie could smell the thick stench of decay that they'd tried to cover up with bushels of dried lavender.

As she was about to knock, a hand came down over her shoulder gently enough not to startle her, and for a split second the smell was washed away by the sweet scent of clean linen.

'Eleanor,' her mother began. Apparently she was back to using her formal name.

When Ellie turned, her mother took a step back, as if blown away by Ellie's stare.

'I know it's hard for you,' Matilde began, her voice as soft as her alabaster skin, 'but it would mean a lot to your father that she sees you doing so well.'

Ellie absorbed her words, realizing with a start that her plan was working – she was actually convincing her parents that everything was OK.

Waiting until Matilde's footsteps had faded down the hallway, Ellie took a deep breath and knocked on her grandmother's door. Pushing her ear up to the door, Ellie heard a faint whimper of acknowledgement, followed by a small cough that let her know her grandmother was waiting for her.

The door creaked as it opened, groaning on its hinges as if the room itself was displeased that she had disturbed its stuffy dark sanctuary.

'Hello, Grandma,' Ellie said, letting the door shut behind her without stepping any further in.

Willemena had always loved the colour purple, and had filled her room with rich plum-velvet upholstery and lilac silks. Once it had been a statement of her royal blood, bold and elegant. But because of the lack of light the colour now seemed inky and muted, more like a bruise.

'Come closer, Eleanor,' Ellie's grandma said with a wheeze from where her small frame was propped up against a mountain of pillows, a Jane Austen novel on her lap. Ellie had heard that people liked to reread their favourite books when they didn't have long left to live.

'Can I bring you anything?' she asked as she approached.

'No, no, just yourself is fine.'

As Ellie stepped closer, Willemena reached out a shaky hand, the joints swollen under cracked skin, and turned up the dial on her lamp.

Illuminated in the milky light, Ellie's grandmother was an ancient being. Her skin was mottled and blistered like a pattern of rot, her lips split and dry, with thin wispy hair falling over her shrivelled body. Yet still she clung to life, despite being confused and unfocused, a withered semblance of the wolf that still barked somewhere behind her yellowing eyes.

'Look at you,' she marvelled, her breath sour. Her face softened. 'At last you are becoming the girl I need you to be.'

Ellie had spent so long hating this woman, and it was only now, at death's door, that she was getting an inch of her approval. All she'd had to do was be everything she wasn't.

'Father wanted me to tell you that I'm doing well at school.'

Willemena didn't appear to register Ellie's words, still admiring the dress-up-doll princess image Ellie had forced herself to wear.

'Yes, yes.' Willemena's voice cracked and she coughed, a nasty brittle sound, as if her insides were grating together.

'Wonderful. So pretty. So sweet.' There was a childish awe to her tone, and her eyes were murky and vague, as if she were not quite there.

'I'll let you rest now,' Ellie said gently, already desperate to leave.

It was as she approached the door, fingers curled on the ice-cold handle, that she heard it: soft mumbling from her grandmother like baby babble. It made her nauseous.

'My perfect little princess.'

10

In a palace filled with precious antiques and dusty corners, Ellie's rec room had always been the one place that was hers. The moment you stepped into the cavernous space beneath the palace, you were surrounded by the electric glow of neon lights, each of them twisted into clouds and thunderbolts that stuck like a kaleidoscopic storm to the ceiling. Lined with vintage rock and indie memorabilia, the walls were dedicated to the music and movies she'd found solace in. Most of the posters were signed by her idols and all of it was worth a small fortune. For Ellie the monetary cost was nothing compared to the way it felt to be surrounded by items owned by people who'd written scripts and music that felt as though they spoke directly to her. This room wasn't just hers; it *was* her. So nicknaming it the Vault had seemed appropriate – a reminder that the storm and fury that came naturally to her needed to be shut away. Which begged the question if she was trying so hard to keep up her princess image, why on earth had she thought the Vault would be a good place to host her party?

'A stairwell to a secret door?' A bleach-blonde girl who had a name like Camilla or Clarissa marched forward. 'This is a lot more ominous than I expected of the Maravish princess.'

'Christabelle!' called a voice. *That was it.* 'Wait for me and Yasmin! We can't do stairs in heels as well as you can.'

They were the first three to show up to Ellie's party – which was more of a small gathering – all in matching black and white and smelling of expensive perfume. They had arrived together in a painfully bright white car. Surprisingly it had been driven by the chestnut-haired girl Ellie had been caught admiring on her first day at school. For some reason she'd assumed every rich Maravish kid used chauffeurs.

Yasmin and Fumiko did a half-trot to catch up with Christabelle at the bottom of the stairs, and together they entered the Vault.

There was silence as the three girls took in the scene.

Fumiko let out a delighted squeal. 'You have enough controllers for a *Mario Kart* tournament!' she said, clapping. Her ebony hair bounced in flawlessly curled ringlets as she rushed over to the sofas at the other end of the room. Within moments she had the TV up and running.

Christabelle was the next to step into the room, a look of awe plastered on her Hollywood-beautiful face. 'Is that a real vintage popcorn machine?' she asked, not bothering to hide her wonder. 'Can we turn it on? Oh my God!' She turned on the spot, taking in the rest of the room. 'This whole place is a collector's dream.'

Ellie couldn't help grinning. She'd only ever had her family and Lottie in this room. To discover that other people actually liked this stuff – liked *her* stuff – was warm and exciting in a way she hadn't felt since she'd lost Lottie and Jamie.

'Yes, everything works,' Ellie said modestly.

As she watched them explore the room, a whisper played over and over in her mind, the confused babble of her grandmother's words making her question her every step. *Perfect little princess.*

A hand came down over Ellie's shoulder, shocking her out of her daze. Her eyes met her classmate Yasmin's, brown, like tempered chocolate.

'This is so different to what I expected,' Yasmin said. 'I'm glad the twins persuaded us to come.' She gave a perfect smile. 'You know, I was worried you were planning to kill us and bury us under the palace.'

'Please,' Ellie chuckled, 'under the palace is already full – I'd have to keep you in the dungeon.'

Ellie was horrified with herself. How could she have let such a completely unprincessy joke slip out? Only Yasmin wasn't disgusted – she was laughing.

'Maybe I wouldn't mind being held captive if it was by you.'

Ellie's mouth fell open. Had this girl just flirted with her?

'I was curious,' Yasmin interjected, pushing a silky strand of mahogany hair behind her ear. 'Are you still in touch with your Portman? You guys must have had a pretty intense relationship.'

There was something unspoken in her words, and Ellie knew that what she really meant was 'Do I have any competition?'

This was not territory Ellie was comfortable with. 'I'm not in touch with her,' she said simply, trying not to let her pain seep into her expression.

A practised socialite, Yasmin caught on quickly, effortlessly turning the conversation back to something lighter. 'Can you play any of those?'

Ellie followed Yasmin's gaze up to the wall of signed guitars. Her trophies. She nodded and turned back to her, already sensing the next question.

'Would you play for us before the others arrive?'

Ellie couldn't stop her lips spreading in a wide smile, wild energy coursing through her – the same energy that made her a terrible princess.

In the back of her mind she could hear her grandmother's words again, but she squashed them down. Ellie smirked. 'Since you asked so nicely.' *Oh my goodness! Am I flirting back?*

Her most prized possession was a guitar owned and signed by Joan Jett. She carefully took it down from the wall, and when Ellie's fingers met the strings she felt the vibration like lightning through her bones. Everything flooded back to her on instinct – connecting the guitar to an amp, the position of her fingers, the hum from the feedback like a deep tender sigh.

This isn't the behaviour of a good princess, she told herself. *This isn't how Lottie would behave.* And then that's all she could think.

Lottie.

Lottie.

Lottie.

She struck the first chord – loud and perfect.

'Woo!' Fumiko appeared from over the sofa, her hand forming little devil horns, but Ellie hardly noticed; her fingers found every chord as though she were searching for a hand to hold.

92

Floating up from a hungry part of her, the melody slipped from her mouth as she conjured up the first verse to a song by one of her favourite bands.

> 'You grew over me, like moss climbs a tree.
> Twisted roots on rainy days and smiling as we pulled away
> . . . Please take my hand run with me.
> Don't look back; come with me –'

Ellie's eyes shot open, the song drying up in her mouth as she took in the sight in front of her. To her extreme mortification the rest of the party had arrived and heard her song.

The amp made a harsh screeching sound and the image of Lottie vanished, the sweet melody replaced by her grandmother's words. This was not the behaviour of her perfect little princess. She was embarrassing herself, and putting shame on the family. How could she be so selfish?

'Nooo! Don't stop!' Yasmin pouted from where she sat cross-legged a few metres away. 'You guys have gotta hear this. Ellie's music! It's so . . . unexpected.'

Gulping down her mortification, Ellie took in the six new arrivals, including the twins. Pushing back a strand of hair, it all came rushing back. Her hair wasn't black any more; it was blonde. And, just like that, she was back to being a princess.

'Ellie, can we speak with you for a moment?' Stella said, fixing Ellie with a serious questioning look.

While the rest of the party greeted one other, Ellie headed over to the twins.

'What are you doing?' Stella squeaked.

'We arranged this for you, convinced your parents to let you have it, and persuade all these people to give you a shot – and you what? Burst into song? Are you a performing monkey now?' Sam looked as if he were somewhere between laughter and screaming.

Ellie tried to look as apologetic as possible. 'I know how it looks; it's just they really seemed to like it and –'

'Don't be so naive,' Stella interrupted. 'They're *humouring* you. You're their princess and they're in your palace. They're not going to tell you that they find it cringe.'

Ellie had rarely been made to feel so entirely stupid. As if on cue, she heard the distinct hoot of Yasmin's laughter. When she looked up, sure enough, Yasmin was looking right at her from across the room. *What would Lottie do?* she asked herself for the hundredth time.

Taking a deep breath, Ellie put her mask back on, allowing her face to settle in an approximation of the serene expression that came so naturally to Lottie. 'OK,' she said at last. 'Let's stick to the plan. You're right. Thank you.'

It was almost physically painful for Ellie to so graciously admit she was wrong, and she felt like she deserved some princess points for that alone.

Stella shook her head in disappointment – but then her expression changed back into its usual toothy grin. 'Good. And, by the way, we asked your maids to bring down the refreshments because we knew you'd forget.'

Ellie didn't know which bit to be more offended by – the fact they'd ordered the house staff around, or the fact they were completely right.

'You just stick with us and look pretty, and, you know, try not to say too much.'

Ellie narrowed her eyes at Sam, her instincts telling her to rip him to shreds, but when she tried to focus on that rage all she found was defeat.

Pretty, sweet, perfect little princess – that's what she was meant to be, and the twins had every right to be mad at her. She'd let them down and made a fool of herself. 'OK,' she mumbled.

There was a sigh of relief. 'Great.'

The twins grabbed a hand each and dragged Ellie over to the sofas where most of the party had congregated round the TV and game console. Some of them were scooping up handfuls of popcorn and candyfloss that they'd got from the vintage machines.

Soon after, Midori arrived with food and drinks for their guests, laying everything out with only a discreet nod of encouragement for Ellie.

With a soft hiss, the door to the Vault eased shut, leaving Ellie to face her guests.

I can do this, she told herself. *I can totally be a princess. How hard can it be?*

For the next hour the twins whispered instructions in Ellie's ear: what to say, how to lose games, laugh at the boys' unfunny jokes, which drink to take. Most importantly, she avoided Yasmin's flirty glances. *Princesses don't flirt.*

None of it was fun.

The party dragged on and Ellie felt like a doll in a doll's house, looking out at the real world while she was stuck forever pretending.

At some point the room started to get hazy.

'You need to eat and drink more,' Stella cooed in her ear. Ellie was grateful that at least someone had noticed. 'You look tired – and it encourages your guests to eat more too.'

'Yes, I'll eat more,' Ellie said on autopilot, taking a plate of party food that Sam held out. Was it Sam? Or was it Stella? It was getting hard to tell; they were both so similar, both so demanding and controlling. Both so entirely sure that they knew what was best.

When she next glanced up from her almost empty plate, the party seemed to have descended into mayhem. Glasses were left overturned, bottles were broken into jagged shards where they'd fallen to the floor, and her guests had become a hazy mass of bodies, tripping over themselves and the furniture as if they were fawns learning to walk.

Ellie was aware of indelicate fingers playing roughly with her prized possessions, and she knew she should tell them to be careful, but something numbed her mind.

How long had they been down there? Was she having fun? Maybe this was *normal*?

As Ellie took another bite of food, a strange smell caught in her nose, conjuring a memory she knew was important if only she could find it in this haze. What was it? It was sweet and sickly, like baby powder.

Ellie burst out laughing at her own mind, but suddenly she couldn't remember what was so funny.

'Drink,' a voice whispered in her ear, and so – yet again – Ellie did as she was told. Ellie had grown very used to taking orders, even from these strange new twins. Because that's what a princess did, wasn't it? Exactly as she was told . . .

11

With the bitterly cold climate, saunas were a staple of most Maravish households. They were also one of the few private places in the open-plan safe house, which meant that Jamie found himself spending more and more time there after using the pool or the gym.

Sinking into the hot steam, Jamie softened into the bench, trying to make his mind melt in the same way. He wanted to let the heat match the wild fire inside him until he was numb to it.

Don't think of Lottie. Don't think of Lottie.

That's all he had to do, and it was easier when he felt dazed from the heat.

The routine was deeply meditative. Usually he could hear someone swimming laps in the pool beyond the door. Occasionally Haru joined him, and they'd sit in awkward sweaty silence. Sometimes he'd find himself so lost in the lonely warmth that enough time would pass for Phi to come and make sure he hadn't collapsed. The sauna was becoming his second home. So when he heard a splash from the pool he was pulled out of his trance.

Instincts kicking in, Jamie rushed to the pool, slamming into the cool air like being violently woken from a dream.

There was a blurred shape at the bottom of the pool, no more than a smudge, but he knew straight away what it was – a body. Not even pausing to think, he dived into the water.

Through the water the blur began to clear and the shape morphed into Julius. The moment Jamie touched him, his eyes flew open, locking directly on Jamie's with an almost irritated look until he realized who he was looking at.

Reaching under Julius's arms, Jamie tried to haul him up to the surface, but he wouldn't budge. It was then he noticed the chain curled round his ankle, a sinister black weight anchoring Julius to the bottom like a kraken pulling down its prey. Diving down, Jamie untwisted the chains. When that didn't work, he grabbed the weight itself, clenching his teeth as he engaged every muscle to lift it up. Bubbles bursting from his mouth, Jamie pulled both Julius and the weight out of the water, ignoring the pain that screamed at him as he dragged them both over the ledge of the pool.

'Are you injured?' Jamie asked, noting that Julius was still conscious.

Julius shook his head before vomiting over the tiles.

Jamie untangled the chain and began moving Julius into a recovery position, careful not to aggravate anything that might be damaged.

But to Jamie's bafflement the other Partizan broke out in a soft chuckle, rolling himself over to get up on his feet again.

'I see you remember the drowning-and-recovery part of our training,' he said, as though nothing out of the ordinary had happened.

Julius was laughing, the sound like a rattlesnake, while holding out a hand to Jamie. He took it, and the two of them stood face to face, their fractured reflections bobbing in the pool water.

With his confident swagger, Julius had all the square-jawed strawberry-blond good looks of a high-school quarterback from the kinds of movies Lottie loved and Ellie loved to hate. Now Julius was split down the middle; the right side of him was still as sharp as a cut diamond and smiling like a crocodile, while the left side, the side he tended not to lean on, was different. His right eye was the crystal of a blue sea, but the prosthetic on the left was a little darker, like he'd swum into a deeper part of the ocean. Somehow it suited him. His left arm was the other noticeable change, with three distinct silver scars from his wrist to his shoulder. They were a souvenir of his car crash in Tokyo, when he had been chasing down Lottie, mistakenly believing her to be the princess.

'What happened?' Jamie asked, and he worried that Julius would think he was asking about the damage to his body. Jamie knew full well that Saskia was the cause of his missing eye.

'Frustration,' Julius drawled, sauntering off to the edge of the pool. 'I was hoping a minute at the bottom of this here pool might kickstart my adrenaline.' He nodded down to the black mass of chain and anchor on the floor. 'Thought I might be able to pull that weight out if my life depended on it.'

'Sounds like self-destructive behaviour,' Jamie said frankly.

Julius smirked. 'That it does.'

There was something odd about the way they were conversing, something Jamie couldn't put his finger on, until Julius jumped back into the water, the great rippling splash sending droplets all the way up to Jamie's face.

Julius didn't speak to him like a prince. There was no pomp, no admiration and no devotion. Frankly it was a relief, so Jamie jumped in after him.

'What are you so frustrated about?' Jamie asked as they both began treading water in the deep end. He wasn't usually one for interrogation, but he felt partially responsible for Julius. They were on the same team now, and Jamie took care of his own.

Julius flicked his hair back and gave a smile that didn't quite reach his eyes. 'This beat-up arm doesn't always do what I want it to.'

'You need to do the right physio,' Jamie said on autopilot, and Julius immediately laughed again, taking off in a back stroke.

'What do you think I'm trying to do right now?'

Jamie was about to reply when the door opened and in walked the most unlikely pair.

'And if I beat you, which I will –' Ingrid was red in the face, while Haru sauntered along beside her – 'then you have to swap rooms with me –'

She cut herself off as she spotted Jamie and Julius.

'Why do you want to swap rooms so bad, Ingrid?' Julius called over, mischief tugging at the edges of his smile.

'What are you doing here?' she practically screeched at Julius, but Jamie was too focused on Haru to care about her question. Jamie knew that look; he was planning something.

A spark lit up Haru's dark eyes and he clapped his hands together. 'If there's four of us here, why don't we play a different game?'

Haru beamed at Ingrid, and it was like looking at the human equivalent of toothpaste and orange juice – two things that absolutely did not go together.

'This isn't a game!' Ingrid said angrily. 'I'm going to prove I'm a better swimmer than you, whether you like it or not.'

Haru wasn't even looking at her any more; he had already turned his summery smile back to Jamie.

Julius tilted his head. 'What did you have in mind?'

Haru's expression turned dark, his smile turning sly, and Jamie knew there was no getting out of whatever he had in mind. Maybe it would be a chance to build bridges with Julius and Ingrid. And that's how Jamie found himself balancing on top of Haru's shoulders, the two of them squaring off against Ingrid and Julius, in a game Haru had explained was called Water Chicken.

Jamie glared down at Haru beneath his legs. 'You knew I was here, didn't you?'

'I hoped,' Haru replied, his freckled face a mask of innocence.

Jamie was acutely aware of the way Haru held his thighs, a supportive squeeze reassuring him that he would not let him fall.

'Well, this isn't fair!' Ingrid hissed the moment she was on Julius's shoulders, the two of them making a surprisingly natural and sturdy unit even if they were about a head shorter.

Without missing a beat, Haru looked up at her. 'Would you prefer to be on Jamie?'

Ingrid glanced away angrily. 'No.'

She still appeared to hate him then.

Jamie glanced at Julius, thinking of the way his arm had trembled. There was determination there, a need to prove himself.

'I think Julius and Ingrid can handle themselves,' Jamie said assuredly, meeting Julius's eyes briefly.

Haru began the countdown, ignoring Ingrid's protests that she wasn't ready.

'Five, four, three . . .'

At one, a demon took over their opponents. Ingrid's tantrum melted away into focus and it almost looked as if she and Julius had melded into an impenetrable wall of human skin. It was unnerving to say the least, and that was even before they charged forward to attack.

The rules were simple – knock your opponent into the water – and if Ingrid and Julius were taking it seriously, then so would Jamie.

Ingrid moved to grab Jamie's dominant wrist, pouncing as fast as a feline.

Haru didn't waver; he angled himself sideways so Ingrid's hand went flying past him. Any normal person would have overshot and tumbled into the water, but Ingrid and Julius were ready, instantly matching Haru's stance so Ingrid could block Jamie's oncoming left hand with an elegant flick of her wrist.

Jamie couldn't help being impressed, even as his hand went gliding upwards, leaving himself open for Ingrid to attempt a chest push.

'I'm not losing again,' Ingrid snapped, pulling her arms back and ready to deal the final blow. Julius smirked from underneath her.

Everything happened in slow motion as Ingrid's hand fanned out, a monstrous crab formed of fingers ready to plough into his chest.

The playful battle triggered a long-buried memory in Jamie. Suddenly he wasn't at the pool. He was a child, deep in the gardens outside the palace where trees grew like giants around him, where his hands were muddy and smelled of the earth, and the air was metallic from panting and running. Before he was a prince, he'd been a boy. And, though he'd never known them as children, he saw it in Ingrid too, and Julius, and Haru beneath him; through the sting of the chlorine he could see all of them running through the woods, searching for a place to call home.

Ingrid's hands came crashing towards his heart, and he held them there, locked in place, sending the two of them flying together.

'No one has to lose,' Jamie whispered in the split second that they were floating, before they all crashed into the water.

Time seemed to stop under the water, as Haru and Ingrid stared at him through the storm of bubbles. Then, as if summoned by a call, all three swam to the surface together, breaking free at the same time.

Ingrid made a noise somewhere between a growl and a shriek, but the sound came out in hiccups, slowly turning into the oddest sound Jamie had ever heard. She was laughing. Not her usual cruel laughter but happy, real.

'There is a problem,' Haru said in that straightforward but pleasant way of his. 'Julius didn't get submerged.'

'Julius needs to be dunked too.' Ingrid spoke as if this were a matter of honour, and all of them turned on Julius with an impish glint in their eyes.

'Hey, now. Wait a second!' Backing away, Julius held his hands up, and then his expression darkened. 'You'll have to catch me first.'

They had made it halfway across the pool towards him when the sound of a throat clearing made them all turn round.

Standing at the edge of the pool, his black robe spilling out behind him like ink, was Claude. There was an affectionate look on his face as he took in the scene, but then it faded.

Phi stood behind him like a guard, but her broad shoulders were shaking, as if she were holding in a laugh, and Jamie wondered how much they'd seen.

'Looks like you're all having fun,' Claude said.

Despite his kindly expression, the pool seemed to turn cold at his words, and Jamie felt like he'd been caught doing something he shouldn't have. The others must have felt it too, because they all stood up straighter.

'I need to borrow you all, I'm afraid.'

They nodded in response, the joy they'd shared dissolving in the water. Claude was upset about something, and that meant they should be too.

Claude departed with a swirl of cloak, leaving Phi to give the orders.

'Lounge, twenty minutes.' After a pause, she addressed Jamie, her expression tempering ever so slightly. 'I'll make sure the housekeepers have something warm prepared for you to eat.'

Jamie could practically hear the unspoken 'my prince' at the end of her sentence and was grateful for the effort she was making. He nodded back an acknowledgment.

Phi didn't smile but her nose twitched, something Jamie had learned was the closest thing to pleasure she showed. It was taking some getting used to, that she found so much joy in serving him.

They changed quickly and headed to the lounge, Jamie arriving at the same time as the other boys. Claude, Phi and Ingrid were already there, his father sitting in the great winged armchair, leaning back into the ebony upholstery. It was hard to see where the chair ended and its occupant began.

There was a magazine open on the coffee table. Ingrid leaned over to avidly read an article, her damp hair dripping.

Jamie caught his father's gaze and Claude gave a short nod. Jamie looked back at Ingrid; her eyes had grown wide with either wonder or horror.

Jamie moved over to the table, Haru following.

It was a photo of a large chaotic room. Bodies moved about in a blur, dancing with abandon. Then he saw her – the girl he'd been sworn to protect – her arms splayed over two other teenagers, their jaws stretched wide in a noiseless cackle.

Ellie.

The name was poison in his mind and the picture a lethal dose. This confirmed his worst fears. Ellie didn't care. Ellie could never take responsibility. While Jamie had to face the horrors of his past, Ellie was laughing. *She's laughing at you.*

Jamie's hand tightened into a fist. How could he ever have thought that she'd changed?

It was an article by Aimee Wu, a name he knew well from her previous takedowns of Ellie.

Concerns rise for the future of Maradova!
Princess caught corrupting the children of the nobility!

He skimmed the story. Ellie had hosted a party that had got out of control, trashing part of the palace and pressing the other attendees into inebriation. It was unclear whether she'd spiked the drinks, but the article seemed to suggest so.

'Say the word, my son, and we'll bring her in.' Claude gave him a reassuring nod. He was talking about Lottie. 'The Portman will be kept safe, as far away from the princess as possible.'

'What?' Ingrid squawked. 'You can't bring the pumpkin in! She's too much trouble.'

There was a twitch in Claude's jaw, and when he finally spoke his words emerged in a low warning rumble. 'You do not speak on this,' he said. His eyes hadn't left Jamie's face. 'This is my son's choice.'

The room went still, waiting for Jamie to answer.

Jamie didn't trust Ellie not to go back for Lottie. None of them, except his father, could possibly understand.

He was being asked to make an impossible decision, to confront a truth he'd been avoiding. If he brought Lottie in, he could keep her away from Ellie and anyone else that might harm her. He could keep her safe – but he knew if he did that, she'd hate him. And the worst part, which he was loath to admit, was that he didn't mind if she hated him, as long as he could keep her close. That was why he couldn't think of her – not now – and why he couldn't say yes – not yet.

'We'll keep an eye on the situation,' Jamie said at last, avoiding his father's piercing emerald stare. 'If something else like this happens, then OK.' He took a deep breath. 'Then you can bring her to me.'

12

Every student at Rosewood had seen the article about Ellie; it was the current hot gossip. How exciting it was for people to know they'd been so close to such a bad girl. But for Lottie it was a nightmare to hear her friend's name whispered in corridors, to see her warped and defamed for fun. This kind of cruel vilification had Leviathan written all over it.

I know who you really are, Ellie, Lottie told herself, *and I'm going to save you.*

But first Lottie had to get well.

'*Atchoo!*' Sneezing into a pink hanky, Lottie cast an apologetic look around the library. This was her fifth sneeze since she'd sat down with Binah, and she couldn't blame the rest of the students for keeping a wide berth.

With her final piece of coursework handed in early, Lottie had flung herself into researching their only lead on Leviathan's plot: Alexis Wolfson. Scattered on the table in front of them were the open pages of every book they could find that mentioned the first Wolfson to claim the throne in Maradova, the saviour of the kingdom. There were only three tomes left to read, and so far they hadn't found anything interesting. Lottie was starting to doubt they'd find any clues to Claude's plan.

It was Ingrid who'd claimed Claude would be welcomed back to the Maravish kingdom *just like Alexis*, so how did he intend to do it? What was he going to do that would make everyone instantly love him as they had Alexis? What had been so special about Alexis? Stuck in this train of thought, Lottie sneezed once more.

'Bless you . . . again.' Binah slammed her book shut. 'You know, Sayuri told me that in Japan they have a superstition that says if you sneeze unexpectedly it means someone is either thinking about you or talking about you.'

Despite her cheerful explanation, Binah cleaned the next book that Lottie handed her with a sanitizing wipe, filling their booth with the smell of sterilized lemon.

Lottie was a living plague, and it wasn't just her cold. The gloom around her was as bitter and intense as the spreading frost. Blue shadows were forming beneath her eyes and it had only got worse since the article about Ellie had come out.

'And what if I can't stop sneezing?' Lottie asked.

Binah giggled. 'Then whoever's got you on their mind is in love with you. But the more important question is –' she casually opened the book at a random page – 'who did you think of when I said that?'

Ellie had flashed through Lottie's mind again. On instinct, she had grabbed the wolf pendant, but the cold metal only dug into her palm, cold and unforgiving. She hid her face inside her purple Ivy scarf. 'I just have a cold,' she said, sniffing, 'so can we please get back to work?'

Binah took the hint and they both returned their attention to the remaining books.

They were no more than a minute into reading when Binah huffed. 'Why is it called a flower festival in the first place?' she asked. 'Odd to call it such a thing in a kingdom that looks like *that* ninety per cent of the time.' Binah pointed at the window without looking up from her book.

Winter break was only a week away, and the early December days were some of the coldest they'd ever had. Lottie was glad to be hidden away in one of the library's nooks with a hot drink to sip and warm her hands on. She was less glad about having to go to sleep alone in her cold room that night, with nightmares about Jamie hovering nearby.

As his name popped into her head, Lottie turned a page to find a man staring back at her – someone who bore a remarkable resemblance to her friend. Beside him was a woman who looked almost the spitting image of Ellie. With bold and roguish expressions, the pair were painted in layers of expensive fabrics and furs, a fire roaring behind them that matched the blaze in their eyes. Strangest of all, they were surrounded by golden flowers – every one of them was alight and glowed as brightly as the flecks of starlight in Jamie's eyes.

Lottie's fingertips traced their faces – the angled brows, the familiar curve of their jaws and the bee-stung lips that teased a smile. These features had been passed down for hundreds of years and been gifted to Ellie and Jamie. But this wasn't Lottie's princess or Partizan – it was a rare painting of Alexis and his wife:

Figure Four: a portrait of King Alexis Wolfson and his wife Inessa Wolfson at the first Golden Flower Festival, originally named Inessa lov Zolotey Prohennya before Maradova adopted the English language (see Gibson's essay 'Facts and Fables: The Lost Folklore of Maradova').

'Inessa's awakening.' Lottie could taste the words on her lips.

'Who?' Binah closed her book.

'The GFF didn't used to be called that.' Lottie drew a careful finger below the lines of text. 'It was originally called Inessa's Golden Awakening.'

'Strange name.'

Lottie hummed thoughtfully. 'It was named after Alexis's wife it seems – and it sounds better in Maravish. It's just . . .'

Lottie felt her heart skip a beat. She recognized the feeling she'd shuddered away from; it was the one that had bloomed inside her when she'd read her English essay question – that prickle when she thought of Sleeping Beauty and the kingdom that fell asleep alongside her. She tried to hold on to the feeling, focusing on the ring's burn. It wasn't painful – more illuminating; it filled her mind with flowers she'd almost forgotten.

The words came out almost against her will. 'It's like "Little Briar Rose".'

Binah held Lottie's gaze, light glinting from her glasses. 'Which part?'

Lottie swallowed. 'I'd forgotten,' she began. 'In the first text I read last year – the one that helped me figure out the date for Leviathan's plan – it said the rumours *went so far as to declare that when Alexis seized the throne, flowers bloomed and the sun shone in Maradova for the first time in ten years.'*

Binah's eyes narrowed in understanding. 'And now this – Inessa's awakening,' she whispered. 'If the two go together, then that means she woke up and the flowers bloomed again.'

This time when Lottie shuddered it had nothing to do with the cold or the feelings she was trying to hide away from. She was afraid because she'd remembered something else.

'Hanna and Midori said there's a superstition –' Lottie felt her breath come out in a shudder – 'that the gardens have grown wild since Jamie was born.'

Simply saying his name brought about a wash of confusion. When she thought of him now it was as the rueful stag prince, antlers growing from his head in a bony crown. With every step he took into his kingdom, flowers came to life beneath him.

'Well!'

Lottie nearly jumped at Binah's exclamation.

'Whatever Claude is hoping to achieve at the ball, it's clear the answer is buried with Inessa. Perhaps fairy tales are more real than you thought.'

Lottie shook her head. 'I can't think like that any more.'

Binah quickly composed herself, hiding her disappointment. 'We'll ask the librarian if they can get us a copy of this Gibson essay, the facts and fables one.'

After the two girls had filled out a form to request the text, they ventured out into the unforgiving frost. The wind felt like it went deep into Lottie's bones.

'It's like the school is angry or something,' Binah grumbled, wrapping her coat round herself tightly and pulling her woolly hat lower down.

Lottie felt apologetic, remembering what Professor Devine had said about her connection to the school; she had suddenly thought the weather might be her fault.

'Why don't you come back with me and I'll make you one of my cold-curing drinks?' Binah suggested.

Lottie was about to reply with an enthusiastic 'yes' when someone called her name.

'Oh, thank God you're here.' Saskia was shivering and looking downright furious. 'The thought of having to look for you two in this weather makes me nauseous.' Saskia was definitely not a winter person.

Lottie groaned, holding back another sneeze. 'Please tell me it's good news.'

'It is!' Saskia said, beaming. 'You have approval to meet the Partizan council. We're going to Paris!'

This was good. This was progress, an actionable plan.

Lottie squealed, throwing her arms round Saskia, who went completely rigid. 'Thank you!'

'Whoa.' Carefully peeling Lottie off her, Saskia grimaced. 'You're welcome, but let's save the affection for when you're not a walking plague.'

Slinking backwards, Lottie laughed, covering her face with her scarf again.

'I've got to head back to Ani, but I'll catch you tomorrow to organize the travel arrangements, yeah?'

Lottie nodded, and they waved Saskia off.

Binah sighed. 'I wish I could come too, but I'm going to visit my cousins in Nairobi.'

Paris. Lottie could hardly control her excitement and she practically skipped up the steps of the Stratus tower. 'Paris,' she whispered, and the word felt like hope on her lips.

'I'll be right back,' Binah said a few moments later, leaving Lottie curled up in a corner of the common room to mull over the good news.

Through the arched window everything looked small and coated in a silken sheet of white. The cold no longer seemed bitter or cruel; it was calming. Things were finally looking up.

Smiling to herself, Lottie looked down at the newspapers scattered on the table, absently picking one up while she waited for Binah and her drink.

She soon wished she hadn't. Plastered across the page was a grisly black-and-white image of Ellie's grandma with a headline above it as simple as it was devastating:

WILLEMENA YELENA ANYA WOLFSON
DIES AGED NINETY-TWO

13

The tabloids said Willemena had died of shame, that she was so wounded by the dishonourable displays of her granddaughter that her heart had given out.

They were wrong – not that it mattered.

The queen mother hadn't heard anything of the news. She'd died peacefully in her sleep believing her granddaughter Eleanor was finally becoming the perfect princess she'd dreamed of.

Ellie wanted to be upset. That would be the appropriate response to having the final nail hammered down into the coffin of her reputation. But it was hard to concentrate on anything right now, not when the palace was filled to the brim with white lilies, now browning at the edges, the scent turning sour in the inhospitable cold. Even the mourning flowers were dying.

From where she was lying on the bed she could see the card of condolence Sam and Stella had sent sitting on the mantel. It was a trite little thing that stated *'thinking of you'* in sickening cursive.

She hadn't spoken to them since before her grandmother had died. Instead she found herself replaying her last conversation with them over and over, the one she'd been having just before the palace guards showed up at school. Just before the headlines broke about Willemena's passing.

The Rat Twins had been completely inconsolable.

'We're such idiots! We ruined everything!' Stella had wailed, pulling away from the crook of Ellie's neck.

Sam had chimed in, his face buried in his hands. 'This is all our fault. Everyone hates you now and thinks you tricked them.'

They were all Ellie had, and they were sorry, so Ellie had patted Stella's head and told her it wasn't her fault – that as the host she was the one who should have been paying more attention to the drinks.

In retrospect there was something odd about the whole situation. Ellie was supposed to be the one crying. Her character had been destroyed by one idiot's idea of a joke. And yet here she was comforting the people who had persuaded her to host the party in the first place.

Of course, the worst news had been yet to come. In some awful way she was glad Willemena had departed when she did, before she could see what a failure Ellie truly was, and even more selfishly because it meant Ellie had an excuse to stay out of school in the days leading up to winter break.

No one at school had spoken to her since the photo had emerged, and no one had come forward to admit they had spiked the drinks. As far as the St Agnus's student body was concerned, the rumours about her looking for blackmail leverage on other noble children was as good as fact.

Taking in a shaky breath, Ellie rolled over to face the ceiling. It was too early to go to sleep, the moon a strange blemish in the twilight sky, so she resigned herself to another lonely night with no one to talk to and nothing to distract her.

Staring down at her, a wooden Wolfson wolf guarded every poster of the bed, its teeth open in a permanent snarl. Only now the wolf wasn't her protector. She was trapped in its jaws, and she could almost hear it growl: *For everything you and your family have done – you deserve this.*

Ellie forced herself off the bed, deciding she needed a change of scenery.

Pushing on the door to her quarters, she was submerged in the candlelight from the hallway, only to be confronted with the last person she wanted to speak to. Her mother.

Sighing, Ellie stepped into the hallway and shut the door behind her.

Ellie's mother was perfectly framed among the heirlooms that decorated the hall – she was not a Wolfson by blood, but she held her ground with poise and elegance. 'Eleanor.' Her voice was as melodic as a siren. 'I was coming to find you.'

She came forward and it almost looked as if she were about to hug Ellie when she stopped short.

'I'm not in the mood for another lecture,' Ellie grumbled, barging past her.

'Eleanor, please. I just want to have tea with you. Can we do that?'

Hesitating, Ellie turned. The queen really did remind her of Lottie, that easy grace and enchanting set of her lips, but it was a hardened version of her carved from marble. It made sense that people had believed Lottie was her real child. Unfortunately for Ellie it only made her harder to look at. Squeezing her fists together, Ellie looked away. 'OK.'

Whatever had been wound tight inside Matilde visibly relaxed, her usual breezy elegance returning. 'Excellent. Come with me.'

Ellie followed the silken tail of her mother's gown through the echoing hallways filled with dust-blanketed antiques. Sometimes, when the light hit a certain way, the dust seemed to turn to ash and the palace looked as if it had been burned alive.

By the time they reached her mother's preferred reception room, Ellie had resigned herself to whatever speech Matilde had prepared. But when the door creaked open, light pooling over them in amber waves from the large bay window, Ellie had to catch her breath.

Above the fireplace, drenched in the evening sun, was a painting Ellie had forced herself to forget, a relic from her old life. With a more powerful reflection than any mirror, the portrait showed Ellie dressed in her pristine fencing gear with all the posture and charm of a true royal. At her side, long and sturdy, was a gold-handled rapier. Lottie had painted this. It was how she saw her princess – not pretty and sweet like her grandmother had wanted, but as a handsome and valiant prince.

'I hope you don't mind,' Matilde trilled as she sat herself down on the chaise longue. 'I simply loved Miss Pumpkin's painting so much.'

Tea had already been laid out for them on the chestnut coffee table in a shining white and gold display. 'Do you take sugar nowadays?' Matilde asked.

The clink of expensive china finally snapped Ellie out of the spell the painting had put her under. 'What are you doing?'

Letting out a sigh, Matilde lay back in her chair, her buttery curls spilling around her. 'I've lost so many people now.' She spoke with a harshness that Ellie wasn't used to. 'I won't lose my own child to whatever this is.' She waved her hands in the air vaguely before taking a sip of tea.

Ellie's expression must have mirrored her confusion, because Matilde shook her head in exasperation. '*This*.' She gestured to herself. 'It's easy for me and I like it. I wake up every morning, put on my pretty-woman suit and it fits like a glove.'

'I'm trying –'

'Well, stop.' Ellie was held in place by her mother's ice-blue stare. Her next words sent a jolt through Ellie's spine. 'What we love and admire in others does not always work for ourselves. Do you understand?'

They both knew who her mother was talking about. Ellie nodded, terrified of the dangerous waters they were treading.

'Now listen to me, Ellie – really listen.' Matilde leaned forward, and Ellie was entranced. Her mother took a deep breath. 'Instead of trying to be like the girl you love, try living up to how she sees you.'

The words struck Ellie like lightning. She felt herself plummeting.

Lottie, Lottie, Lottie.

What Lottie had was so rare, so precious.

Blinking back tears, Ellie focused on the painting again. 'I don't understand,' she said, trying to hide her confusion. 'I thought you wanted me to be the perfect princess?'

Matilde shook her head. 'I want you to be the best ruler you can be, and it's up to you to figure out what that looks like.'

'But Grandma said –'

'She's gone.'

Any remnants of the sweet and graceful Matilde had burned away, and Ellie was staring at a mother wolf, who would rip the throat out of anyone that got in her way. For the first time in Ellie's life she could recognize something of herself in her mother.

She didn't realize she was crying until a tear hit the hand curled in her lap. She wasn't sad; she felt seen.

'Ellie,' her mother breathed softly. 'Willemena was a very old and very scared woman clinging to rotten and sickly beliefs. I won't let her mistakes become our mistakes.' She leaned forward again, but this time she reached out, bringing her hand up gently to wipe Ellie's cheek. The touch felt like a kiss goodnight – comforting.

A strange calm enveloped Ellie. 'Then I have something I need to do.'

Matilde narrowed her eyes, a smile creeping across her face. 'I can't wait.'

Later, marching down the palace halls, Ellie knew exactly what she was doing. Her breath came out in hot gasps as she started to run, desperately trying to keep up with the girl from the painting. She was just out of reach, just round the corner, just behind the door, and Ellie was going to catch her.

A ghost of a laugh escaped her lips when she tumbled into her bathroom, amazed by her own mistake. All this time the question should never have been *What would Lottie do?*

It was obvious now. It should have been: *Who does Lottie think you are?*

Ellie fumbled for her magic potion and a pair of scissors at the back of her bathroom cabinet behind the piles of make-up and primping equipment prescribed to her by the king's advisor.

Once she was sure she had everything she needed to summon the girl in the painting, she began. She rubbed away the sticky make-up that covered her face in a pretty mask, and when she looked up at her reflection – at that strange plastic princess with the dull brown eyes – she knew . . .

She had to free her.

After the news about Eleanor Wolfson, Ingrid was sure something was wrong with her own body. So she had checked her temperature, taken her blood pressure and even asked Julius to do an eye exam. But apparently nothing was out of the ordinary.

Frustrated by her heart flutters and the twisting feeling in her stomach, she threw herself into training, spending as much time in the gym as she could in the hopes of levelling her mind and fixing her body. *So why*, she thought, furiously bouncing up and down on the cross trainer, *do I keep doing such stupid things?*

Her traitorous mind kept replaying her argument with Claude. Letting out a furious grunt, Ingrid jumped off the cross trainer, the steps still turning. She stormed up to her room to shower, hoping hot water might scorch the memory away.

Water spilled over Ingrid's face. *Why* would Claude want to bring in that bratty Portman? And, worst of all, why would she question him about it?

Tilting her face into the spray, Ingrid imagined herself submerging, and without warning the memory shifted, stars coming to life in the emerald eye of her master until that punishing look melted away and she was dreaming again of her prince. How odd it was that a father and son could be so different. Jamie never raised his voice. He never made her feel beneath him. Jamie was kind to everyone. *Jamie thinks you're delicate.*

She violently turned off the water and, grabbing a towel, rubbed herself dry. Then, shaking her damp hair, she stared at her reflection. Everything was going according to Leviathan's plan. Ellie was disgracing herself. Willemena was dead. And the plan to put Jamie on the throne was so close she could almost taste it. They were finally getting what they wanted. Yet all she could do was sulk.

'Spoiled girl,' Ingrid snarled at herself in the mirror. 'Ungrateful, stupid thing.'

She needed to stop feeling sorry for herself and find a way to make it up to Claude.

How many times are you going to have to make it up to him?

Ingrid blinked, shocked that she'd had such a thought.

She was ready to tell herself to shut up but stopped before the words left her. She was truly losing it. Instead of letting her mind unravel further, she grabbed her gown and headed to her laptop.

Crawling under her duvet, Ingrid flipped open the laptop and used her special code to access the back end of the Partizan council website, checking as usual for any sign they might know Leviathan's plan.

Once upon a time she'd had her own login, but now she had to make do with pages of HTML and unformatted text as she trawled for the bones of the scheduling page. She scrolled down to December and found a meeting planned at their headquarters in Paris. She told herself not to get excited until a name flashed on the screen that made her vision turn red. That Portman had somehow managed to convince the council to hear her speak. Flexing her fingers, Ingrid visualized her prey – a little mouse walking into the perfect trap.

She didn't know what the bumpkin planned to tell them, or what she knew, but Ingrid was absolutely certain about one thing. Whatever the Portman had to say to the Partizan council, Ingrid was going to hear it too.

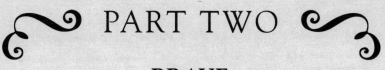

PART TWO

BRAVE

(adjective)
Showing courage in the face
of danger or difficulty

14

Christmas was fast approaching, and Paris wore the merry season with class and elegance. Beneath the sprinkle of snow, the city was delectable – a feast of festivity, glitter and gold threading the Roman columns. This late in the year the sun faded by mid-afternoon, and when Lottie, Saskia and Anastacia reached the Partizan headquarters Christmas lights lit up every cobbled street. And then it ended. At the steps up to the Partizan council premises, the festivities stopped dead. As grey as old meat, the tall building swayed in Lottie's vision until she narrowed her eyes and ascended the steps.

At the heavy doors, a woman dressed in monochrome with a matching suitcase passed them and Lottie attempted a smile. 'Merry Christmas,' she said cheerily, holding the door open for her.

The woman stared at her blankly before muttering something under her breath and continuing on her way.

'I see my fellow Partizans still haven't quite discovered the concept of Christmas cheer,' Saskia grumbled.

'Nor central heating,' Anastacia added, pulling her white cloak more tightly round her shoulders.

Lottie followed them into the reception, the three of them passing a large marble sculpture of a sword and shield that stood proudly in the middle of the frigid room.

She didn't feel anything ill towards the woman who'd passed them; in fact, quite the opposite. She'd had a hardened look, a burden of responsibility that pulled down her brow, which sent a pang through Lottie's heartstrings. It was the same expression Lottie had seen so often on Jamie, and looking around the reception she could see it on half the people in the room.

In a building filled with the severe and focused glares of trained killers, Lottie and Anastacia stood out like blood in water. They didn't belong.

Saskia marched up to the front desk and flashed a card.

The receptionist turned to his computer to check them in. 'They're expecting you in Conference Room Three,' he relayed without looking up. 'You need to be checked by security in the left hall before you enter the main building.'

With a grin, Saskia turned to Lottie with their passes, spreading them out like a suite of winning cards. 'Ready to meet the beasts?'

Lottie grabbed her lanyard and draped it round her neck. 'Let's do this.'

How scary could the Partizan council be anyway?

Conference Room Three turned out to be more of a courtroom. It was curved in a half-crescent, with three tiers of oak benches arranged round a circular desk and chair on a platform.

Lottie was escorted up to the dais and was surprised when the attendant who'd shown her the way offered to take her coat and get her a drink. She declined both, hoping that once she'd told the council of the imminent danger facing the Wolfsons, they'd be quick to jump to action.

When the attendant left, Lottie only had a few moments to gather herself before the rear door burst open and Lottie realized how accurate Saskia's description had been, because in marched three beasts in human form.

At the head of the group emerged a tall dragon of a woman with flowing auburn hair and a silver gash over her left eye. She took a seat in the centre of the tiered bench in front of a gilded plaque announcing her as GARWEN BOWEN.

Next was a tall thin man, whose dark hair was tied elegantly in a slick topknot, his sleek black-leather coat giving him the streamlined appearance of a barracuda. Taking a seat in front of a plaque reading LANCE CHOI, he watched Lottie through eyes that were scowling, dark and calculated.

The final person had snow on his shoulders and was wearing a muskrat hat, the white and beige a stark contrast to his dark skin. The furs he'd wrapped himself in rippled with every step, like the bulk of a polar bear, and he stomped into the room with a huff, making it clear, as he sat in front his plaque which read ARTHUR SOLOMON, that he felt he had better places to be.

Trying not to fidget, Lottie stared at the three heads of the Partizan council. They shared that same look: brows furrowed, weighed down by a heavy beast of responsibility.

'Let's get this over with then,' Arthur grumbled. 'We're told you have information regarding the upcoming Golden Flower Festival at Wolfson Palace in Maradova.'

Lottie nodded, pulling a file out of her bag. 'Yes. I have evidence that Leviathan intend to execute their final plan then.'

Lance waved away the file. 'This is the group headed by the disgraced Claude Wolfson – the one who's been recruiting our Partizans?'

Lottie felt herself light up. They understood! 'Yes,' she said.

The three council members looked at one another, until finally Arthur let out a grunt.

'And do you know what the plan is?' Garwen asked.

'Well, no,' Lottie admitted, 'but I'm sure we can figure it out in time to prevent it.'

'So let me get this straight,' Arthur began. 'You've arranged this meeting to tell us that there's a *suspected* threat?'

'I wouldn't say it's –'

With a laugh like velvet, Lance pinned Lottie with a condescending look. 'There are always insurgent groups. And there are always threats to the Maravish annual ball,' he explained like she was a child. 'It's an affluent event filled with influential people, a lot of people who themselves have Partizans. The council has always worked closely with the Wolfsons to assure these events are secure. This is no different.'

'It *is* different,' Lottie insisted. Heat crawled up her neck. 'Leviathan has been planning this for a long time. It's personal, and the Wolfsons are in danger. If you could just find a way to –'

'We understand you were the Wolfson princess's Portman,' Garwen interrupted. 'I know it's not uncommon for Portmans to become quite involved in their roles. Perhaps we can lend one of our therapists to help you move on from your duties? Partizan and Portman transition periods are not that dissimilar; it might help you –'

'I . . . *What?*' Lottie spluttered. 'I don't need a therapist. I need you to take this threat seriously.' But in a flash Lottie realized that they never would. To them she was just a sad little ex-Portman who couldn't move on.

Lance was first to break the quiet. 'We cannot put you in touch with the Maravish royal family.' Lottie was at least relieved for his honesty, even if the words crushed her heart. 'What we can do,' he continued, 'is assure you that the Golden Flower Festival will be under the strictest and most thorough security. We promise you no harm will come to your previous employers; the Wolfsons, and all who attend the ball, will be safe under our protection.'

All three of the council members smiled.

Part of Lottie wanted to refuse to leave, to dig her heels in and demand they take her seriously, but Garwen beat her to it. 'If you change your mind about the therapist, don't hesitate to contact us again.'

The words were laced with genuine concern, the kind that made Lottie suddenly see herself as they did. *Pitiful.*

She took a deep breath and walked to the door. 'Thanks,' she muttered as she let herself out, making sure she was down the corridor until she let herself sniff back angry tears.

Aggressively rubbing her eyes with her coat sleeve, she was halfway down the corridor when she bumped into a huge woman.

'I'm so sorry, I –'

Lottie took in sun-kissed skin, honey-brown eyes and golden hair that spilled over her muscular shoulders with all the majesty of a lion's mane.

With a slight tilt of her head, the woman held Lottie at a distance. 'Easy now,' she said, and tutted.

That voice. Deep yet mirthful. Lottie knew exactly who this woman was.

'There you are!' Saskia and Anastacia barrelled down the hall, before stumbling to a halt.

'Lottie,' Saskia said breathlessly. She held out a hand. 'This is Marta San Martin – my mother!'

15

'No, no, Mama, let me!'

Lottie watched in astonishment as Saskia fussed around her mother, pulling her seat out for her in the restaurant.

From the way Saskia had avoided the topic, Lottie had assumed Saskia's relationship with her mother must be a sore spot. Now she realized that she couldn't have been more wrong. Saskia was a complete mama's girl. What was more interesting, though, was that Saskia's mother seemed completely oblivious to it.

'Sit down, Saskia,' she ordered.

Saskia immediately complied.

In many ways Marta was a sized-up version of her daughter. But, despite their similar shape and feline facial structure, Saskia's mother had had her wildness tamed. With not a hair out of place and an immaculately cut suit, Marta oozed control from every pore. Beside her, Saskia had never looked more like a little girl.

With a tight-lipped smile, Anastacia leaned over to whisper in Lottie's ear. 'She'll be so embarrassed about this later.'

Lottie stifled a giggle. But her frustration was starting to bleed into fear the longer they sat in the cafe. The festive

135

lights that had seemed so joyful now flickered like winking eyes, and everything reminded her that Leviathan were out there and no one was taking it seriously.

It must have shown because Marta turned on her. 'What are you so afraid of?' she asked Lottie directly.

'I'm sorry?' Lottie spluttered.

'Saskia – what's got your friend so jittery?' Marta demanded. 'She should have nothing to be scared of when she's with two trained Partizans.'

Lottie bit back the temptation to remind her that most of the Partizans she knew had betrayed their masters.

'I'm just worried about the meeting,' Lottie said instead.

'It wasn't the outcome you wanted?' Marta asked, stirring a sugar cube into her coffee.

Lottie didn't want to seem rude. 'They reassured me that there are always threats to the ball, and that this is no different.'

Anastacia scoffed. 'Very reassuring indeed, I'm sure.'

'It might not be what you wanted to hear, but I hope it's put your mind at ease,' Marta said, wearing the same hardened expression as the council members had.

Tearing off a chunk of French bread, Saskia laughed. 'You should have reminded them that I nearly kidnapped you with entirely no help only a few years ago.'

Marta scowled. 'Saskia, please. *No me parece graciosa.*'

Saskia turned to her mother and suddenly did the most out-of-character thing Lottie had ever seen. Like a wounded puppy, she hunched over. 'Sorry for being so rude,' she said, practically snivelling.

Marta nodded at the apology but looked far from pleased. 'I hope my Saskia is not too much trouble for your parents,

Ani.' Marta turned away from her daughter and towards Anastacia. 'It was generous of your family not to remove her as your Partizan. After all that time and effort we put into her training, grooming her for such a privileged position – she allowed herself to become compromised.'

It was like watching a silent tug-of-war between them, with Saskia in the middle.

Anastacia took a small sip of her tea, the ring Saskia had gifted her glinting. 'Saskia's been an incredible Partizan.'

Marta narrowed her eyes.

'We actually have something to tell you,' Anastacia continued. 'Something we think Lottie should hear as well.'

For the first time Lottie started to question why she'd been invited to Paris. 'You knew the council wouldn't do anything, didn't you?' she said.

Neither of them answered.

'Mama, I'm actually . . .' Saskia took a deep breath, spurred on by a reassuring squeeze of her hand that was intertwined with Anastacia's on the table. 'I'm not going to be a Partizan.'

The colour immediately drained from Marta's face. 'You're joking.' Saskia shook her head, and Marta stared at her daughter with a furious scowl. 'But what about Anastacia?' She gestured across the table with such force she nearly knocked over a glass. 'Don't you care at all about your –'

'Please, Mama,' Saskia interrupted. 'I have no intention of leaving Anastacia's side.'

'What are you saying?'

'Anastacia and I . . . we're together,' Saskia said simply. 'I love her.'

'That's –' The word escaped her like a lone air pocket bubbling up through water. 'That's fine –' Marta shook her head. 'No, that's good. Great. I'm . . . I just wish you'd told me sooner.'

It was the most unkempt Lottie had seen her; a single strand of hair had come loose from where she'd rubbed her forehead.

'You're OK with this?' Saskia asked.

Lottie watched Marta reach out and cradle her daughter's chin gently. It was the first time she'd seen them touch. 'Yes,' she said, then quickly pulled back, that stern look creeping back. 'You'd better have a plan, though. I'm not letting you leave until I know this isn't some silly idea you've just thrown together.'

Anastacia immediately put her cup down, sitting up straight. 'Saskia will be applying to the University of Paris with me to study international relations, and we'll be taking a gap year to travel East Asia. We'll be together – but as partners now, rather than Partizan and master.'

Lottie felt an emotion choke her, writhing round her like clinging ivy. She realized it was jealousy.

Marta laughed throatily, snapping Lottie from her thoughts, but before anyone could say anything else, an alarm went off inside her bag. 'That'll be work,' she said, placing a crisp pile of euros on the table. 'My treat.'

'Thanks,' Lottie murmured, still dazed.

They followed Saskia's mum out on to the street, Lottie and Anastacia standing to the side as mother and daughter said goodbye.

'Saskia,' Marta began, hesitating, 'let's make sure we meet up regularly from now on, to avoid too many more surprises.'

Laughing, Saskia leaned in as her mother ruffled her hair, and Lottie saw the glint of joyful tears in her eyes.

The moment she was out of sight, Saskia let out a huge sigh of relief. 'That went so much better than expected.'

'I know, right!' Anastacia agreed, the two of them in borderline hysterics. They'd done such a good job of keeping calm that even Lottie had been fooled by their performance. But Lottie couldn't join them in their thrill.

'Why would you do that?' she asked, her voice barely a whisper, her red fingers fidgeting in the cold. 'Why would you orchestrate this whole thing when you knew the council wouldn't help me? What? Just so you could rub this in my face?' She swallowed hard, trying to remember what it felt like to be kind, how important that feeling was – but she couldn't find it. 'I'm sorry,' she tried to say, but it sounded insincere. 'I don't want to ruin this moment for you. I just don't understand. Why would you want me to hear that?'

A flash of sympathy passed over her friends' faces.

'Let's go for a walk,' Anastacia said.

Side by side, they walked the short distance to the canal, snow melting without a trace where it landed around them.

Anastacia's words pierced the air. 'We know you're scared of seeing Jamie again.'

'It's OK,' Saskia added, as Lottie flinched. 'We're all nervous about how it will go down when we find him.'

Lottie clung to the word 'when', knowing that it was both absolute and inevitable. They'd find him or he would find them. It had to happen surely?

'But we also know that's not all,' Anastacia said. 'There's something else you're not admitting you're afraid of.'

'I-I . . .' Lottie stuttered, taking a step back.

'We see how you look at us.' Saskia spoke softly. 'We try not to show too much affection around you. Not since, well . . . Not since Ellie left.'

Rubbing the bridge of her nose, Lottie tried to make sense of what she'd heard, but her head was cloudy.

Anastacia spoke up, her voice as clear as a bell. 'It's time for you to say it out loud, Lottie. Say what you feel.'

Lottie didn't even realize she was crying until she felt dampness on her cheeks.

Kissing Ellie on the balcony, the bitter taste of coffee on her lips.

The knife cut of Ellie rejecting her.

Jamie's promise to come back for her.

Ellie, Jamie, out of reach, yet always with her, like a shadow.

'I'm terrified,' Lottie whispered. 'I love her.' The moment she said it, a dam broke, and a sob racked her. 'I'm so scared to see either of them again.'

Lottie melted into Anastacia's embrace. 'But what if I'm completely wrong? What if they're all right, and I should just leave them alone and stop trying to save everyone?' Lottie paused, a last sob emerging. 'What if Ellie sees me as a burden?'

Anastacia held her at arm's length, and Saskia leaned in, the two of them looking her dead in the eye.

'Listen to us very carefully, Lottie,' Anastacia said. 'We have never seen anyone so smitten with another human as Ellie is with you. She can try to bury it, but she loves you, and she wants you to save her.'

Lottie hiccupped another sob. The idea that Ellie could love her, that it could be real, not just a dream she clung to . . . It ached in the most perfect way.

'Really?'

'Absolutely.' Saskia said. 'And wouldn't the ultimate lesbian couple know a thing or two about sapphic pining?'

Lottie laughed, at once embarrassed and relieved. 'I'm a bisexual disaster,' Lottie grumbled, hiding her head in her hands.

'That's the other thing, Lottie,' Anastacia said with a sigh. 'It's not just Ellie.'

Saskia finished her thought. 'It's Jamie. We think the reason you're so afraid is because you don't know what to do about his feelings for you.'

The words hit Lottie like a shuddering wind. Somewhere inside her, a thought buried deep in ice was melting, and a feeling once frozen now trickled through her, threatening to flood her system. Cradling her left hand, Jamie's ring clinked against the wolf at her neck.

'What do you mean?' she asked. Yet she already knew the answer. She knew it from the fire that burned in Jamie's eyes with a promise to keep her safe. She knew from the way his skin sought hers, coveting any touch. She'd always known exactly what she was to Jamie.

Oh.

'He loves me,' Lottie whispered. She'd just never wanted to admit it to herself.

Saskia and Anastacia shared a concerned glance.

'Of course he does. The only question, Lottie,' Saskia said quietly, 'is what are you going to do about it?'

16

The vertical tower of hexagonal rooms that made up the safe house unfurled in Claude's office, a cut right through the centre, laid bare like a split hive. If he were to step on to the landing, he could see right down into the lounge where his Leviathan were currently perched. Licking his lips, Claude moved closer to the flickering screen of the security footage, pixels coming together to show his son leaning back, a silent laugh bubbling from his throat, a response to some presumably crass comment from Julius.

At some point, without Claude becoming aware, Jamie had begun to assist Julius in his physiotherapy sessions. An unlikely friendship was blossoming between them. Even Phi wasn't immune to the strange effect Jamie had on those around him, and Claude caught the twitching smiles she tried to suppress whenever his son accepted food she had made him or simply wished her good morning.

Jamie was so beautiful, as Claude had once been, a creature of effortless charm and eloquence. Unlike Claude, he was also righteous and gentle, and it was easy to see why they adored him. The natural way he collected love and devotion, royalty at its finest, that was what Claude needed if he were going to convince the Maravish people, and the world, to welcome them home. To welcome him back as the true king of Maradova.

But it was also a problem. As if on cue, Haru entered the room, placing himself beside Jamie, and even through the static of the screen he visibly softened when Jamie met his eyes.

Claude was not surprised that the obsession he'd encouraged in Haru had turned to something more simple. Offering Haru – a boy who fancied himself a hero but felt disconnected and unwanted by his master – a prince for him to rescue had seemed a foolproof plan, but now, watching him fuss about Jamie, he understood his mistake. All of Leviathan were falling for him in their own way, and Claude had to make sure it never crossed a line. He wanted them to love Jamie, but he needed them to remain loyal to him first and foremost. They could love Jamie, but they must revere Claude.

With Ingrid he felt he'd found a good middle ground. Too stupid to understand her feelings, all she could do was turn to Claude to ground her. It was almost amusing to watch her vie for his son's attention, and Claude was sickly fascinated by what she'd do when she realized Jamie would never love her like that. He was sure it would only drive her to him.

He watched her on the screen wandering into the lounge before pausing.

Claude was meant to be having a meeting with her, and, glancing up at the clock, he saw she was already a few minutes late.

Ingrid was never late. And yet here she was, stopping to loiter, keeping him waiting, because she was distracted by his son.

Claude moved closer to the screen, watching with growing irritation as Ingrid blushed at something Jamie said and then laughed. Her face cracked into a smile like he had never seen on her, bright and strange on her usually stony features, and she laughed and laughed.

When she finally pulled herself away, it was ten minutes past the time they were scheduled to meet, and Claude realized how hard he was gripping the table. When a knock finally came at the door, he took a moment to compose himself, flicking off the screen and taking a calming breath before he called, 'This'd better be good news.'

Appearing before him with no trace of the bright smile he'd just seen, Ingrid let herself in, shrinking in on herself in that way she did in his presence.

'It is sort of,' Ingrid said quickly, giving a slight bow as she spoke.

'Go on,' Claude intoned, not convinced she could say anything to fix his foul mood.

'I managed to eavesdrop on a recent meeting with the Partizan council.'

In spite of his annoyance Claude lifted an eyebrow, his interest piqued. 'Oh?'

Ingrid took a cautious step further into the room. 'They met with the Pumpkin girl.' Claude's eyes narrowed. 'She knows we intend to execute our plan at the Golden Flower Festival.'

Claude felt fire flare inside him. 'Does she know what the plan is exactly?'

Ingrid was clearly thrilled to tell him the next part. 'No. And the council rejected her; they told her they were handling security for the event and that there was nothing to worry about.'

Claude let out a cackle, his emerald eyes lighting up like they'd become radioactive. The universe really did want him to rule; why else would it bend so conveniently to his plans? He hummed, swirling his drink. 'The Portman is skirting dangerously close to finding out our plan. It seems we finally have a reason to bring her in.'

Ingrid let out a choked sound like a cat coughing up a hairball.

'Is that a problem, Ingrid?'

Ingrid hesitated, her mouth opening and closing like she was swallowing down what she wanted to say, until finally – timidly – she shook her head.

'Good, then let's begin arrangements.'

'Right away,' she replied, and rushed out of the room in an attempt to hide her frustration.

Claude didn't care. He'd been given the answer to all his problems. Bringing in the girl would be the ideal way to stop her meddling and drive a solid wedge between Jamie and the rest of Leviathan.

Downing his drink, Claude turned the screen back on and watched his son and Haru once more, the two of them edging closer to one another, before shutting off the monitor.

Jamie could have his little Portman, and Claude would have everything else.

17

The great vigilant eye of the St Agnus's clock stared down through the frosty morning. It was always watching, and today – on the first day back after winter break – Ellie was going to give it a show.

Arriving an hour early, there was only a limited audience, but Ellie had something important to take care of before debuting her new self to the school.

Pulling open the heavy door and marching into the mezzanine, Ellie relished the whispers and glances sent her way by the other students. Their reactions felt like little rounds of applause.

'Is he new?' one student asked.

'That's a girl.'

Another gasped. 'No it's not. That's our princess.'

Ellie bit down on a smirk. Sweeping through the hall, she felt like a storm blowing everyone aside. Nothing could touch her.

'Oh my God!'

Right on cue, the Rat Twins skittered out from where they'd agreed to meet her, their faces stretched wide in shock. 'What did you *do*?'

Ellie gave a curt bow. 'You like?'

Grabbing her by the elbow, the twins pulled Ellie into an empty classroom and slammed the door behind them.

'You look like, like –'

Cutting off his sister, Sam marched forward. 'You look like everything they accused you of being.'

Ellie couldn't help it; she threw her head back and laughed.

'This isn't funny!' Stella's voice went up several octaves. 'You're only going to prove them right.'

Ellie shrugged, turning away. 'Well, maybe they are right.'

Catching sight of herself in the window, Ellie grinned. God, it felt so good to finally see herself, not some fake plastic doll-girl. Cut short, her hair was slicked back like a wave of midnight as dark as her eyes. Discarding the prim skirts and blouses, Ellie now wore the boys' uniform – a stiff jacket and belted trousers that accentuated her sharp features. It made her look taller, more poised. Regal in a way she was born for – not as a kindly princess but a charming prince. This was how Lottie saw her. This was Ellie at her best.

'I'm tired of pretending. It clearly wasn't working to play the princess, and it's not like I can possibly do any more damage than I already have.'

'But, but . . .' Stella looked completely at a loss, her outrage melting into confusion. 'What would your grandmother think?'

Ellie froze, waiting for the question to sting, but it never hit. The words rolled off her like water off a duck's back. 'I don't think the dead think anything at all.'

If the twins were shocked before, now they were ready to depart their own bodies.

'Anyway, I can't talk right now.' Ellie shook them off, walking through the door and down the corridor. 'I'm signing up for the fencing team.'

The squawk that came from behind her almost stopped her in her tracks. Almost.

At her heels the twins fired off a string of desperate protests. 'This is a terrible idea!'

'Yep,' Ellie agreed.

'You're going to make everything worse!'

'Probably.'

'Just stop and talk to us about this for a second.'

'No, thank you.'

Ellie reached the gym and paused with her hand on the door handle. She could hear the rhythmic twang of bouncing rubber balls and the breathy shouts of team enthusiasm. Beyond that was the irresistible sound of singing metal – swords at play.

Ellie pushed on the door, slamming it shut behind her and drowning out Sam and Stella's words.

Every student in the hall came to a sudden halt and turned to the newcomer.

One side of the enormous hall was currently in use by the girls' volleyball team and the other – the whole reason Ellie was here – was crowded with the white homogenous forms of students in fencing uniforms. Ellie realized that none of them recognized her.

That was until Yasmin stepped forward in her volleyball gear, her chestnut hair tied up in a high ponytail. 'No way,' she said in awe. 'Is that you, Ellie?'

Ellie had had no idea Yasmin was on the team or would be in the gym at all, but she sauntered over, glad that someone had recognized her, even under her new mask. 'Actually I'm her evil twin.'

To Ellie's relief Yasmin laughed, and this seemed to encourage some of the other girls to join in.

'You look so . . . tall.'

'I – what?'

With a ball tucked under her arm, Yasmin placed the flat of her palm against the top of her own head then pushed it out in a straight line through the air, her hand level with Ellie's mouth.

'I never noticed before,' Yasmin said, taking a step back and looking her up and down. 'It's like you've been hiding.'

Ellie blinked. Had she really been trying to shrink down into herself all this time?

'Nice to meet you,' Yasmin continued. She smiled. 'The real you, that is.'

A smile spread over Ellie's face before she took Yasmin's hand. 'Sorry for deceiving you,' Ellie said. 'It's nice to meet you too.'

'You're forgiven. That is –' she glanced back at her team – 'as long as you're here to play volleyball.'

With a move like lightning, Yasmin threw the ball above Ellie's head, which she managed to jump up and snatch out of the air.

'Good reflexes,' Yasmin said, nodding, and then added with a laugh, 'I can't believe the perfect middle blocker has been right under our nose this whole time.'

Ellie handed the ball back to her. 'I'm afraid I'm not here for volleyball. Although it was a lovely surprise to find you here.' Patting her on the shoulder to lessen the blow, Ellie turned to find her real target and made her way to the other side of the hall where the fencing team were laying mats out.

'I want to join the fencing team.'

She couldn't tell if the faces hidden behind mesh looked shocked or pleased. In unison they turned to the tallest masked figure. The captain, Ellie imagined.

The mysterious figure reached up to pull his helmet off, and she was confronted with her worst nightmare. Chocolate-brown hair, a face shiny with sweat, a perfectly chiselled jaw and the classic Maravish heavy eyebrows and strong nose. It was the grinning prince of the school himself, Leo Gusev. 'Do you now?'

Ellie had to bite the inside of her cheek to stop herself from saying something she'd regret. 'I'm good. I was best on my team at Rosewood,' she said instead, confident in her own ability.

'You're so funny,' Leo said with a laugh. 'You think you can dress up like Prince Charming and win over the whole school after that fake act you pulled?'

Ellie took a bold step forward. 'You're right. I was being fake, but those news reports were all lies. I know who I really am better than anyone else and I'm ready to show you all.' Ellie loved the way truth seemed to knock Leo off his pedestal. 'I want to be honest now,' she continued smoothly. 'And I can honestly say I would kick your ass in a fencing match.'

Leo flinched, but Ellie made it clear that she'd spotted it, and the challenge ignited something in him. A look that sat somewhere between bloodthirsty and excited spread over Leo's face. Ellie felt it mirrored inside herself, and the two of them found common ground in how badly they wanted to prove the other wrong.

'OK,' he said at last. 'You can join the fencing team.' But before Ellie could get excited, he held up a finger. 'First you have to beat me in a match.'

Ellie shot her hand out for him to take. 'Deal.'

18

Hope was a funny thing. Lottie had now had hers dashed more times than she could count, and yet here she sat in the library waiting for the Gibson essay, as if this one booklet would hold all the answers she needed.

This time it's different, she told herself. *This hope is special; I can feel it.*

When they'd arrived back at Rosewood after Christmas, grey slush and puddles dotted the grounds. Everywhere was sodden and the earth smelled stronger and more vibrant with the promise of spring.

With the weather changing, Lottie felt every minute ticking away – the Golden Flower Festival was constantly looming in the distance. They were running out of time, but she wouldn't give up – not now that Lottie understood what she wanted. *Who she wanted.*

The librarian lay the Gibson essay down on the table, snapping Lottie out of her thoughts. Lottie's last hope of figuring out Claude's plan was a thin hand-bound document with a pretty emerald and gilt title:

FACTS AND FABLES: THE LOST FOLKLORE OF MARADOVA

Gold and green, just like Jamie's eyes. A shiver ran through her and wouldn't go away.

'You got it?' Binah asked as Lottie left the library. Lottie grinned back and patted her bag. 'Then let's roll.'

By the time they arrived at Liliana's study, Banshee were already up on the big screen, Miko and Rio locked in another battle of wills with Saskia and Ani, this time apparently over just how useless the Partizan council was. Anastacia and Miko were in the midst of stringing French and Japanese phrases with increasingly more venom when Binah cleared her throat, announcing their arrival.

'Lottie – thank goodness!' Sayuri and Wei swayed into view, forcing Rio and Miko out of the way.

'Is that the Gibson essay?' Wei asked.

Nodding, Lottie took a seat in the centre of the room beside Percy.

'It's pretty!' the twins cooed in unison.

'Indeed,' Binah agreed. 'Let's hope it's not all form and no substance.'

Lottie flipped to the beginning where Gibson had written out the story of Alexis's claim to the Maravish throne in the language of folklore. Tracing the text, her skin fizzed, the same feeling she used to get from her tiara. She squeezed her hand into a fist, Jamie's ring glinting in the fairy lights, grounding her. She didn't want to be lulled into any more fantasies; yet here she was again delving into a fairy tale.

'I only skimmed it on the way over, but if you don't mind,' Lottie announced, 'I'd like to read this first passage to all of you. It's the story of how the Wolfsons became the rulers of Maradova, and I think it might give us a clue to Claude's plan.'

Raphael perked up from where he was lounging opposite her. 'Amazing. I love story time.' He rolled over, propping his chin in his hands.

Looking up at the screen, Lottie waited for Sayuri to give her the signal to start. As soon as she nodded her approval, the pages came to life and Lottie was sinking down, down into the depths of the story, Maradova unfolding in front of her as though she'd stepped into a fantastical pop-up book.

'*Once upon a time*,' Lottie began, and she heard her own voice ring out, melodic and distant, '*the kingdom of Maradova lay trapped in an eternal winter. No crop could grow or flower could bloom and the people prayed for sun.*

'*At this time Maradova was ruled by a cruel and unpredictable king, Agvan Roanov, who was dubbed the Mad King. King Agvan was a strange and twisted man, with skin so pale that when he stood in the snow he glowed like a wraith. He had a ghastly temper and everyone in the palace hid when they heard him shout, terrified of the cruelty he would enact upon them in his rage. And he was greedy, hoarding food, happy to let his people starve and freeze.*

'*Unlike Agvan, his sister, Princess Inessa, was beloved due to her generosity and kind nature. Despite growing up in the winter-locked land of Maradova, her skin shone gold like she'd been kissed by the sun, and whenever she entered a room the air turned sweet like summer flowers.*

'*Inessa would try to calm her brother whenever he flew into a rage, but one day a scream rang through the palace and poor Inessa found her parents had been slaughtered by none other than her crazed brother. Sure she was next, Inessa fled the kingdom,* running into the wilderness. Everyone thought her dead, but Inessa was strong, clever and quick, and the wilds could not claim her.

'One day she was found by a pack of wolves that had been watching her. They led her to safety, and Inessa discovered a village hidden deep within the wilds, a village of wolf people. Their leader was Alexis Wolfson, a powerful man with a soft smile, who covered himself with pelts and was always warm. Inessa stayed with Alexis and his people, learning how to live off the snowy land and hunt like a wolf.

'After a year together Inessa discovered she was carrying Alexis's child, and decided it was time for her to go home. Together Inessa and Alexis worked in secret to spread the news of their plan to return and save the kingdom of Maradova from Agvan's maniacal rule. They told the people she was carrying their new prince, and that he would be a kind and benevolent ruler.

'When Alexis Wolfson and his army stormed the palace, the Maravish soldiers bowed low, welcoming Inessa home with her warrior wolf at her side and their baby prince in her arms. Agvan tried to hide within the bowels of the palace, but Alexis sniffed him out and dragged him to the steps of the ballroom where he tore his throat out in front of a cheering crowd.

'As the sun rose behind them, Alexis and Inessa sat together on the throne, the blood of the mad king decorating the hall like petals. And with Inessa finally in her rightful place a miracle happened for the first time in ten years – the snow melted and flowers bloomed in the palace gardens. One such flower had never been seen before, blossoming gold like it had been kissed by the sun. It was named Inessa's Gold. With sweeping gilded petals and a scent like spiced wine, Inessa's

156

Gold became the sacred flower of the kingdom, representing hope, truth and love.

'The people declared Alexis Wolfson their saviour and new king, for he had returned Inessa and their true prince to the palace and ended the eternal winter. To honour their saviour every year in the summer they held a Festival of Flowers and every ten years, when Inessa's Gold bloomed, they held a Golden Flower Festival, when all Maravish people could come and explore the palace, inhaling the scent of the miraculous blooms to bring them good luck.'

When Lottie had finished, the world crashed back into focus. The damp earthy smell of Liliana's study, the gentle glow of the fairy lights and the faces of her friends all pulled her back to reality. She slowly became aware that Jamie's ring was scorching her finger.

Through the speakers Rio let out a long whistle. 'Badass.'

'Yeah!' Saskia cried. 'Maradova has some tight history.'

Lottie spoke again. 'Well, it's not necessarily history – more like folklore. Just a fairy tale,' she half whispered to herself.

From across the room Binah pulled a face at Sayuri, the two of them exchanging something wordless that was definitely about Lottie.

'It's still important,' Sayuri said. 'This has to be a clue to Claude's plan. We just need to figure out what it is before the ball.'

Everyone grunted in agreement, and Lottie looked up to find they were all staring at her.

Anastacia rolled her eyes. 'Lottie, what are you going to do about getting an invitation?'

'I, umm . . . I was thinking of asking the guy I went to the first ball with if I could be his plus-one . . . You know, Edmund Ashwick?'

Saskia, Anastacia and Binah spoke at once.

'No way!'

'*Absolument pas.*'

'Are you crazy?'

'Well, what would you suggest?' Lottie said huffily, hands crossing her chest, but mostly she was just embarrassed about suggesting someone as slimy as Edmund might be able to help.

'You could try claiming your heritage?' Anastacia suggested.

Lottie froze, sure the room had turned colder at Anastacia's suggestion. Then her nose was filled with the scent of roses. She heard Percy's words from the start of the year: *I think if we're going to beat Claude, we need to know exactly who we are.* When had she become so disconnected from herself? Kind, brave, unstoppable – it all felt so far away, so childish. The chill spread through her bones, an image of Liliana in her mind like a scorch mark in her vision, but she turned away from it. 'I . . . I can't!'

'I have a suggestion,' Sayuri said calmly, noticing Lottie's discomfort. 'But you're not going to like it.'

'At this point I think any suggestion is better than nothing,' Binah said, and everyone nodded in agreement.

'Emelia, my best friend, the one who solved all this last year . . .' Sayuri waited for everyone to register who she was talking about, and all eyes turned to Percy, the only one of them who'd ever met her.

'*I didn't get to talk to her much,*' he signed.

Micky reached out, squeezing his boyfriend's hand.

Lottie thought back again to her conversation with Percy. Leviathan had kidnapped Percy and Emilia to test out the Hamelin Formula. Emelia was the opposite of Lottie in every way, completely infallible. What was it like to know exactly who you were?

'Yes, well,' Sayuri went on, pushing forward, 'she has a plus-one.'

Lola clapped her hands together, squealing. 'Oh my God, that's amazing. This solves everything.'

But Lottie wasn't getting her hopes up yet. She knew Sayuri well enough to see there was more to come.

'But she doesn't want to give it to you,' Sayuri said plainly. 'She doesn't trust you.'

Raphael was the first to speak, gesturing wildly towards her. 'How can anyone not trust Lottie? She's the sweetest person in the world.'

Sayuri stayed perfectly calm. 'I've told her she's wrong, but I'm afraid she thinks Lottie won't be able to think clearly when it comes to Ellie and Jamie.' There was a low murmur that Lottie chose to ignore. 'She thinks Lottie won't be able to control her emotions when she sees them again and that it might end up jeopardizing all of us.' Sayuri turned her focus directly on Lottie. 'She wants you to prove yourself.'

While her friends broke out in protests, Lottie stayed silent. 'What can I do to prove she can trust me?' she asked eventually.

A smile spread over Sayuri's lips. 'She wants you to meet her and prove yourself in person,' Sayuri said after a moment.

Lottie nodded. 'Just say where.'

159

'Next Wednesday, she wants you to sneak out of school and meet her at the statue of "he who kills the lost" – her words. I don't know what they mean, but she says you will.'

Lottie bit her tongue to stop a cynical laugh escaping her. She knew exactly what Emelia meant, and she realized that no matter how much she tried to distance herself from the girl she used to be, magic and stories would always be part of her. 'OK,' she agreed, determination flooding her. 'For Ellie and Jamie – I'll do it.'

19

The fencing match was scheduled for after school the following week. By the time it rolled around, the whole school knew about Ellie and Leo's deal, and she'd be lying if she said it wasn't a little thrilling to finally feel like part of the school – even if it wasn't in the way she'd planned.

By the way Leo had St Agnus's wrapped round his finger, Ellie had expected some curiosity around their showdown. What she hadn't expected was for the entire sports hall to be filled with students screaming for blood from the benches.

A roar echoed through the gym as Ellie sauntered in, her helmet tucked under her arm.

'Well, this is quite a turnout,' Stella marvelled, carrying her rapier at Ellie's side.

'Don't let it intimidate you,' Sam added, and there was a surprising amount of fire in his eyes.

Despite their initial protests, the Rat Twins had organized a schedule of intense practice to get Ellie back up to speed. She'd spent every free moment training with them, glad of their friendship and support.

Leo was chatting to the rest of the fencing team, and Ellie's gaze snagged on a group of girls carrying handmade posters. They squealed when she noticed them, holding up a sign that read TEAM PRINCESS.

In shock Ellie realized the sign was for her and that several groups in the audience were not just there to support Leo. She turned to the part of the crowd with posters for her and gave a melodramatic bow, lifting her head to wink at them as though she were some kind of Casanova. A ripple of fresh cheers and boos broke out, along with quite a lot of swooning.

Stella rolled her eyes, but there was the tiniest hint of a smile on her lips. 'You are incorrigible! Now come on. You need to get your head in the game.'

Scurrying about her, the Rat Twins continued fussing, making sure her suit was done up properly and that she was well hydrated before heading on to the mats.

Ellie felt warmth spread through her, the kind that normally only Lottie could cause. She smiled when they were done. 'Thanks, guys.'

Sam looked surprised, as though he had never received gratitude before. 'No problem.'

'Seriously,' Ellie told them, 'I know I dropped this new look – and the new plan – on you out of the blue. I really appreciate your support.'

Stella and Sam scrunched up their faces, looking like they didn't know how to reply, and Ellie couldn't believe she'd actually found two people worse at social cues than herself.

Laughing fondly, Ellie pulled them into an embrace, squeezing them tight even as they went rigid. 'Thank you for being my friends.' She really meant it.

When she pulled away, the two of them were stiff as boards, their arms pressed into their sides.

Stella was in a daze, her hazel eyes glazed over. 'Sure.'

Ellie grinned, her blood already pumping with adrenaline. 'I'd better get out there. Stella?' Holding her hand out towards Stella, she waited. 'Stella . . . my sword?'

Stella didn't move – her fist had tightened over the weapon. Then she swallowed down whatever worry had been bothering her. 'Right.' Stella shook her head, holding it out. 'You'd better win, OK?'

Ellie gave her a reassuring grin. 'Don't worry. I'll win – since you asked so nicely.'

It was time to face her enemy.

Waving to his adoring fans, Leo barely registered when Ellie approached the mat. Even from a distance she could smell expensive men's cologne.

'Ready to be humiliated?' Leo asked, his voice light and playful, making it clear he wasn't taking her seriously.

Ellie grinned. 'Sure. But first let me win this match.'

Leo's cocksure attitude faltered. 'Let's just get this over with,' he grumbled, turning his back to her.

To keep things simple the match was going to be a best out of three, both of them using épée-style swords, the fencing co-captain acting as director.

Once they were ready at opposite ends of the strip, Ellie saluted her opponent as she was trained to do, half expecting Leo to forfeit the match by refusing to do so back. But she had no such luck, although his returning salute came across as stiff and reluctant.

Barely registering as the co-captain announced, '*En garde!*' all Ellie was aware of was her own breathing. They pulled their masks in place and Ellie felt herself come to life.

Everything about the fencing gear heralded freedom – from preconception or judgement. Ellie was no longer a princess or a schoolgirl. She was a weapon, and she was going to win. And when the call was made to fence, she was ready.

It shouldn't have come as such a surprise but Leo was good. He didn't charge forward as Ellie had expected, and his lunges were well timed; he never let his bloodthirst turn into a rushed move.

Unfortunately for him, Ellie was better.

Partly to wear him out, and partly because she was feeling generous, Ellie allowed them to spar for a while, their weapons singing a metallic duet. Getting a feel for his style, Ellie did some fancy footwork, much to the thrill of the crowd, who let out a resounding gasp as she almost gave Leo the change of a successful parry, only to quickly turn it back on him, their blades slicing across each other with an ear-splitting sound.

The crowd cheered at the unexpected move. The game was turning in Ellie's favour.

Grinning under her mask, Ellie's sword struck his thigh, an undeniable hit executed to perfection.

The crowd were cheering again, and somewhere in the noise she could hear a chant. 'Go, *Princess! Go, Princess!*'

They were cheering for her! They had faith in her!

Only something was wrong.

As Ellie's sword hit Leo's thigh, it didn't stop or bend as it was supposed to, it kept going, and she found herself falling forward with it, her blade sinking into the white.

It wasn't until Ellie heard him scream that she even realized what had happened.

Leo fell back, his leg giving way beneath him, and she watched in horror as a bright crimson flower bloomed. Blood.

Ellie tried to make sense of what she was seeing, when someone in the crowd cried out. 'She stabbed him!' the voice bellowed, and with it came a crescendo of dismayed screams.

'Get her away from me!' Leo roared, pulling his mask off.

Everything erupted into chaos while Ellie stood completely frozen, students rushing from the benches and crowding round while the co-captain hurried to Leo's side to put pressure on the blossom of blood.

'Get a teacher!' someone shouted, and from the other side of the room came another voice. 'Call an ambulance!'

'It was an accident,' Ellie whispered, but no one could possibly hear her above the commotion.

Bodies pushed past her from all sides. Still she couldn't move. Looking down slowly, Ellie saw the tip of her sword and the world drained of colour – except for the vibrant scarlet smear along her blade.

'Get her out of here!' barked someone, and before Ellie could find where it came from, hands were curling round her wrists and forearms, pulling her out of the room.

'It was an accident,' she said again.

'I know,' someone said into her ear, as they dragged her away. 'I'm sorry.'

20

There was only one person with a statue Lottie could think of who '*kills the lost*', and she was itching to seek out the book on the shelf in her dorm room to confirm her theory.

Lottie's battered copy of *Peter Pan* was an old favourite, the pages furled at the edges from water damage, the insides musty and scored with annotations that spilled across the margins. It didn't take her long to find the passage she was looking for, and despite being short it had stuck with her forever.

> The boys on the island vary, of course, in numbers, according as they get killed and so on; and when they seem to be growing up, which is against the rules, Peter thins them out; but at this time there were six of them, counting the twins as two.

The casual horror of it had haunted Lottie since she was a child. It was Peter Pan's childishness that allowed him to do such awful things and not understand the severity, so it made sense that Lottie would only truly grasp it when she was older – something Peter had never been able to do.

Cast in bronze, Peter Pan lived in Kensington Gardens, trapped forever in eternal youth. All Lottie had to do was get to him at the time Emelia had specified, and she would be well on the way to saving her own lost friends from their impending doom.

Sneaking out of Rosewood in the middle of a school day was one of the easier parts of Lottie's mission. As it turned out, when you're a model student and a target for awkward sympathy because you were abandoned by your best friends, teachers were very lenient.

All it took was a white lie about an important meeting with her solicitor in London with some well-timed lip wobbling, and she had permission to leave the grounds on Wednesday morning as long as she was back at Rosewood by curfew. The hard part, unfortunately, was her own stubborn fears.

On the train a trembling started that she couldn't control, and her hands shook when she tried to turn the pages of her book. Every unexpected sound made her jump; every unknown face looked suspicious. There were so many people, and yet she felt alone and defenceless.

By the time she reached Kensington Gardens her hand was firmly lodged in her bag, clinging desperately to her tiara, and she whispered her mantra over and over. '*I will be kind, I will be brave, I will be unstoppable. I will be kind, I will be brave, I will be unstoppable. I will be kind, I will be brave, I will be unstoppable.*'

Had Emelia been right not to trust her? How she'd managed to get herself all the way to London was beyond her.

That was it! Lottie stopped abruptly, the solution hitting her so hard she almost stumbled. She knew exactly what to say to make Emelia realize she could count on her.

This time her trembling fingers didn't feel like a sign of weakness; they felt like the opposite – physical proof of how strong she was. Her fear was proof of her strength.

Just as she thought this, she saw him. Peter. Carefree and oblivious to the worries that came with growing up. The statue was almost black under the dark clouds and the tree stump he stood on was like a twisted shadow, raising him up to play his merry pipe.

While Peter floated above, beneath him, sitting just as still as the statue, was Emelia Malouf. She was dressed impeccably, her burgundy school uniform paired with a rose-gold hijab that gave her dark brown skin a warm glow. She was a lot shorter than Lottie had expected.

Lottie had only seen her once before on a TV screen, staring daggers at reporters. Now she seemed to have none of that fury. She looked serene, and waited calmly with something cradled in her arms. This was a girl who knew who she was, a girl who was so sure of herself that not even Claude could break her.

When she turned to Lottie, she didn't smile, not at first, and Lottie paused.

'You figured it out,' Emelia said by way of greeting.

Lottie shrugged. 'It was the least I could do.'

Emelia smiled and stood up. Lottie could see now that she was cradling a violin case. As she took a step closer, Lottie could smell cocoa oil too, sharp and sweet – an inescapable reminder that Emelia was heir to the Hubbub Corporation,

169

one of the world's most powerful cocoa-bean harvesters and chocolate manufacturers. Her status was the reason Leviathan had targeted her in the first place.

Lottie had done her research and learned that Hubbub represented the marriage of two great companies, making for a deliciously romantic story. It was a perfect match. Emelia's mother, Daraja, came from Nigeria where her family owned a cocoa plantation. Her father, Hassim Malouf, the inheritor of the Emirati confectionery company Hubbub, used to do business with them. The two of them had fallen in love and combined their businesses, remarketing their products as the most passionate chocolate – chocolate so rich and sweet it would make a person instantly fall head over heels for you.

Lottie would be lying if she said she hadn't fantasized a few times about receiving one of their heart boxes from Ellie, but she quickly shook off the thought.

'Sayuri says she filled you in,' Emelia began, cutting right to the chase, 'about not wanting you to get in the way of our mission to stop Leviathan.' Lottie nodded. 'Good, because I don't have a lot of time,' Emelia said, checking her watch. 'I have a violin lesson I need to leave for in ten minutes, and my dad will be furious if I'm late.'

'That's fine,' Lottie replied. 'I only need a minute to prove I'm trustworthy.'

Emelia raised an eyebrow, but Lottie didn't let that deter her. Taking a deep breath, she held out her hand, which was shaking so much that she practically rattled.

Emelia took it. 'You're trembling?'

'I'm terrified,' Lottie admitted. 'Ever since my princess and Partizan left, I'm scared of everything – open spaces, being alone, the dark. I'm even scared of my own reflection.' Lottie listed each symptom, becoming increasingly aware that her teeth were also chattering. She tried to laugh. 'In fact, I was so terrified coming here I thought I was going to be sick.'

Emelia gazed at Lottie, her chocolate eyes narrowing to crescents. 'How is this meant to prove that you won't let your emotions get the better of you?' she said and dropped Lottie's hand. 'Leviathan tried to ruin my life. If I want to get revenge on Claude, I can't have someone on my team who's going to freak out like this.' Emelia looked as if she were preparing to leave.

'But I still came,' Lottie said, not caring that her voice wobbled. 'Don't you see? I'm the most scared I've ever been in my life. I have no idea who I am or what's waiting for me any more, but when it comes to my friends I will always find the strength I need. Claude has to pay for what he did, and that means I can't let his plan succeed.'

Emelia opened her mouth to speak. 'Even if that means fighting Jamie?'

Lottie should have known this question was coming; she'd asked herself the same thing over and over. Every time she had a nightmare, every time she looked at his ring.

She finally had an answer. 'Whatever it takes,' Lottie repeated, and she meant it.

Emelia gazed at Lottie. After a long moment she drew a breath. 'OK.'

'Really?' Lottie squeaked, then quickly coughed to mask her excitement, but it was too late – Emelia was already smiling.

'You have that same look in your eye that Sayuri gets.' She spoke fondly, but there was an edge to her words. 'When she swore she'd take down Haru if she had to.'

Swallowing hard, Lottie realized what that said about all of them. 'Three girls connected by vengeance.'

Emelia laughed. 'Sounds like the start of a beautiful friendship.' Then she checked her watch, and the smile disappeared. 'Damn, I'd better go. Ever since I got brainwashed by my father's secret evil business partner, he's become painfully strict.'

'See you at the ball?' Lottie asked, smiling.

'See you at the ball,' Emelia echoed.

As she left, Lottie turned for a final look back at the statue of Peter Pan, thinking of the poor lost children that had been lulled into his world and she swore to herself that she would find the people who'd become lost to her before they were stolen away for good.

21

Since arriving at the safe house, Jamie had found himself waking up later and later, a side effect of having little to do and no one eager to disturb him. Sleeping in had always been a luxury he didn't much care for; he preferred to rise with the sun. Perhaps it was something to do with the blanket he'd stolen from Lottie's study as he left, but his bed was becoming harder and harder to leave.

Still hazy with sleep, Jamie rolled over, pulling the blanket up to his face. Lottie's scent had long since faded, but the soft texture had become so entwined with his memory of her sweet rose fragrance that he could just about imagine it from touch alone. Through a crack in the curtains snow was silently falling, and he was sure if he pulled them open, he'd see nothing but cold white.

When he eventually pulled himself out of bed, he felt groggy and dehydrated and headed to the kitchen in search of water and caffeine without even checking the time. So it came as a shock when he found Haru scraping a plate of sandwich crusts into the bin.

'You just woke up?' Haru asked, raising his eyebrows.

Jamie only grunted in response, watching curiously as Haru popped a sweet in his mouth.

Haru grinned. 'Want one?'

He held out the box of Maravish honey candy, every sweet nestling in a pretty yellow wrapper, sparking a strange nostalgia. Jamie had eaten these as a child.

He put his hand out as Haru shook the box and two sweets landed on his palm.

'You're still half asleep,' Haru chuckled. 'Where did you get that blanket from?'

Jamie looked down at himself to see he'd ventured downstairs in nothing but his silk pyjama trousers, Lottie's blanket draped round his shoulders. 'Good grief,' he muttered, as he pulled the blanket off and carefully began to fold it. 'I need to stop oversleeping.'

'I can always come and wake you if you'd like,' Haru offered oh-so helpfully, smiling.

Jamie didn't miss the catch. '*If I'd like?*'

Haru's smile grew wider. 'Oh yes, you only need to ask me.'

Jamie sat on the table and laughed, shaking his head as he unwrapped a sweet, before tossing it into his mouth, flooding it with the taste of memory.

'I wasn't sure you liked sweet things,' Haru said, coming to sit beside him.

'Sometimes, I do.' Jamie glanced around. 'Where's Ingrid and Julius?'

'They had some important new information to look over in Claude's office so I offered to stay here and wait for you to wake up. So what other sweet things do you like?'

Jamie desperately tried to think of anything other than *Lottie, Lottie, Lottie,* when he caught a whiff of the increasingly familiar toasted-marshmallow scent that Haru seemed to carry around with him. 'Well, I like you, Haru.'

The significance of his words didn't even occur to him until he saw the look on Haru's face, and then Jamie was suddenly aware of how close they were. He felt the spider-silk brush of the hairs on Haru's arm and smelled the lingering sweet on his breath.

'Jamie –' he whispered the name – 'I would like to kiss you if that's OK?'

Jamie had never thought about his romantic preferences or any romantic endeavours at all. He had stayed focused on protecting his princess and paying back the crown for taking him in. When he'd started to care for Lottie, he'd called her a distraction, using his duty as an excuse to avoid thinking about his attraction to her, even when his own princess selfishly explored it herself.

He didn't have that excuse any more. And for the first time in his life he wanted to know what his truth was. Swallowing his sweet, Jamie stared at Haru's parted lips. 'Yes.'

Time slowed down to the gentle rhythm of a beating heart as Haru leaned in, his fingers tracing the shell of Jamie's ear, until he held his face in his palm, the pad of his thumb molten on Jamie's cheek, every touch a scorch mark.

Haru tilted Jamie's head until he was gazing up into those stardust eyes – and then he kissed him. As smooth as satin, Haru's lips burned with a fire that matched Jamie's own.

It was as if Jamie had never been touched before. The burning morphed into a hunger, the heat not enough, and he clung to Haru's shirt, terrified to lose the feeling.

He'd been so wrong; the fire inside him had never been more than a match flame. Now it had found something incendiary, something that spun him like a Catherine wheel.

But it was nothing like what he felt for Lottie.

As her name drifted through his mind, he pulled back. Haru's lips followed him, but he pushed him softly away. Jamie rested his forehead against the crook of Haru's shoulder. Even in his confusion he was not ready to forfeit the warmth of Haru's skin, and he trembled when Haru's fingers ran through his hair.

'Are you confused?'

'Yes,' Jamie confessed, still not looking up.

'Do you not like boys?'

'I liked that,' he said simply, because it was the only thing he was sure of right then.

Jamie clung to Haru and looked at him dead on, searching for an answer that he knew he wouldn't find. 'I like someone else.' He said it as though to remind himself.

Haru pulled away. 'You like the Portman.' It wasn't a question, so Jamie didn't answer.

For a moment they sat in silence until Haru tilted his head, a vulnerability there that felt secret, something only for Jamie. 'Can I ask what it is that you feel for her?'

Jamie knew he owed him an honest answer, but he wasn't sure himself. 'I don't know.' He spoke in a hushed tone. 'I don't understand it any more.'

Haru remained silent. Even though they were no longer touching, his presence grounded Jamie.

'I thought I loved her, but it feels more selfish than that,' Jamie went on, running his hands through his hair. 'It's like I want her light to shine on me always, no matter what I do, and I don't want anyone else to dim it.' Jamie sought out the blanket, as comforting as a mother's lullaby. 'I want so much from her.'

'I see.' Haru's voice was mellow; he seemed pleased by the answer. He gently laid his hand upon Jamie's. 'Unconditional,' he murmured.

The word rang like the chime of midnight in Jamie's head, but he couldn't quite make sense of it. He was about to ask Haru what he meant when they heard a commotion on the stairs. The two leaped from the table as Claude swirled into the room.

Compared to the sterile kitchen, Claude was all animal. He smelled of spice and pine and brought the wild in with him, his steps like a war drum. There was no way of knowing what he might have seen or whether he even cared, but all Jamie could think of was how empty he felt now that Haru wasn't close to him and how desperately he wanted to feel that fondness again.

Claude gave Haru a look sharp enough to cut glass. 'Don't worry, you haven't done anything wrong, Haru,' he said, and Haru seemed to relax – unlike Jamie, who could feel every muscle in his body tighten. 'I simply need to speak to my son alone.'

Haru swiftly left, Jamie's eyes following him.

The second they were alone, Claude moved in on Jamie, looming over him in his silk suit. Jamie was painfully aware of how underdressed he was.

Claude sighed, a remorseful sound, pulling his wildness back under control, and his hand came to rest at the back of Jamie's neck, pulling him forward, and Jamie realized with a start that something had always been missing from his father's touch. There was no affection there.

'Come with me.'

Jamie found himself steered to the dining table in the next room. On its top lay a tablet with yet another article about the princess of Maradova.

'There was an accident, or so they claim – look.' Claude pointed at the graphic depiction of the injury Ellie had caused – a jagged crimson thing.

Jamie followed the words of the article, thinking only of Lottie, how important it was for her not be exposed to this . . . to any of this . . .

'I worry she is going mad,' Claude said, cutting off Jamie's train of thought. 'It runs in our family you know, madness.'

'Then she needs help,' Jamie replied, unable to believe that the king and queen were failing so spectacularly to see what was staring them in the face. He could tell Claude had something else to say. 'What is it?' All thoughts of Haru had vanished.

With just one look, Claude reminded him that they were the same, that he was the only one Jamie could trust to make things right. 'You must forgive me,' Claude began. 'Ever since you expressed concern for the Portman, I have been keeping track of her.'

'What have you found?'

'She plans to attend the Golden Flower Festival.' Jamie opened his mouth to speak but his father stopped him. 'I can arrange a temporary base if you feel we need to intervene.'

All Jamie could think was that he must not let Ellie and Lottie see each other again. He knew he was being selfish, but he didn't care. When he'd let Haru kiss him he'd discovered a truth about himself that, until now, had always been just out of view. Lottie meant something to him that he could not explain, and in the same way one must know what flower one is tending in order to help it grow, he had to know what she was to him so he could keep her safe.

'OK,' he said, calm and focused. 'But I want to be the one to bring her in.'

22

With Emelia on her side and an invitation to the Golden Flower Festival successfully acquired, Lottie was further along in figuring out Claude's plan and putting a stop to it. So why was it turning out to be the most impossible task ever? She felt like Sisyphus. Every time she thought things were finally turning round, the boulder would roll back down the mountain.

Claude wanted to be welcomed back, which must mean he wanted to be king again, but how did he expect to have the people declare him their ruler? It didn't make any sense.

Lottie exhaled noisily, closing the pages of the Gibson essay and watching Alexis's name disappear. 'Urgh, what are you planning, Goat Man?'

Binah looked up at her from where she was filling a tote bag. Slowly but surely Liliana's study was being stripped back to the way they'd found it, as everyone removed their belongings before study leave. It was a reminder that Lottie's time at Rosewood was coming to an end.

Binah's and Lottie's things were the last to go, as everyone else had already left. Lottie wasn't sure how long she'd be able to handle being in there alone, with just her and the memory of Liliana.

'Still no luck?' Binah asked, carefully encasing a china cup in bubble wrap.

'It just doesn't make sense.' Lottie's words were slightly muffled as she nibbled the end of her pen. 'If Claude plans to remove Ellie's parents, then he'd be the villain of the story; there's no way they'd accept him back on the throne.'

Binah gave one last look over the room, before tapping her bag, satisfied she'd got everything. 'Why don't you take a break and we can pick this up tomorrow?'

'Can't,' Lottie announced, carefully placing the essay in her bag and trying her best not to look too hard at the room around her. 'I've got a train booked for Cornwall in two hours.'

'You're seeing Ollie?' Binah's eyes seemed to grow two sizes bigger and she grinned at the mention of Lottie's childhood best friend.

It was no secret that Binah and Ollie had developed a deep platonic partnership, and Lottie would be lying if she said it didn't make her feel a little weird to think of Ollie being anyone's soulmate.

'Yeah, it's a surprise actually.'

'That's great, Lottie.' Binah sounded genuinely thrilled. 'I'm glad you're visiting home again.'

Flinching at the word *home*, Lottie tried to cover up her response by throwing her bag over her shoulder.

'Well, if you're leaving tonight, I'd better show you *your* surprise now.' Her friend flitted over to an antique armoire and pulled open the rickety doors. There in the old dusty oak cupboard was a dress on a mannequin.

'We mice have been very busy,' Binah announced, bringing it out.

The dress was a simple shape but its cloud-puff sleeves were folded into a flowerbud of white, while the skirt was delicately appliquéd with pink and gold roses. It was cute and chaste, exactly what people would expect from Lottie – the perfect dress for a kind, brave and unstoppable princess.

'When did you do this?' Lottie asked in astonishment, touching the material.

'Anastacia organized the whole thing, but, wait, look at this.'

Lottie took a step back as Binah picked up the entire mannequin and placed it on the floor with the poise of a magician preparing for a magic trick. 'All your dresses – Sayuri's, Anastacia's, Emelia's and yours – have a rather complex feat of fashion engineering if I do say so myself. If you pull hard on these two cords, the fabric unravels – watch.' With the dress still on the mannequin, Binah tugged the ribbons on either side of the bodice and the shape transformed. The delicate bud of a flower was now blooming, snowdrop wings expanding at the back to reveal a flytrap centre: Liliana's sword.

Lottie's breath caught in her throat, her eyes trained solely on the sword as it peeled itself from the gown. The dress was a mere cocoon, and now its venomous stinger was exposed.

'Don't you like it?' Binah asked worriedly.

'I do. I love it.' But Lottie had backed away and her foot struck one of Liliana's covered paintings, the dust sheet falling away to reveal her ancestor's face in all its fiery glory.

It was a face very much like Lottie's and her mother's, but there was one major difference. Liliana was furious.

The painting had clearly been done in anger. The wild in her eyes was palpable, and whatever sat beyond the frame had made her violently mad. The portrait was a mirror image of everything Lottie had never let herself feel. She quickly covered the image again. She was sure for a split second that Liliana was mad at *her*.

Lottie quickly apologized, grabbing her bag again. 'Sorry. It's not the dress. I love the dress. It's me. I just . . .' Lottie checked her watch. 'Sorry. I'm going to be late for my train.' Before Binah could stop her, she ran to the door, only looking over her shoulder to call goodbye. 'I'll see you next week to finalize our plan, yeah?'

Narrowing her eyes sceptically, Binah slowly nodded. 'Lottie –' she said her name like she was pulling on a leash, demanding Lottie's attention, and it worked – 'take the dress.'

Lottie let go of the door handle and turned back to the gown. She immediately thought of Liliana again, the savage beauty of the dress a reflection of the lost princess. How could someone so bold and frightening be her ancestor? What would it be like to let herself feel that sort of rage, the sort she could see in the painting? She was always kind, brave, unstoppable, but certainly never furious.

Lottie acquiesced with a sigh and stepped forward to retrieve her gift.

'Give it time,' Binah said, calm and certain. 'You'll grow into it.'

*

The train ride was a blur, the world zipping past too fast as Lottie went over the tale of Inessa and Alexis again and again, trying to find a clue to Claude's plan while staving off the uncomfortable memory of her experience in Liliana's study. She'd packed away the dress and sword in her dorm room to be collected before the ball, telling herself it was better to simply lock it away. Binah had said she'd grow into it, but how could she be so sure?

By the time Lottie reached the station she was no closer to understanding Claude's plan. All she'd succeeded in doing was giving herself a headache, and when she reached for her train ticket, her hand brushed Liliana's tiara box and its velvet made her shiver. She shoved it further into her bag.

Sighing, Lottie stepped out into her old town, the fresh smell of the sea clearing her thoughts, a lone drop of rain urging her towards Ollie's before the storm hit.

It was just as she headed into an alley, remembering a shortcut up the hill, that someone spoke her name.

Everything froze, as Lottie turned to the owner of that wonderful and awful voice. His scent floated in the growing wind – cinnamon and spice.

She'd forgotten the thing she was supposed to be most afraid of.

Looming over her was Jamie Volk.

'Sorry,' he whispered, and then everything went black.

23

Kiss the princess to wake her up.

Wake up . . .

'*Wake up!*'

The first thing Lottie became aware of was the bad taste in her mouth. And she must have been sleeping at an odd angle because her neck ached.

'*Wake up.*'

Lottie blinked herself awake, slowly battling through the fog and rolling her neck from side to side. Then everything flooded back and she took in the strange room in wide-eyed horror.

'Jamie,' she croaked.

To her relief she was alone, but she was tied to a chair. In the dim light she made out what looked like a hotel room; the carpet was squishy beneath her bare feet. She decided not to dwell on the fact that they'd taken her shoes, making escape even more difficult. Instead she turned her attention to her restraints.

Violently tugging her wrists, Lottie tried to move, but the rope burned as her desperate pulling increased. It didn't budge.

Frustrated, she tried to get a better look at the knots when she saw something she recognized. On the desk to her side was a green pamphlet that seemed to suggest she was in Bay View Hotel, which would mean she was only about a mile or so away from her old house. This was where she'd grown up. If she could escape, she could run to safety. *If*.

But nothing even slightly close to a plan formed in her head, and then Lottie heard the door rattle and saw the handle sink down. Light suddenly poured in, and the nightmare she'd spent so long running from walked right into the room.

Lottie forgot to breathe. She stared as Claude Wolfson stalked towards her, his shadow stretching out ghoulishly.

He was older than the painting in the Wolfson ancestral hallway had depicted him. His face was scored with frown lines and crow's feet – mementoes of every furrowed brow and cruel smile.

'Ah, wonderful! You're awake.' His tone was infuriatingly casual.

She noticed two figures behind him – hotel staff. 'Help me!' she screamed, trying to tilt her chair to get a better view and nearly toppling over. 'What are you doing? Stop him! Can't you see I'm tied up?'

To her horror, they simply continued to watch from the corridor, expressionless.

'Oh, they won't help you,' Claude explained, closing the door behind him. 'They have strict orders not to interfere.'

Lottie scrutinized Claude, and what stood out the most was that he was nothing like Jamie. While the green and gold in Jamie's eyes always reminded Lottie of a starlit meadow, Claude's emerald eyes were the sickly green of greed and envy.

'You used the Hamelin Formula on them,' Lottie said, amazed at how level she managed to keep her voice.

'Well, of course.' Claude laughed, a sound as dark as his tendrils of black hair. 'I wanted to make sure we had somewhere comfortable to let you rest while we make arrangements to take you back with us safely.'

Lottie managed to hide her repulsion and asked, 'Where's Jamie?'

'He will speak to you momentarily,' Claude reassured her, the knowing edge to his voice making her wish she could wipe the smirk from his face. 'If I am to undo the damage that has been done to you, first I must see what poisons the Wolfsons have infected your mind with.'

Lottie tried to think of something – anything! – she could do to give her an advantage. But the other half of her brain begged her to be polite and not to make things worse.

'If you're so concerned about my well-being, perhaps you could untie me?' Lottie tried in her most saccharine tone.

She immediately regretted her words when he stalked towards her with tangible bloodlust. As he came closer, she smelled spiced wine, like the sweet cinnamon she could always detect on Jamie but with none of the warmth. It was another thing that set father and son apart. She braced herself, but Claude didn't lay a finger on her. Instead he knelt beside her, eyeing the ropes that held her wrists. 'I will make sure you're treated,' he said, his voice full of concern. 'As soon as I've figured out what lies my family has hurt you with.' Looking up, with their gaze level, he rested a hand on her knee and whispered, 'Let me help you.'

For a terrible unforgivable moment Lottie felt herself fall for his hypnosis. Perhaps it would be easier if she played along? If she could persuade Claude she was not a threat?

'I-I . . .'

It was then that she saw it, a light so bright it was like catching the sun in her eye, and, as fast as she'd seen it, it winked away again, but she already knew what it was. In the corner, spilling open, was her bag, and nestled among the contents glinted her family's tiara, Liliana's tiara.

No! Lottie told herself, and she was sure the room turned colder; her breath rolled out in wisps like a ghost curling inside her. *No!* she thought again. The voice in her head was louder this time – except it wasn't her voice. It was Liliana's.

Right now was not about being kind and brave. Sometimes you had to be angry. Sometimes you had to be furious and wild, and instead of reasoning with villains you had to go for the jugular.

'I'm not as naive as you think I am,' she said at last, feeling something build inside her, a feeling she'd denied for so long. 'I know what you're planning to do and you can't trick me.'

'Oh, do you now? And what – pray tell – do you think this great plan of mine is?' He tried to keep his tone casual, but she wanted to push him further, wanted to see him crack.

Lottie's mind raced, Inessa and Alexis sprinting along the edges like wolves on the hunt. She had to say something, anything, so she took a stab in the dark, hoping to hit her mark.

'You're going to kill your brother and his wife.'

When Claude laughed it was a great booming sound, his head leaned back like he was howling at the moon, and she cringed, knowing she had got it wrong.

'I have no intention of killing anyone,' Claude said through his laughter. 'If anything, I will be saving Maradova from mad rulers.' Tapping the back of her chair, he walked

190

away. 'There would be no point in ruling my country if the people hated me, would there?'

Lottie froze, sensing something in his words. She needed more time to pull the answers into the light.

'You could be a part of it too, Lottie,' Claude went on. 'You could help me save your princess from herself.'

Whatever had been building inside Lottie crested and burst out. Ellie – her princess, her best friend and the love of her life. She would not let anyone talk about her as if she wasn't absolutely perfect just the way she was.

'Don't you dare talk about my princess. You can't trick me, Goat Man,' she said abruptly, relishing the way his face contorted at the name. Powerful anger burned inside her.

It hit her like lightning: everything she'd been missing sparking inside her, awakening a long-slumbering part of herself. She knew exactly who she was. She was the ancestor of a formidable princess and a descendant of Rosewood itself; it was in her blood – strong, unstoppable and smarter than this spoiled royal.

'Your stories might work on other people, but I've lived and breathed fairy tales my whole life, and I know evil when I see it,' she growled, hardly recognizing her own voice. 'I will never let you win.'

Even though Lottie was tied down in a chair, she felt herself loom over this man, a pathetic creature who could only rely on lies and tricks to get what he wanted.

Claude sighed. 'A pity. For Jamie's sake I had really hoped not to have to use the formula on you.'

Lottie's anger stalled, as she realized what Claude intended to do.

He smiled, sharp-toothed and cruel. 'Don't worry. I'll make sure to keep you mostly intact; we wouldn't want to break the little prince of Maradova's favourite toy.' Then he left, as calm and composed as he had entered.

The second the door clicked shut, Lottie began to throw herself from side to side, hoping to break the chair. But with a pathetic thump she toppled over almost immediately. She screeched like a banshee, trying and failing to yank herself free from where she lay sprawled on the floor.

Claude's plan was just out of sight, hiding in his cryptic words.

Inessa, Alexis, Agvan, Jamie, Claude, Ellie.

The names went round and round her head, their roles blurring, until they were like a prophecy – Jamie and Claude standing in a bloodied hall and meeting with adoration. Panic bubbled inside her. If she only had a little more time –

The door creaked open again and Lottie started to panic as footsteps came towards her. She'd fallen with her back to the door and couldn't see who was approaching. 'Wait, you –'

But Lottie stopped short as the ropes round her wrists slackened and fell to the floor. When she twisted round, she saw someone she'd never have expected.

'Haru?'

He was already grabbing her stuff from the corner of the room.

'I'll make it look like you wore the ropes down yourself,' he explained, his voice level as he methodically went about his task. 'Now come with me – we don't have a lot of time.'

'You're helping me?'

'No,' he snapped with a look of disgust. 'I'm helping Jamie.'

24

Nothing was unfolding in the way Jamie had anticipated – but he should have guessed that would be the case, seeing as he was dealing with Lottie.

When he'd approached her near the station, he'd expected her to look terrified at worst, furious at best, but she hadn't looked at him with either of those emotions. Instead she almost seemed to have been expecting him. That had made him more confused than ever.

Pacing back and forth in the stuffy single bedroom, Jamie tried to walk off some of his frustration, trying and failing to understand why he wasn't allowed to see Lottie yet.

Rain tapped at the window, and the wind picked up, promising a storm. A clock ticked away on the mantel, every minute passing making him feel wilder – less a pacing human and more a stalking creature.

He'd held her tiny frame in his arms, the dizzying smell of roses and lavender shooting through his system with every breath. What he wanted was locked away in her, in the softness of her smile and that scent that was so comforting it made his mind go quiet. But he'd let his father take all of it away again.

Now he'd had enough of waiting. When it came to Lottie he had no patience.

Marching to the door, he prepared to storm down the corridor and have his first argument with Claude. He would do it if it meant knowing Lottie was safe. But as he flung open the door, another figure was already on the other side.

He took hold of Lottie by the shoulders to make sure she was real, squeezing tighter when he realized how cold she was. 'Did Claude let you out?'

He could feel her trembling and her pupils were large. She was in shock.

'No.' Appearing round the corner, Haru tossed Lottie's bag towards him. 'I did.'

Haru ushered them back into Jamie's room and carefully shut the door behind them. 'We don't have long,' he said in a hushed tone. 'I can distract Claude for ten minutes, but when I give you the signal your time is up.'

Jamie shook his head. 'What's going on?'

Haru laughed wildly. 'I don't know.' The threads that were usually wound so tight and kept him so composed were coming loose. 'All I know is you're my prince. You're everything to me, and I want you to be able to make the right decision. Whatever you decide, I'll trust you.' Haru bowed his head, gazing up through heavy lashes with a look of such utter devotion that it made Jamie's body sing. 'I'll always follow you.'

Then he turned and was gone, leaving Jamie and Lottie alone. The moment he left, wind screamed through the sash window. The storm was breaking and Jamie couldn't escape the building pressure of his guilt, the shame of what he'd done rumbling like the thunder outside.

'Jamie.' The sound of his name sent a spark through him. 'Jamie, look at me.'

Jamie obeyed. He anticipated fear or anger, for her shock to have crumbled into the painful sting of disappointment. But, of course, Lottie never did what he expected. In the silver moonlight her skin glistened like carved marble, her face as serene as mercy.

'I'm so sorry.' The words felt rigid in his mouth, but a weight that he had not realized he'd been bearing lifted. He waited, terrified of her reaction, and then she smiled and the world lit up with forgiveness.

'It's OK. I understand,' Lottie replied, her voice brimming with compassion.

Jamie was pulled in by the vortex of what he felt for her, and he was desperate to know where it would lead.

'You had to find out who you are. You've been deprived of that knowledge your whole life.' Lottie said it so simply, absolving him of things he'd convinced himself were unforgivable. 'And, I can't believe I'm saying this, but Haru's right – you need to have all the information if you truly want to find your own path.'

There was a flash, this one followed quickly by a rumble; the storm was getting closer. But he couldn't let Lottie go yet; he needed her for a little longer.

Lottie turned to the sound, the wind from the window sending her white dress and golden hair flying around her like a flurry of birds taking off. 'We don't have long.' She stretched up to push the window fully open, and when that failed, the window too high up for her tiny frame, she climbed on the table. 'Claude is going to use the Hamelin Formula on me.'

Jamie choked. 'What? No. Why would he –'

Lottie turned back, and the fury in her eyes made her look ferocious. 'He's not who he says he is, and you're nothing like him,' she growled, and with a start Jamie realized she was trying to protect *him*.

'He's my father –' Jamie began, but Lottie wouldn't let him finish.

She leaped off the table. 'Look at me.' She took his face between her hands. 'I know you. You are nothing like him.'

Her conviction felt as firm as her grip on him. Eventually he relented, nodding once, and she let him go.

'I have something for you before I go.' She grabbed her bag and threw it out of the window, ready to follow it.

He knew he should tell her to slow down, that she was in shock, that he couldn't let her go without Claude's permission – but it all felt useless. She'd already made up her mind.

Lottie came back to him, and there was something in the way she pinned him down with her gaze, as though she believed everything was riding on this moment.

He believed it too.

Gently, as if she were presenting her own heart, Lottie slid a band of gold from her finger and held it out in the centre of her palm.

There was another flash of lightning. It bounced off the ring, and the stars etched into the precious metal sparked into life along with the looping foreign script written inside the band.

Jamie knew that whatever message the ring carried, it was only meant for him.

Lottie spoke softly. 'Your mother left this for you when you were a baby. You were supposed to receive it when you were eighteen. The king and queen were going to tell you everything, about Claude and Hirana, but they became scared, trapped by their own mistakes.' Now she reached for him, beckoning him towards her, until they were so close he could smell roses and lavender again.

'After you left to find your father, Hanna and Midori entrusted it to me. They care about you, Jamie.' She smiled again, and it was full of kindness. 'I hope it can guide you – just as your mother wanted.' She placed it in his palm.

'My mother?' Jamie whispered, and when the words left his mouth they sounded like a prayer.

Suddenly there was a knock at the door. Three hard thuds – their time was up.

Breaking away, Lottie ran to the table again and hoisted herself up. 'Even if you don't trust Ellie and the Wolfsons, please trust me.' Lottie's bare feet were pale against the wooden desk as she straightened up. 'I know what I'm doing and who to put my faith in.' She pushed the window open higher and leaned into the wind, her golden hair flicking back like angel's wings.

'I do trust you,' Jamie called over the howling gusts. He reached up to grab her wrist. 'You're about the only thing left I really believe in.'

With a crack, the sky illuminated with another flash, and Lottie lit up as she turned to him. 'Jamie . . .' She breathed his name, leaning down from the ledge, the billowing fabric of her dress enveloping him. He reached up to meet her until she had cradled him in her arms. He felt small and cherished, like an infant.

Fluttering down as fragile as spring blossom, Lottie's lips were two perfect petals, and when he met them with his own he expected another incineration and waited for the surge of burning fire he'd felt with Haru. But all he felt was peace and quiet. That flame that had always flickered within him dimmed to embers with every chaste press of her mouth against his.

'You are loved,' she whispered, with a single kiss to his forehead. 'Believe in that.'

He saw himself then as the lonely little boy wandering through a palace that was not his home. Darkness pooled around him until a crack of light broke through, a hand reaching out with a scent like roses and a warmth as unstoppable as the sun. It wasn't until the pad of her thumb gently wiped his cheek that Jamie realized a solitary tear had escaped him. It was a truth so pure and simple it made him feel reborn, and that word Haru had used came up from the shallow waters of his mind. *Unconditional.*

The sky lit up once more as Lottie pulled herself over the ledge. Jamie loved her; he loved her in a way that made him want to lay himself at her knees, for her to sing him to sleep, as he basked in the sunlight of her smile, glad that he'd made her proud. She was the affection he'd sought his whole lonely life – loving, kind, brave, unstoppable. Just like a mother.

'Thank you,' he half whispered, but the sound was whipped away on the wind as Lottie disappeared. Jamie understood – in the same way he knew now what his heart felt for her – that she had to leave. The storm was calling.

25

The storm was exactly the kind Ollie hated. It rattled the windows and howled through every crack it could find. To cover up the sound of the wind he had the TV playing reruns, something mindless that he could pretend was just background noise for his biology revision if his mum got home early.

There was another loud bang and Serena van der Woodsen's face lit up on the TV screen along with the rest of the room and Ollie jumped. 'This is ridiculous,' he said to no one at all, wrapping his blanket round himself. 'How am I meant to go adventuring around the world with Binah when I can't even handle a storm?'

Trying to ignore the rolling thunder, Ollie headed for the kitchen, switching on as many lights as he could on the way, telling himself it had nothing to do with being afraid of the dark.

Kettle switched on, he went to the fridge to hunt down the *moqueca baiana* his mother had left for him to eat, thanking whatever god was listening that he at least had some comfort food to tide him over. It was just as he was spooning some of the stew out into a bowl that the doorbell sounded, quickly followed by a violent knocking. Ollie went very still, as the knocking and then the bell went again and again. Whoever it was, was absolutely desperate to get inside.

Picking up the ladle from the counter and, careful to be as quiet as possible, he crept into the hallway. A shadowy figure lay on the other side of the mottled glass of the door.

Inching closer, he held the ladle over his shoulder, preparing to whack whatever nightmare creature could possibly be out in this storm. With his heartbeat so loud Ollie was sure whoever was on the other side could hear it, he placed a tentative hand on the doorknob and opened the door.

He immediately dropped his ladle with a clatter. Barefoot, a once-white dress clinging to her, filthy with mud and rain, stood the last person Ollie had expected.

'Lottie?'

Ollie grabbed her under the arms, before she collapsed. 'What happened?'

'Hello,' she said ever so politely. 'May I come in?'

'What happened?' Ollie repeated, attempting to carry her in, but she shrugged him off and marched forward unaided. Where did she get the strength from? She looked soaked to the bone and was pale with fatigue. She didn't even have any shoes on, and her feet were red and bloody. She looked like she'd crawled out of her own grave.

She went straight to the kitchen where she grabbed the kettle and began making herself a cup of tea as if this was all very normal.

Ollie offered her his blanket, which she took wordlessly. 'I'll go and get you a towel,' he said before running upstairs.

By the time he got back she had two cups of tea laid out for them along with two bowls of stew. He recalled the part in his biology textbook about shock responses, and her eerie calm made sense.

As gently as he could, Ollie wrapped towels round her shoulders and over her head, then placed a pair of big warm slippers on the floor in front of her and was relieved when she slipped her feet in them, thankful at least that she was warming up.

Taking a sip of her tea, Lottie looked at him again. 'I met Claude.'

'Holy –'

'It's fine,' she interrupted, and looked off into the middle distance. 'I'm fine.'

In the silence that followed, the room filled with voices floating in from the living-room TV, the sound barely dampened by the screams of the storm.

Lottie's nose scrunched up in concentration, and then she asked, 'Are you watching Gossip Girl again?'

They stared at each other for a moment until something cracked – the absurdity of the situation getting to them – and they burst out laughing. Tears ran down their faces, both of them struggling to catch their breath, and the sound started to twist, becoming more and more feral.

'You know your life is completely unhinged, right?' he asked between gasps.

'I'm not the one blasting out Gossip Girl because I'm scared of storms,' his old friend countered, drying her hair with the towel. This only set them off into more fits of laughter.

When they finally calmed down, she leaned into the table with a great sigh, exhaustion starting to take over. Her shock was subsiding.

'I know how to beat him,' she said with a yawn, downing her tea.

Ollie raised an eyebrow. 'Why do you think that?'

Her mouth was set in a thin line of determination. When she spoke, her words were heavy with foreboding. 'Because I know what his plan is.'

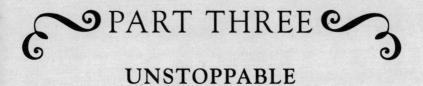

PART THREE

UNSTOPPABLE

(adjective)
Impossible to hold back or stop

26

In the weeks leading up to the Golden Flower Festival, Binah and Lottie spent every day and night until the early hours in Binah's family library forming a plan.

Ollie visited sometimes, staying over, but he knew well enough not to disturb them other than to keep them hydrated and to occasionally fall asleep with his head in Binah's lap and her fingers in his hair as though he were her personal house cat. The easy affection between the two of them was something Lottie was still getting used to.

Nothing could be left to chance. Lottie now knew the exact moment during the Golden Flower Festival when Leviathan would execute their plan – and an execution was exactly what she feared it would be.

Binah turned to Lottie. 'So, the dress,' she said abruptly.

Lottie saw in her mind's eye the deadly beauty of the dress – the way the soft fabric transformed into predatory wings, the sword stinger at the back. It was her mother, and it was Liliana, and it was her. She was all of it. 'You were right,' she said casually. 'I grew into it.'

Grinning, Binah opened the video feed, and everyone's faces appeared on the screen, eager and ready, while Lottie pulled up a shared screen for visuals and speech-to-text for Percy.

'OK, everyone,' Binah said, 'please listen carefully and keep your gasps to a minimum. Thank you. Lottie?'

Sliding into view, Lottie pulled up her notebook. It was now or never. 'So, I had a run-in with Claude –' she began.

The video conference immediately erupted into confusion and shouting.

Binah leaned into frame again, eyes narrowing. 'I said "gasps to a minimum",' she reminded them firmly.

Lottie started again, as everyone forced themselves to calm down. 'I had a run-in with Claude, plus Jamie and Haru.' Sayuri and Emelia went noticeably rigid at this but didn't say anything. 'I don't entirely understand what happened, only that Haru and Jamie let me escape.' A grin spread over Lottie's face; that part of her was Liliana – the part that craved retribution. 'But that wasn't before Claude's ego made him reveal what I needed to figure out his plan.'

His hubris played over and over in Lottie's head. *I have no intention of killing anyone*, he'd said, laughing. Lottie finally understood the joke.

'Is anyone gonna die?' Saskia asked frankly.

'Well, we got the murder right but not the execution, so to speak,' Binah explained, adjusting her glasses casually, as if she weren't in the process of explaining a royal assassination plot. 'Do you remember in the Gibson essay, when it told the story of Inessa and Alexis, how the people of Maradova were on the side of the invaders?'

'Well, duh,' Anastacia said. 'Because they were being rescued from the Mad King. I think anyone would be happy about that.'

'Exactly! And this got me thinking about Ellie's reputation.' Lottie held up a recent magazine to the screen, the one depicting Ellie as having gone wild at her own party and putting other people in danger. 'All the major Maravish newspapers have featured Ellie in the past year – and this isn't entirely new. There were rumours, even when she was a child, about being wild and unstable.'

Binah pulled up an old Maravish article on the screen as a case in point. 'This has been a plan long in the making – a plan to set Ellie up as the Mad Princess of Maradova, just like Agvan was the Mad King.'

'We think – no, I'm *sure*,' Lottie went on, 'that Claude is going to use the Hamelin Formula on Ellie to make her kill her parents at the ball. Just as Agvan did to his own parents.'

Everyone went silent, and Lottie would almost have believed the video had frozen if not for the face Emelia pulled, her thirst for revenge as palpable as Lottie's own.

She was the first to speak up, pulling everyone else out of their shocked stupor. 'OK. So if Claude wants to make it look like history is repeating itself, who's playing the roles of Inessa and Alexis?'

Now Miko chimed in, chewing on one of her decorated nails in thought. 'Well, obviously Jamie is Inessa's baby, right? He's the prince that they bring home?'

'Which means Inessa is Hirana, and Claude is . . .' Micky trailed off.

'Oh, crumbs,' Lola said.

'Yep,' Lottie confirmed. 'Claude will be their saviour – the one to bring the rightful ruler back and rescue them all.'

'Hmmm. *Just like Alexis*,' Anastacia said. 'Exactly what Ingrid said.'

Lottie nodded again, glad everyone was catching on so quickly.

Wei, who'd been deathly still in the corner of the screen, mulling it over, went straight for the most important question. 'When do they plan to do it?'

'In the story, Alexis kills Agvan on the steps of the ballroom,' said Lottie, shuddering. 'More specifically he rips his throat out in a violent display of dominance, and, well, the only time the Wolfsons will be a significant distance away from their guards and the hired Partizans is when they are presented to the guests at the GGF. So we think they'll do it after the presentation, right in front of everyone.'

Wei was taking notes, the lenses of his glasses flashing.

Binah shrugged. 'It makes the most sense, especially considering this is also Ellie's first time being officially presented at an event.'

Raphael finally spoke up. 'Talk about a bad introduction.'

A dark chuckle echoed through the speakers as Rio leaned forward. 'Right, like, *Hi I'm your future ruler. Oops! Just murdered my family. Anyway, nice to meet you.*'

Both boys cracked up, their laughter slowly fading as they realized no one else was joining in.

Rio huffed, leaning back again. 'Tough crowd.'

'Anyway . . .' Anastacia gave an eye-roll as she quickly moved the conversation on. 'What's *our* plan?'

Binah pulled up a blueprint of the palace. In the centre of the image, circled in red, were the steps of the ballroom with 6 *p.m.* written above it. According to the event information, this was when Ellie and her family would be presented to announce the start of the festivities.

'Our main goal is to make sure we get to Ellie first,' Lottie explained. 'If she steps out to be announced, we've failed.'

I've failed, she repeated internally.

Everyone nodded, the importance of the situation dawning on them.

'That gives us sixty minutes from when guests arrive to get to them – Binah?'

Binah leaned into frame, tightening both her space buns like she was preparing for a sprint. 'I propose we split into four groups.' There was a contagious excitement to her voice that made everyone instantly trust the plan. 'The first group will be me, Percy and Wei. Our job is to head to a private room, hack into the surveillance and relay to you guys where the royals are so that we can make sure you have a beeline to them without bumping into Leviathan. We can't waste a second.'

She waited patiently while everyone jotted down the info, and then Lottie took over again. 'The second group will be Lola, Micky and Miko.' Lottie let them register this before continuing. 'You will search for the king and queen in the right-hand antechamber with Binah and Wei's guidance.'

She paused to zoom in on the blueprint. The ballroom had an antechamber that acted as a dressing room on each side for royals to enter from. From Lottie's memory of being presented, the king and queen always came down the right staircase, and the princess came down the left.

'As long as one of us reaches one of the Wolfsons before they are presented, we can warn them and stop them.'

The group jotted down notes, and Lottie felt proud. 'The third group is Saskia, Anastacia, Rio and Raphael.' Their faces lit up with excitement. 'You have the most dangerous mission. With Saskia's knowledge of Leviathan, we need you to hunt down and halt any members you find, using any means necessary. You cannot let them get to Ellie.'

Saskia smirked, holding a thumb up to the screen. 'Beat Leviathan up. Don't get caught. Easy!'

There were only three people left unaccounted for, and Lottie stared at two of them intently. 'The final group will be me, Sayuri and Emelia.'

They both nodded, expecting this. Lottie knew she could trust these girls with her life. They would all do whatever it took to bring Claude down.

'We will make straight for the left antechamber, which is where Ellie will be waiting to be presented,' Lottie went on. 'We'll try to get there before the Hamelin Formula is used but we can't rule out the idea that they will already have used it. Emelia, with your previous knowledge of the effects of the formula we can help bring Ellie out of it should that be the case.'

Emelia pursed her lips, but whatever worries she had, she didn't voice them.

'Does everyone understand?' Binah asked.

Every member of their group gestured or vocalized their support. The sounds were like a suit of armour deflecting attacks – trustworthy and strong.

'OK!' Lottie announced. 'Then we're ready to save our princess.'

27

The safe house had become oppressive. Everyone was on edge. Ingrid cowered whenever Claude was around and Julius jumped at every small sound. Even Phi was stiffer than usual, and when they sat down for dinner Jamie was sure she cut her food more quietly than normal, careful not to even scrape her fork on the plate. All because Jamie's father hadn't got what he wanted – Lottie.

Haru had taken the brunt of the blame for Lottie's 'misplacement', as Claude had taken to calling it, mostly because the only other person who could be responsible was Claude himself, and apparently that was impossible. One thing was absolutely clear, though: Haru had meant every single word he'd said about where his loyalty lay.

His words echoed in Jamie's head. *You're my prince. You're everything to me.*

For the first time in his life Jamie didn't cringe away from the title. The words finally felt real.

Jamie had taken to spending even more time in his room, hoping his father would assume he was sulking. Better Claude think that than discover that Jamie was secretly researching the ring Lottie had given him.

Lottie had said Hanna and Midori had entrusted it to her, and even that had made him question everything he thought he knew. That the maids, who had taken care of him as a boy, still had faith in him and still thought he was worthy of redemption after everything Claude had said. He'd been made to believe they all thought him unworthy and feared he would take after Claude. Now none of that made sense.

For hours Jamie had analysed the ring, even the weight of it in his palm – something small and precious. Stamped with a pattern of scattered stars, the gold ring's surface contained a whole galaxy to explore and etched inside was a message for him.

ਤੁਸੀਂ ਆਪਣੇ ਖ਼ੁਦ ਦੇ ਹੋ

It hadn't taken long to translate the text, and when he attempted to speak it out loud, the language rolled off his tongue – not quite unfamiliar, more like a distant memory.

'You belong to yourself . . .' Jamie turned the words over in his mouth – words that Hirana had had inscribed for him to find.

It was an uneasy feeling at first, but he soon found a strange power in questioning everything he'd known to be true. He'd thought he belonged to the Maravish royal family and that had been wrong. He'd thought he was only a Partizan – and now he was a prince. He'd thought he was in love with Lottie, but he'd only been searching for his mother. And he'd thought himself his father's child, destined to become an extension of him. But he had a ring that said otherwise.

It had him wondering what else he had got wrong, and who had really been keeping him in the dark? With the Golden Flower Festival mere days away, when they would make their claim to the throne, he knew he couldn't stay in the fog any longer.

He now stood before his father's closed office door and raised a hand to knock.

'Come in, Jamie,' Claude called from the other side of the door. He hadn't even had time to bring his knuckles down against the polished wood. How did he do that?

When Jamie entered the dim office, Claude was in the process of inspecting his suit choices for the ball. He was dressed in a robe that pooled around him on the floor, as though he were emerging from a bottomless lake.

Two mannequins were propped against the window wearing almost identical ensembles – embroidered black velvet with red-silk lining that glistened like blood. In the half-light the smaller one – Jamie's – looked darker, swamped by the shadow of Claude's.

Claude opened a box on the mantel and presented Jamie with a crown of bones, or so it seemed. The silver-white of the metal made Jamie flinch, the design monstrous, all of it slotting together like the intricate pattern of a skeleton. From each side ascended jagged jewel-topped ridges that protruded like horns. 'This is for you. What do you think?'

Jamie knew this wasn't true. This crown was not for him; none of this was for him. This was Claude's vision, and somehow Jamie had become convinced that this was who he was meant to be – that becoming Claude was inevitable. What would happen if he defied that vision?

'It's certainly striking,' Jamie said, taking a closer look. He could feel the power radiating from it.

Letting out a self-satisfied hum, Claude went back to his own suit. 'I was hoping a glimpse into what your new life holds might lessen the blow of losing your little Portman.'

Jamie had to use all his willpower not to wince. Lottie had given him so much more than a ring; she'd given him clarity, and he was thankful Claude was too preoccupied to see his hand involuntarily squeeze into a fist. The gold band pushed into his flesh, throbbing with his heartbeat, and the fog shifted a little more with every pulse – the enigma of his father cracking.

He'd come looking for Claude because he thought he'd find himself there, but he was starting to realize that he had been looking in all the wrong places.

'What if I wore white?' Jamie tried, wandering over to one of the other suits to feel the fabric, avoiding eye contact with his father. He could sense Claude's gaze on his turned back and he used his Partizan training to keep his breath even.

Claude laughed, low and cold like a grave. 'You are my son, Jamie, and we do not wear white.'

Jamie breathed a quiet exhale of relief that Claude had decided not to pounce. He tried again. 'I was only thinking it might be more appealing to the Maravish people –'

A hand came down on his shoulder. How had Claude crept up on him?

'What is this really about?' Claude asked, his breath hot on Jamie's neck.

216

These were dangerous waters. If Jamie so much as let a drop of sweat form on his brow, Claude would know he was harbouring doubts.

Jamie needed to be everything Claude wanted him to be, and he was starting to realize what that was – a son as spoiled and temperamental as himself.

With a sigh that Jamie hoped sounded moody, he put on his best impression of a sulky teenager. 'I know you want us to come forward at the ball to expose what they did,' Jamie muttered, fiddling with the sleeve of the suit in front of him. 'But how can you be so sure the people of Maradova will adore me, or that they'll welcome me home?'

The grip on Jamie's shoulder immediately relaxed, and a chuckle rumbled from his father's throat. 'You have nothing to fear, my son. You are their prince. Of course they will adore you.'

'How can you know they will?'

Claude broke away. 'Because I have made sure of it.'

There was a finality in Claude's words; there was something Jamie didn't know, a crucial part of his father's plan.

Jamie acquiesced, putting the horned crown back in its box. 'I trust you.'

Claude turned him round so he was forced to look into his father's face and at the manic grin, wild and expectant. But, despite recognizing that feral edge in himself, Jamie could only see differences. Claude's skin was paler than his, his lips thin and cracked with lies, and the green of his eyes was as cold as money, while Jamie's were warm like a meadow.

'Is all this because your little Portman escaped us?' Claude asked. 'There will be other chances to bring her in once you

217

take your rightful place.' He reached out to stroke Jamie's hair in open adoration, and Jamie forced himself not to back away.

'You are just like me,' Claude mused. 'In the end we always get what belongs to us.'

Jamie felt sure the room turned colder, though the ring on his finger burned. 'What?'

Claude smiled fondly. 'You are my son. You were always destined to come back to me so that we could put things right.'

Claude had it all backwards. Hirana had already won. She'd stamped her words into gold to make sure Jamie would know, forever and always, where to find himself. *You belong to yourself*.

Though Claude was right in a way. Jamie would get what belonged to him; his life had always been his for the taking. He was not fated to be or do anything except live how he chose. He had to claim himself and his own destiny.

Jamie's ring sent electricity up through his veins to his heart. He could no longer see any of himself in Claude – any of that monstrosity he'd thought he was predisposed to become. He only saw a lie, one that Jamie was guilty of feeding himself. 'Thank you for putting my mind at ease,' he managed to say at last.

Claude patted his head and stepped back to the mannequins. 'You still have much to learn.'

Jamie did have more to learn. But at least now he knew there was one person in the safe house who he could trust, someone who had always let Jamie be true to himself without judgement or expectation. Haru.

28

Ellie must have heard the phrase *unfortunate accident* at least a hundred times now. Adamantly from her mother and father, reassuringly from Sam and Stella, whispered in the corridors by students, as well as headlined in every Maravish newspaper – and a few international ones. But it didn't matter that it was an accident; it didn't matter that Ellie hadn't meant to hurt anyone – Leo had still been badly injured. If she hadn't been so stubborn, so sure she knew what she was doing, Leo would be OK right now, and she wouldn't be having to prepare to be presented at a ball where everyone hated her.

A knock at the door pulled her out of her downward spiral, and Hanna and Midori carried in trays of tea and finger sandwiches. 'We thought you kids might want some fuel to help you prepare for the ball. Wow!'

Midori immediately stopped short and Hanna came up behind her. The two of them stood gaping, thunderstruck by Ellie's get-up.

'We thought you'd decided you wouldn't wear dresses any more,' Hanna said, peering over Midori's shoulder.

Scurrying back into the room with rows of necklaces draped over her arm, Stella scowled at Ellie's maids. 'Is there a problem?' she asked stonily. 'Ellie asked us to help her prepare. You shouldn't doubt her choices. She's your princess.'

Hanna and Midori sheepishly shared a glance.

'If that's what she wants,' said Hanna.

After setting the trays down, they loitered by the door, waiting for Ellie to say something, but she couldn't bring herself to add to the conversation. Every choice she made only made matters worse. She was tired of thinking for herself.

'Inform my parents that I'll see them at the ball,' she said eventually.

Then they left and Ellie was alone with the twins once more.

They were right to find it strange, of course. Ever since Ellie was little, wearing ball gowns had always been unpleasant. She liked them well enough on other people, but to her they felt claustrophobic – like wearing an iron maiden, the spikes piercing her skin – reminders of everything expected of her, everything she couldn't be.

But this was different. It was her last chance to redeem even a molecule of her reputation. And if that took metres of organza and velvet, she'd do it.

'You look beautiful,' Stella said, as she fanned out Ellie's skirts. Piles upon piles of flowing silver and black gossamer hissed and whispered with every move Ellie made.

There was something punishing about the dress; its shoulder pads stuck out into sharp points and a long ebony cape traipsed behind her, darker than any shadow. She caught her reflection in the mirror and thought she looked like misfortune personified. She pitied anyone who might brush up against her, as though her own misery could be catching.

'I feel like I'm going to my own funeral.'

'With your luck it'll end up being someone else's funeral.' Sam snickered from where he was draped sideways over the armchair, but quickly shut up when his sister hurled a cushion at him.

'Sam! That's not funny.' Stella quickly went back to humming a happy tune as she picked out accessories and fascinators to pair with Ellie's ghoulish ball gown.

With their mousy hair curled up in victory rolls like horns, the twins were matching in olive-green silk and bronze jewellery. They looked like woodland sprites, Stella scampering around Ellie with busy little fingers while Sam lounged about, nibbling on the occasional grape while he watched his sister work.

Unlike Ellie, the twins looked perfect in their garments; they'd even received a nod of approval from Simien, only confirming that Ellie was right to let them help her.

Stella tutted, holding up a gold feather earring to the side of Ellie's cheek. 'You mustn't pull that face.'

Ellie sighed, trying to smile. 'I know, I know. I should have listened to you guys from the start, then I wouldn't be in this mess.'

Stella's nose scrunched up and Ellie wondered if she was feeling guilty. She'd spent hours crying about what happened to Leo, convinced that she should have checked the blade more thoroughly. However, Ellie knew it was her own responsibility – and once again she'd dragged someone else into her problems.

Instead of bringing it up, Stella smiled, leaning in to gently rouge Ellie's cheeks. 'You really don't want to be a princess, do you?' she asked.

'No,' Ellie replied honestly. 'I think it was a mistake.' Then she thought of Jamie and just how much of a mistake it really was. 'There's someone else out there I think would have been much better at all this than me.' The words pulled her deeper into thoughts she didn't want; thoughts of Lottie, and how even on the other side of the world – even when she hadn't seen her in over a year – she was still failing her. Clutching the wolf to her chest, Ellie exhaled slowly. 'There are other people this all comes so naturally to.'

'How so?' Stella asked, pausing with a make-up brush in her hand. Little particles of scented powder danced in the air.

There was only one person in Ellie's mind, the powder's smell reminding her of roses. Lottie's roses.

Ellie's heart cracked. 'Kind people. I don't think I'm a very nice person, you see. I get angry a lot and lose my temper, and I'm stubborn and selfish, and I end up hurting people like Leo, and –' She stopped before she mentioned Jamie or Lottie. 'It's why I like kind people. I admire them and I hope some of their light can shine on me.'

Absorbing her words, Stella stroked the soft brush against Ellie's cheeks. 'Then why do you let us hang out with you?'

Ellie was surprised. 'You and Sam are kind too.'

Stella made a face that showed she thought that was ridiculous.

'You are,' Ellie assured her. 'Both of you have stuck by me, and I know it can't be good for your reputations no matter how many future benefits you think you'll reap. And besides . . .' A whisper of her old smirk formed, an instinct to try to cheer up the only people who'd stuck by her the past year. 'You'd have to be kind to put up with me.'

Stella's face softened in a way Ellie hadn't seen before, and she almost looked sad. 'I don't think you're as terrible as they say.'

It felt as though Ellie were hearing her clearly for the first time. Behind the words there was something real. It was the closest to vulnerable she'd ever seen Stella, and it made her falter, as if the two of them had just fallen out of rhythm in a dance Ellie hadn't known they were performing.

With a clatter, Sam appeared at their sides, setting down one of the trays Hanna and Midori had brought in. 'I think it's time we ate something,' he suggested, raising an eyebrow at his sister. 'We have a strict schedule and we don't want you forgetting to eat.'

Ellie leaned forward for a sandwich, but Stella grabbed her wrist, squeezing a little too tight. 'Let's take some pictures first,' she said, looking up to her brother. 'I think we have enough time for that.'

Checking his watch, Sam shrugged. 'If you want to.'

'I do,' she replied firmly, and Ellie wondered if the twins had recently had an argument she didn't know about.

'Pictures sound good,' Ellie said, and Stella immediately lit up again, the serious look replaced by her usual playfulness. She reached into her bag to pull out a Polaroid camera.

Stella had Sam take a few photos of them in their dresses, posing Ellie first with their arms linked and then turning ones making a little heart with her fingers like she'd seen pop stars do. Feeling completely ridiculous, Ellie focused on the smile it pulled out of Stella, remembering how Lottie would get excited over things like photos.

'OK, everyone, get in tight,' Stella called, pulling Sam and Ellie in for a selfie. 'I've always wanted to take a photo like this – say cheese!'

Exhaling sharply, Ellie thought of the only thing that could ever make her smile, and her head filled with Lottie again. She let the sweet roses and lavender wash over her as she imagined the only girl she'd ever loved, pink-cheeked and grinning before Ellie had ruined everything – before that lovely round face had been stained with tears.

'Cheese!' Ellie called as the memory cracked and she saw Lottie crying on the balcony, her chapped skin pressed against cold stone, as Ellie cut her with every wretched lie.

You're doing the right thing, Ellie reminded herself.

Sam held out the tray of food again, and this time Ellie took a sandwich and a flute of mimosa, swallowing down every miserable feeling.

'Shall we play a game while we wait?' he asked, pulling out a deck of cards.

'Crazy eights?' Stella offered, looking at Ellie for approval.

Ellie nodded, nibbling at her food as Sam dealt out the cards.

They were a game in when the edges began to fade and the numbers on every card turned hazy. Ellie wondered if it was the drink. She didn't mind; the world was turning soft, and every card she put down brought the calm closer. A welcome fog was claiming her, and she felt like a doll, her limbs turning plastic, her bones folding into ball joints, her brain melting, until she was no longer plagued by her own thoughts. A distant voice told her this was wrong, that something wasn't right, but she pushed it away with one last sip of her drink.

The cards slipped through her fingers along with the last remnants of herself. And just like that she was gone – finally free of the burden of making any more decisions. Now she would be quiet and complacent, do as she was told, all choice and desire melted away.

Stella came over to place a tiara on her head. As dark as night, the tiara was made of interlocking onyx and diamonds, the black metal fanning out like snow crystals, icy and unfeeling. It felt as heavy and cold as a curse.

Somewhere in the back of her mind she thought of another tiara's opal, a crescent moon shining from its centre, and a name popped into her mind. *Lottie*.

'Ellie,' Stella whispered, 'you really do look beautiful.'

They were such sweet words, but they must have been painful to say because when Stella pulled away, tears brimmed in her eyes. Ever so gently her brother placed a hand on Stella's shoulder, comforting her.

Why is Stella crying? Ellie wondered, confused.

Her last conscious thought before everything turned black was that she had a bad habit of making her friends cry.

29

As was traditional in Maradova, the Golden Flower Festival was met with snowfall. It was as though Lottie had stepped into a toy globe and every soft kiss of snow made her exposed skin hum with nostalgia. The palace that had once felt like a second home now loomed over her in a white flurry, beautiful people in flowing ball gowns running up the steps to the open door where golden light spilled out. The scene came straight from a fairy tale.

And, just like the fairy tales from her childhood, there was a princess that needed saving and evil that needed defeating, and Lottie Pumpkin was there to make sure this story had a happy ending.

Lottie and Binah headed up the steps to enter the ball and find the others.

'Thank you again for my dress,' Lottie said, feeling the hilt of her sword at her back. It was her secret stinger, ready, waiting.

Binah grinned back. 'You're most welcome. You need the right disguise after all.'

Lottie's white skirts twirled around her as though she were part of the snowfall. The gold and pink roses embroidered along the hem of her dress winked in the moonlight, as if she were scattering flowers with every step. Binah wore a yellow beaded gown with the skirt flaring out below the knees in a dramatic mermaid cut. Together they looked like the sun and its adoring flowers. Lottie's tiara nestled in her curls, the crescent moon glowing as they approached the candlelit entrance, warming her with its strange power – it was a reminder of who she was and where she came from.

'Ready?' Binah asked as they reached the open doors, where a snarling wolf was engraved into the handle.

Lottie stared at the creature's bared fangs. 'I'm ready.'

Stepping into the light, her heels clipped on the marble like the desperate beat of her heart. There was no thunder, no explosion of feeling, just the familiar echoing quiet of the palace. Somewhere inside was a princess and a prince who held the key to ending this eternal slumber.

They made their way down the hall with the other arriving guests. Lottie turned to Binah. 'We need to head straight for the hall where –'

Lottie stopped short. She was relieved to see that Claude's portrait was no longer displayed. What she hadn't expected, though, was the painting that had replaced it.

It felt like a lifetime ago that she had seen this painting of Ellie – an impeccable rendition of everything Lottie knew she could be, and so very different to the strange plastic girl she'd recently seen plastered on magazine covers. There was a possibility tonight, she knew, that Ellie would have changed, that her wildness would be tamed. But Lottie knew who she really was. She was the girl in this painting. A prince – her saviour, valiant, brave and handsome, and perfect just as she was. She knew because she'd painted it herself.

Their invitations were checked three times and Lottie was acutely aware of the guards stationed each side of the double doors of the ballroom. The shield emblem she'd seen at the Partizan council was displayed on their breast pockets. But not a single one of them clocked Liliana's sword in the back of her dress. The blade was wound up tight and held her back straight and her head high.

There was an arrogance to the guards that meant she was able to walk past them with a weapon, which only confirmed to her that she was right not to trust that they could handle the situation.

Delicate fingers threaded round Lottie's and Binah pulled her towards the ballroom. 'Here we are.'

Music swelled, vibrating through Lottie's bones, and, when the white doors parted, Lottie stepped inside without fear or reservation, ready to revive the palace's heart.

'Utterly splendid!' Binah said as she took in the sight, bunching up her skirts in her fists as she swayed across the marble floor in time with the plucked strings of a distant harp.

The summer ball had been stained for Lottie by their first run-in with Leviathan, the first of many. And now, as she wandered the ballroom again, having sustained more welts at Claude's hands, she expected the sensation to sting, like pressing on a bruise, but all she felt was a childlike thrill. 'Magic,' she whispered.

Painted cherubs lounged on the ceiling on clouds of hydrangea, wisteria and grape, in blooms of lilac and blue, the painted paradise spilling out through every vine and branch. If Lottie could only reach up and pluck one of the fruits, she was sure she would taste heaven. But it was all fake; the wonder, the beauty, every piece above her had had to be imported, shipped in from a land that was warm and alive. Every person in the room, dressed so elegantly, dancing so joyfully – they were celebrating an empire on its last legs.

Stepping further in, Lottie searched for her group, but, before she could find them, a vanilla swirl in human form grabbed her.

Wrapping her arms round Lottie's side, Lola spun her in a frilly sweet-scented twirl like they were strings of sugar in a candyfloss maker.

'Holy chocolate biscuit, Lottie!' she chirped happily. 'This place is amazing. Have you seen the cakes?'

Lottie untangled herself from Lola's grip. 'When we succeed we can eat all the cake we want,' she said with a smile.

Micky perked up at this from where he had his white-suited arm hooked round his boyfriend's, a serious look taking over his usually saccharine expression.

'*We've been waiting for you,*' Percy signed. '*Come on.*'

Lottie followed Percy, who was difficult to lose in tails and a top hat, and then she saw her – hair as black as night and skin like plum blossom, dressed in a kimono of red-painted silk. She looked like a single glowing ember still alive in the grey ash of a dying fire.

Sayuri turned, her dark eyes slicing across the room. When she spotted Lottie a sly smile slid across her lips.

Lottie ran towards Sayuri and threw her arms round her, breathing in that calming scent of lily that she'd missed so much.

'Is that a sword in your dress or are you just pleased to see me?' Sayuri asked.

'I could say the same,' Lottie mumbled, as her fingers brushed something hard – the sword that matched her own, the one that connected them.

Lottie turned to the rest of the group. She checked that none of the other guests could hear them and said in a low voice, 'How many of us have . . .' Lottie cupped her hand over her mouth and whispered, '. . . have weapons?'

Anastacia's entire group raised their hands, while Emelia shrugged in her nonchalant way as confirmation.

'We can't go up against Leviathan with just our bare hands now, can we?' Anastacia said.

Lottie was about to laugh when she saw Emelia's face. She was biting the inside of her lip like she was trying to solve a problem. When she caught Lottie watching, she sighed and gestured her over.

They walked away from the group and Lottie admired the gossamer cape fanning out like iridescent wings from Emelia's gold abaya-style dress and the jewel on her forehead like a third eye at the edge of her hijab. Lottie almost felt as if she were by the side of an angel – one with a very serious expression.

'I wanted to talk to you about the formula,' Emelia said when they were out of earshot. 'I want you to be prepared in case we get there too late.'

Trying to smile reassuringly, Lottie kept her voice calm and measured. 'It won't be too late. As long as she hasn't gone out to be introduced yet, I can snap her out of it.'

Emelia shook her head, her honey-flecked eyes anxiously looking into the middle distance, clearly seeing things that Lottie couldn't.

'But that's it – you can't just shake someone out of it.' Her voice was high and tight. 'If they use enough of it –' she swallowed hard – 'it pierces through everything that makes you who you are, until you're trapped in your body without a soul.'

Lottie couldn't imagine Ellie as anything but wild and full of life. If only she could show Ellie how perfect she was in her eyes, how much she loved her just the way she was.

'If that's the case,' Lottie said carefully, knuckles turning white as she squeezed her hands, 'I'll just have to go in even deeper to pull her out of it.'

Emelia was very still, her eyes flickering as the clouds of her nightmare parted and vanished completely. Her lips twisted up in a smirk. 'You really are just like Sayuri said.'

'And how's that?'

'Unstoppable.'

Just then across the room a set of trumpets sounded, and sauntering in from the upper right staircase, stick-thin and dressed impeccably, was a man Lottie knew all too well.

Simien, the king's advisor – her old mentor on all things appropriate for a princess – took his place at the top of the centre staircase, extending his arms in a sweeping motion as if he were about to sing. 'Distinguished guests, we welcome you to another Golden Flower Festival,' he announced, his

232

voice ringing with authority. It pained Lottie to think how clueless he was about the imminent danger. 'This is a time for the people of Maradova to celebrate the royal family and reflect on our vast and rich heritage. We hope you will enjoy the festivities, and we look forward to presenting each one of you to our great monarchy later this evening.' The trumpets blared once more and he bowed. 'Enjoy your evening.'

Then to the sound of applause Simien disappeared up the left staircase into the room where Ellie would currently be waiting. Lottie wished she could follow him. How simple it would be if she could just break through the crowd and run up the steps to her princess. How painful it was to have her just out of reach.

Turning back to her friends, Lottie looked over their group. All of them were here for the same reason.

'Is everyone ready?'

They nodded.

'Then let's go save Ellie.'

30

'Over there,' Binah announced, gesturing to her companions. They were stationed on the terrace, the party glowing behind them through glass double doors while they shivered their way down to an appropriate hiding spot.

'This will do,' Binah announced, squeezing herself between two of the stone pillars that held up a balcony on a higher level. Clinging to the dark, the others followed and the light of the party vanished as they became one with the shadows.

They each took a seat on the stone slabs beside her, Wei carefully placing a handkerchief down beforehand so as not to dirty his white suit. Binah decided not to take offence that he didn't whip a handkerchief out for her or Percy too.

They'd wandered out to the near-deserted gardens, and Binah was relieved when Percy had handed her his jacket. The heaped snow was a clear indicator of just how frigid the night was.

'Aren't there supposed to be guests appreciating the gardens?' Wei asked, already pulling his phone out and taking the back off to reveal a collection of wires and chips.

Binah chuckled to herself as she reached into her purse. 'A rather hopeful idea,' she said, taking out a monitor that by the look on Wei's face he thought was much too large to have been able to fit inside. 'They keep this area of the gardens open as part of the tradition, you see,' Binah explained. 'The idea was that the guests could come and view the flowers, but it's been a long time since the weather permitted such a thing.'

Like a strange mechanical spider, the finished device had eight colourful wires stretching out from it, each attached to a tiny hard drive.

'Monitor,' Wei requested, holding his hand out.

Binah passed it to him, watching as his long thin fingers hooked it up while Percy double-checked the connections.

By the time they were done, it was simple enough to run the code Wei and Binah had written to bypass the login to the network's security system and pull up the palace's internal security-camera footage. There was approximately a fifteen-second delay, but it would be enough time for them to send a warning.

Flicking through the images, the reflection of the screen glinted in Percy's eyes. Then he paused, his jaw dropping. Binah and Wei leaned forward to look.

'Interesting,' Binah mused, taking in the familiar figures arriving through the back garden. It was Leviathan, of course. She wasn't surprised; she'd known they were coming. What was strange was that they weren't doing a very good job of avoiding the cameras.

Well, most of them were. The figures stuck close to the shadows, but every now and then Jamie or Haru would flash across the frame almost by mistake. Yet there was something else – the way their hands moved.

'Are they trying to get the attention of the security camera?' Wei asked.

'*It certainly seems so,*' Percy signed.

They looked at one other, none of them daring to voice their hope.

'Regardless,' Binah said quickly, 'we still need to warn the others that Leviathan are here and that they're coming in from the back –'

Just then Binah and Wei froze, turning slowly to the approaching sound of boots.

'Hands against the wall – now!'

Binah gestured to Percy while she lay the screen on the ground, and the three of them immediately did as they were told.

It was a woman and a man. She was short but built like a house, while he was tall. Both of them sported a shield emblem on their jackets.

Wei spoke up first. 'You're making a mistake.'

The woman came up behind them, cuffs at the ready. 'We had a tip-off about your little Leviathan group,' she said. 'Not as much of a threat as we were led to believe.'

The two guards chuckled to themselves while on the screen beneath her feet Binah saw Jamie and Haru slip inside the palace. With handcuffs firmly round her wrists, she sighed. 'This is my fault. I always forget to factor in other people's incompetence.'

*

237

Beyond the glitter and spectacle of the ball, Miko found herself in a strange place.

It was dark and spooky, and painted eyes followed a person across icy corridors, candles flickering in impossible breezes. Everything Miko loved.

'It's like a haunted house,' Lola grumbled.

Miko grinned back. 'I know!'

Shuddering, Micky wrapped his hand round his sister's, as they turned into a long corridor. 'Here,' he suddenly announced, holding a lollipop out towards Miko. 'Sweets make everything less scary.'

Miko took the red lollipop, but watching the twins in the dark hallway, Miko felt as though she were seeing two worlds collide. The twins were wrapped up in frilly white, yellow and pink outfits – looking like mascots for a Japanese brand of candy – with shadows nipping at their legs. It was almost comical. A nagging voice tried to remind her that they were in the middle of a serious mission, but Miko couldn't help herself. 'You know I heard there's a ghost.'

The twins cuddled in closer to each other and Miko had to hide her laugh.

'What kind of ghost?' Micky asked.

'Agvan, of course,' Miko explained. 'Every year during the Flower Festival, he wanders the halls looking for revenge on anyone that celebrates his demise.'

With perfect timing, one of the windows gave a ghostly rattle.

'How do you know if he's coming?' Lola whispered.

Twirling a strand of her blue hair round her finger, Miko thought. 'You hear him gurgling, trying to scream through the endless blood spilling from where his throat was ripped out. Wait, listen. Do you hear that?'

There was no sound, but Miko delighted in the way the twins stopped deathly still and leaned forward to listen.

'What's that?' Lola asked.

Furrowing her blue brows in confusion, Miko listened too. And there it was: a distant methodical *crack, crack, crack*.

Miko took a step back, pulling the twins with her against the wall.

The sinister sound grew closer.

The lights went out abruptly, leaving only a single candle flickering.

'It's Agvan's ghost,' Micky whimpered, clinging to Miko.

The clacking was close now, just round the corner.

Miko spat an expletive in Japanese before turning to the twins. 'OK, listen – we need to run back and –' Her breath caught in her throat. She watched her own nightmare reflected in the twins' faces. She heard the click again, and now she could hear it properly. It was the distinct static of a walkie-talkie.

'Yep, I've caught them. Over.'

Miko spun to face their captor, a huge man with eyebrows so thick they looked like hay bales. She had just spotted the shield emblem on the giant's jacket before Lola's sweet voice added, 'Would you believe us if we said we were . . . lost?'

The man's grasp tightened on Miko's wrist. From his expression the answer was clearly . . . no.

*

239

In another universe Anastacia was enjoying a pleasant evening in the ballroom, showing off her new Chanel gown, drinking champagne cocktails and taking selfies with her girlfriend who'd agreed to wear a colour-coordinated tux.

Unfortunately this was not that universe, and instead she'd had to switch out of her Louboutin stilettos into Keds of all things behind a statue of some long-dead royal so she could run down stupidly long corridors while listening to Tweedledum and Tweedledee go on about their failed love lives. She was definitely going to make Claude pay for this.

'What I need is a girl like Emelia,' Raphael said with a sigh.

Raising a heavily pierced eyebrow, Rio threw a knife in the air and caught it absent-mindedly. 'You barely even know her.'

Raphael shrugged. 'She just has that takes-no-crap attitude, and I mean, come on . . .' He gestured at his own face. 'We'd look really good together.'

Turning to her girlfriend as they continued to jog, Saskia made a gagging gesture.

'As much as the lesbian in me loves hearing you two go on about hot women who are way out of your league,' Anastacia muttered, 'shouldn't we have heard something from Binah's group by now?' She checked her phone again. Not a single message.

Raphael shrugged. 'No news is good news, right?'

'Yes, but she's supposed to be –'

They stopped abruptly as they turned a corner, Anastacia's trainers squeaking against the marble as she collided into some party attendees. Or at least she thought they were party attendees, but from the way Saskia was staring at them it was clear something wasn't right.

'I think you two must be lost,' Raphael purred. 'I can take you back to the party if you – hey!' He let out an indignant sound as the girl swatted him away.

'Playtime's over, guys,' Anastacia hissed, reaching to the back of her dress. 'I don't think they're here for the ball.'

Saskia blinked. 'Sam, Stella, is that really you? Wow, you guys have really grown since I last saw you, although I see you still haven't grown out of your braces, Stella.'

'Oh, I see.' Rio grinned, catching on immediately. 'They're from Leviathan, huh?' He looked thirsty for a fight.

Stella narrowed her eyes. 'And I see you still haven't grown any common sense.'

'Guards!' Sam screamed. His voice was so loud Anastacia nearly had to cover her ears.

Within seconds footsteps could be heard thundering down the corridor.

'Wait, what?' Saskia turned to her old comrades. 'Why would you call the guards on yourselves?'

Sticking her tongue out, Stella let out a blood-curdling scream.

'What the hell? Get off me, you little rat.' Saskia tried to push her away, but Stella clung on, digging her claws into her arm.

Growling, Anastacia had stepped forward, trying to pull Stella off her girlfriend, when the guards arrived.

'That's them!' Sam screeched again, running off to safety. 'Help! They have my sister!'

'Wait, *what*?' Saskia hurled Stella forward, who, despite being perfectly capable of holding her balance, did an entirely ridiculous display of toppling to the floor.

Stella put on a twisted grin before she pointed at the group. 'That's Leviathan,' she declared. 'Get them!'

Something was wrong . . . Actually something was the opposite of wrong. Ingrid had put together a plan to make sure they got into the ball without being noticed, and yet not a single guard was where they were supposed to be. It was almost an anticlimax.

'Did one of us schedule a diversion?' Julius asked Ingrid as they flooded through the back entrance that was *supposed* to be guarded.

'Not me,' Ingrid said with a pout.

She'd been really looking forward to taking out those guards and showing Claude how good her plan was. Now they were waltzing in as if they'd been invited. *Stupid Maravish royal family can't do anything right*.

They were all dressed impeccably. Claude had gifted each of them an outfit so lavish that Ingrid didn't feel worthy. Hers was a long black-velvet dress with a slit up the side of the leg for easy mobility, but it sat too tightly round her chest, the fabric itchy.

Haru and Jamie stuck so close together they might as well have been holding hands.

'You OK, buddy?' Julius asked, patting Jamie on the back. 'Must be weird being back.'

Jamie patted Julius in return. 'Yeah, I'll be all right.'

He smiled, and Ingrid muttered, 'Definitely weird.'

'OK,' Phi murmured, looking over the group, 'now remember – outside this door is the meeting point if anything should go wrong.' They all nodded, then Phi did a final scan of their surroundings before heading in. She looked like a tank in a suit, her silk tails tailor-made to fit her.

Ingrid's breath hitched as she realized this was it – they would finally put things right and bring Claude's plan to action. Jamie and Claude would be where they were supposed to be, and they'd –

'Ingrid,' Claude snapped, 'stop loitering and concentrate.' He leaned down, and for a split second she didn't recognize him. His green eyes had narrowed into slits like a snake's. 'I won't have you ruining this like you ruin everything else. Not again.'

'Sorry, Master,' she whispered.

Quickly following him, she couldn't remember what she'd been so excited about.

31

Silence tracked Lottie through the palace.

'Is it true you spoke to Haru?' Sayuri asked out of the blue, throwing a lock of her silky hair over her shoulder.

'He helped me,' Lottie said. 'And there was something different about him and Jamie.'

'How so?' There was a hint of hope in Sayuri's voice.

'There was something between them, and whatever it was felt strong enough to overpower Claude's hold.' And then almost to herself she murmured, 'It made me wonder if something had happened between them.'

Emelia and Sayuri shared a sideways glance.

'It doesn't change anything,' Lottie said, as though she were trying to persuade herself. 'If Jamie and Haru are here for Claude's plan, we have to stop them.'

'Whatever it takes,' Emelia vowed.

'Whatever it takes,' Lottie echoed, and although her voice came out steady, her mouth felt dry with fear.

Wordlessly they continued down the corridor, all three listening out for any sign of other people, but the palace seemed entirely still.

Emelia leaned over to Lottie and whispered, 'You're not shaking.'

Lottie looked down at her hands and saw a stillness to rival the quiet palace, almost as though they'd found a truce. She shrugged. 'I know what I have to do.'

The part of her that was Liliana, fierce and fearless, had now been awakened and would never leave. And it was all because of Ellie that she'd unlocked this part of herself.

'It's just down here,' she breathed, terrified and exhilarated at the same time.

The three of them drifted round the bend in the corridor. Heavy mahogany doors with golden handles were Lottie's last hurdle before she reached the part of the palace where her heart lay. Where she'd find Ellie.

But she wasn't the only one. Coming round the bend were Jamie and Haru.

Both groups skidded to a halt outside the door, each of them panting, hearts racing, confusion growing. All Lottie could do was stare into Jamie's eyes, searching, hoping beyond hope. He stared right back, the two of them alone in this tiny moment before it burst around them.

Hands reaching behind their backs, Emelia and Sayuri moved to arm themselves. They transformed in front of her, the fabric of their dresses hitching and giving way to sheathed swords, both girls turning from elegant to deadly in seconds. But, despite herself, Lottie hesitated and to her surprise so did Jamie.

Lottie could feel him across from her like the pull of a powerful tide, but she clenched her fists. *Whatever it takes*.

Emelia stepped forward, her blade outstretched. 'Back away from the door.'

'Put your weapons away,' Jamie retorted. His hand hovered over his pocket, and Lottie saw something glitter there. His mother's ring winked at her from its rightful place on his finger.

Hope surged through her, and she willed herself to believe he could still change his mind.

'Sayu?' Haru's voice was soft like melted butter. 'You have a sword?'

'Catch up, Haru,' Sayuri spat back. 'There's lots we've been keeping from each other.'

Emelia and Sayuri looked between Jamie and Haru, giving each other a knowing side-eye. Lottie regretted telling them about what she'd sensed between them in Cornwall.

Jamie shook his head. 'I'm sorry . . . Who are you?'

Emilia's look of fury was strong enough to knock down a building. 'I'm one of the people your hideous father tried to use.' She strode forward, ready to strike.

Her sword sang against the steel of Jamie's knife, clanging in the air like a warning bell.

Sayuri pushed Lottie away. 'Leave us! We can hold them off.'

Lottie rushed to the door.

'No! Wait!' Jamie called after her, but Lottie slipped through anyway. Jamie had picked his side, and she had to go and save hers. 'Goodbye, Jamie.' She slammed the door shut behind her and went to find her princess.

At first sight the plush dressing room appeared to be empty. The lights were low. Everything was silent. Beyond

247

the door she could faintly hear the sword fight continuing, but she couldn't think about that now. 'Ellie . . .?' she called anxiously.

There were no guards anywhere, so Lottie wandered further into the room, heading towards a walk-in wardrobe where the light was dazzling, illuminating boxes of expensive jewellery.

'Ellie . . .?' she called again.

Then she saw her. Her princess was sitting at the dressing table, her back towards her.

I made it, Lottie wanted to sing, her feet carrying her forward. *I made it! I made it!*

Everything was OK. Ellie was safe. She just had to –

Lottie froze. The figure sat facing the mirror, wearing a tiara that sparkled like a cluster of jagged black stalagmites. It was impossible to see where the girl ended and the tiara began. But, worst of all, she could smell that familiar sickly aroma – the venomous bite of the Hamelin Formula.

'Ellie,' Lottie tried again, firmer now. 'Look at me.'

Slowly Ellie turned her head ever so slightly.

Lottie's heart nearly stopped. Many years ago, at Rosewood Hall, Lottie had seen a girl who was a storm, a hurricane in human form, who had whirled into her life with a smile that flashed as white as lightning. In contrast, the person in front of her now was an empty shell. She reached out and tenderly cupped her friend's face in her hands. 'Ellie, I'm so sorry. I –'

Then hands wrapped round Lottie's arms, jerking her backwards, and she screamed, reaching out desperately for her princess. Ellie hadn't even taken her hand.

248

'So you're the pumpkin princess we've heard so much about,' a girl's voice whispered in her ear.

'Don't worry,' a boy echoed just as insidiously. 'We've been taking good care of your friend.'

'Get off me!' Lottie growled, biting down on the hand that trapped her.

The boy howled and pulled back, but his hand was only replaced with another, and now another wrapped round her mouth like a muzzle.

The reception door behind Lottie opened, and two sets of feet made their way in.

'Stella! Sam!' Ingrid's familiar voice purred. 'Put her up against the wall there. I want her to hear the crowd scream when we win.'

They threw Lottie against the panelled wall hard enough that she felt the sword against her spine. If she could just reach for it . . .

'No moving,' Ingrid said menacingly.

With Sam and Stella holding her back, Lottie saw Ingrid's spider knife glinting and noticed Julius just behind her.

Ingrid prowled towards her. 'You're lucky our prince has forbidden us from harming you.' She allowed the cool point of her weapon to run down Lottie's jugular.

Lottie fought back tears. 'You don't have to do this!'

She was so close. Ellie was so close.

'You can stop this,' Lottie tried again. 'Ellie's a good person.' She looked desperately over at her friend, who was still sat silently before the mirror. 'Claude's been lying,' she said. 'To all of you!'

At Lottie's side Stella's grip softened and her jaw unclenched. But only a breath away, Sam moved her princess to the door to the ballroom, preparing to send her out to her doom.

Julius carefully retrieved a knife from his jacket. The handle was a wolf's open snarl, the blade a hideously beautiful obsidian that glinted like blood in the light. It was the perfect weapon for the black wolf of the family to wreak his revenge.

'Ellie!' Lottie screeched, desperately trying to break through the princess's fog, but there was no reaction. Ellie didn't even seem to recognize her own name.

Lottie tried again, clinging to the hesitation she'd felt from the girl on her left. 'Claude doesn't care about any of you.' She could taste the cruelty in her own words and kept going. 'He's *never* cared about any of you. Deep down you all know this. You're better than this. You're better than him.'

Ingrid paused after slipping the knife into the folds of Ellie's dress. She was trembling.

'Don't let him win,' Lottie urged.

There was a sudden growl and, out of nowhere, a glass smashed on the floor. It took her a second to realize that Julius had thrown it.

'I'm sick of this!' He rubbed his face in frustration. Then he turned to Ingrid, and shook his head, conflicted. 'What do you want to do?'

Lottie held her breath and Stella's grip tightened. Everything seemed to depend on Ingrid and Julius, and whatever they decided to do.

At last, Ingrid let out a hiss. She looked at Julius, her eyes swimming with tears. 'What else do we have?' she asked him helplessly.

Julius closed his eyes, a deep regretful breath leaving him as he made his choice.

'OK.' He nodded. Their decision was made; they would stay with the Goat Man.

Lottie felt her heart almost break – not just for Ellie, but for them too. 'You don't have to do this!' she cried in one last desperate plea, but Ingrid had made up her mind.

'What is your objective?' Ingrid asked Ellie.

The shell of Ellie smiled. When she spoke it sounded like decay.

'Once I finish my speech,' she intoned dully, 'I will kill the murderous Wolfsons.'

Then Lottie watched her princess disappear through the doors, her skirts frothing around her, an obsidian blade tracing a path at her side. Lottie squeezed her eyes shut as she heard the thunderous applause that greeted her friend.

Lottie had failed, and now Ellie was set on a course of death.

32

Being back at the palace was disconcerting. It had always been a strange sort of prison for Jamie, even if he hadn't been aware when he was a Partizan. But with what he knew now – everything he'd learned about his mother and his title – he'd thought that to return here would be a nightmare. After all, what animal willingly walks back into their cage?

So it was puzzling that as they walked through the palace grounds, his feet crunching on the frosty grass, his mind went completely calm. There was no instinct to run, no sense of claustrophobia. Instead he found himself drawn to the evergreens, his fingers tracing snow-covered privet, the petals of the *Camellia oleifera*, which survived stubbornly in spite of the climate. It was a garden his mother had laid the foundation for, and every frost-tipped kiss on his skin felt like a welcome home.

But inside the palace his calm had been completely shattered outside the door to Ellie's dressing room.

'We're not letting you through,' Emelia said, as she blocked him from following Lottie.

His mind was moving a mile a minute, and still it couldn't make sense of what had just happened.

They'd expected Lottie to show up. In fact, they'd been counting on it, but to come with Haru's master and the girl Leviathan had kidnapped two years ago! He reminded himself that Lottie never did what he expected.

Jamie let out an exasperated sound, effortlessly deflecting Emelia's sword with his own and sending her stumbling into the wall, the painting above her head clattering. 'Will you just listen to us?'

'Sayu, please, I know this is a lot to take in,' Haru said from further down the hall, visibly bemused. '*Watashi o shinjite.*'

'You expect me to trust you?' Sayuri roared, her kimono fanning out like insect wings as she narrowed in on her target.

They switched to speaking Japanese, Haru's soft tone echoing down the hall as Sayuri deflected every warning swipe of his sword. Her sword rang with a fury grown from the bitterness of betrayal. The two of them were stuck in a stalemate – neither wanted to hurt the other, neither ready to back down.

With a violent strike, Sayuri went to disarm her Partizan, but he neatly stepped to the side, tripping her over in one swift move.

In the meantime Emelia had recovered and was back at her spot, protecting the door.

They clearly needed a different approach. If Jamie could just find some common ground – something that linked them. And then it hit him. The one unstoppable person they had in common, a light so rare no one could resist wanting to protect it.

'Lottie's in trouble.'

Immediately Emelia faltered and Sayuri looked up from the floor.

'Most of Leviathan are already in there,' Jamie said, being careful not to make any sudden moves. 'She won't be able to stop them on her own.'

Emelia raised an eyebrow, but she didn't raise her weapon again.

Haru sighed, holding his hand out to his old master. 'We're here to sabotage Claude's plan.'

With one easy move, Haru lifted Sayuri up from the marble floor, her sword discarded.

Both girls scrutinized Jamie. Whatever he said would determine what happened next. Would he inspire their trust or their wrath?

'I want to save Ellie,' he said simply, letting his weapon drop. 'Not as her Partizan, but as her friend.' Swallowing, he looked each girl directly in the eye. 'I have to do this – to prove to Lottie I'm what she believes I am.' He waited for them to make their decision.

'She really got through to you too, huh?' Emelia snorted, shaking her head in disbelief. Jamie's shoulders dropped in relief. 'Does Claude know anything about this?'

Haru stepped forward, picking up Sayuri's sword. 'Nothing,' he said. 'To him we're still his loyal pawns.'

'And what got through to you, Haru?' Sayuri asked as he handed her the weapon, her voice low.

Haru glanced away from Sayuri and his eyes came to settle on Jamie. Haru's aching devotion of unspoken love was louder than words, more nourishing than any food. And it was Jamie's, only his.

A smile settled on Sayuri's face. 'I see.'

Emelia interrupted, picking up Jamie's knife to pass it to him, and with no warning she ran to the door. 'Grab your weapons. We have a princess to save.'

With a powerful kick, she sent one of the double doors flying open without a single part of her outfit falling out of place.

The door slammed shut behind them, but what lay on the other side was everything Jamie had feared.

Ingrid turned violently from where she was holding Lottie back, her grip loosening enough in her shock that Lottie had a chance to wriggle free. In her flowing white dress Lottie looked like a painted angel, something holy sent to save them.

Lottie's eyes, red and swollen, locked on his. He found himself reflected in their deep blue and saw himself at last – the best version of himself, the version Lottie had always known he was. Lottie nodded once and ran for the door to the ballroom.

Ingrid didn't even try to grab her. Her feline eyes flickered from Haru to Jamie, and Sayuri to Emelia, and back again, the situation dawning on her. She had been betrayed. She stamped her foot. 'You're meant to be *ours*.'

Before Jamie could move, Sam and Stella rushed forward, grabbing Lottie before she could reach the door.

'Get off me,' Lottie growled at them, more ferocious than Jamie had ever seen her. 'You have to let me go.'

'There's four of us and four of them,' Emelia said calmly, eyeing Ingrid who was approaching with a furious look.

'Haru and I will take Ingrid and Julius; you two take the twins,' said Jamie in a low voice. He had just enough time to spin out his blade before Ingrid smashed it down, completely bypassing him to go for Haru. In perfect synch Jamie and Haru deflected her knife and twisted it from her grip, sending it flying across the room where it embedded itself in the wall.

Ingrid was unarmed and clumsy with fury. Haru easily grabbed her, pulling her wrists behind her back while she scratched and hissed in protest.

'You did this! You took our prince for yourself!' she screeched. 'You've ruined everything.' Practically spitting venom, she thrashed in Haru's grip, but she was completely trapped.

Now Jamie could turn his attention to Julius. Only Julius stood stock-still, no weapon to be seen, his arms already above his head. 'I'm sorry, Ingrid,' he said. 'I won't fight.'

The words hit Ingrid like acid and a scream emerged from her that was so blood-curdling and desperate that everyone in the room turned to her.

In that split second of distraction Emelia and Sayuri gained the upper hand on the twins, as their swords came up to their throats.

'Lottie, go!' Jamie called, as he turned back to Ingrid.

Lottie ran for the door but it opened as she reached it and a long wide shadow snuffed out the last of the light. Phi.

With terrifying strength, she grabbed Lottie's arm and pulled it back hard.

'No!' Lottie screamed, half in desperation and half in pain.

Phi towered over Lottie, not even breaking a sweat, and carefully took in the scene.

Kicking uselessly at Phi's legs, Lottie was so small in comparison she looked almost like a child, and every protective instinct told Jamie to dive on Phi and save her. But he knew better than that. He knew that was not the way to defuse this situation.

'What exactly is going on here?' Phi asked, her voice as deep as a grave. The question was aimed at Jamie. Phi barely paid attention to the squirming girl in her vice-like grip.

Ingrid's hair spilled out of its bun, the inky strands tearing up her face like black gashes from ferocious claws, her eyes smudged into shadows by the make-up that ran down her cheeks.

Jamie knew this pain, and when he turned to look at the rest of Leviathan it was in them too, each of them still desperately clinging to the home they'd made for themselves from the dirt they'd been dealt.

'Haru.' Jamie spoke softly. 'Let Ingrid go.'

Haru did as Jamie asked, trusting him completely.

It was Ingrid who looked confused. She stumbled forward, rubbing her wrists.

The room held its breath.

'Why?' she whimpered, and her eyes clouded with a hopelessness that Jamie knew all too well.

He strolled over, placing a hand on her head, letting his touch calm her. 'Because . . . no one has to lose.'

The hopelessness vanished, a spark taking its place that lit Ingrid up, as bright and surprising as a firework in an empty night sky.

'Do you all trust me?' Jamie asked, turning to the rest of the room.

A choking sob struck them from the side of the room, where Stella rubbed her eyes desperately while her brother tried to comfort her. 'Ellie's a good person!' she howled, her face a mess of snot and tears. 'She's my friend and she doesn't deserve this.'

Jamie held back his surprise as he stared down the rest of them.

The next to speak up was Julius. He leaned back in his chair. 'I sure trust you more than Claude. You're kind, Jamie, and honourable. You've shown us what that really feels like – what Claude has never been.'

Phi still clung to Lottie until, as easily as setting a dove free into the sky, she let go and fell to her knees. 'My prince,' she said, bowing low. Jamie embraced the title. He felt it burn deep inside him, righteous and true. He was truly home. But there was no time to bask in the feeling, as a collective scream flooded through the door to the ballroom.

Jamie turned to Lottie, but she was already running.

'Go!' he called to her. 'Save your princess.'

33

The ball was spectacular. Claude had to commend his brother for hosting such a wonderful party. With bouquets of flowers sculpted from ice at every table and snarling wolf heads cast in gold standing guard at the stairwell, the festival was everything Claude thought of when Maradova came to mind: fierce, cold, wild. It was the perfect stage for Claude to reclaim his rightful place on the throne.

Making his way through the crowd of beautiful and well-dressed guests, the kinds of people Claude should have spent his life surrounded by, he procured himself an ideal location as the speeches went on. He was near the back, by the bar, with an exquisite view of where Princess Eleanor would plunge the knife into the necks of his hideous usurping family.

'Champagne, sir?'

Claude smiled at the waiter and took a glass.

Homing in on the princess as she made her way to be presented, he saw her hollow eyes; his poison had stripped away her entire being. It was a blessing really. She would be free from the burdens she hated so much. If anything, she should be thanking him.

As he took his first sip, his brother's welcome speech came to an end, and he watched, delighted, as Ellie dipped her head low, the shadows distorting their precious princess into the monster she really was.

In one swift movement Ellie reached into the folds of her dress and pulled her hand out hard and fast, the knife's black obsidian glinting with deadly promise. The crowd broke out in panicked screams as she turned on her family and drove the blade towards her father's chest.

The screams exploded through Lottie's mind. The world zipped past in a blur – the door, the stairs, the ballroom. Lottie's attention honed in on Ellie, charging forward as she brought the black knife towards her father.

Lottie didn't think. There was no time. Running to intercept, she pulled the cords at the side of her dress, the fabric unfurling as she ran, white wings spilling from round the blade at her back. She felt sharpened with the change, like an arrow aimed at the heart of the ballroom.

The room was blurred at the edges – with only her princess and the deadly glint of Ellie's raised blade in focus.

Faster, faster!

Rumbling deep as thunder inside her, the call to her princess surged, and she leaped over the last steps, reaching behind her to grasp her sword, and with a sing of metal she set it free. Whipping herself round, Lottie threw herself in front of the king.

There was a clang, a screaming hiss of metal on metal, and when Lottie looked down, Ellie's knife was centimetres from her heart, King Alexander safely behind her.

Lottie let her gaze travel up slowly; her breathing was ragged but her stance was unwavering, and she stared into the dead eyes of her princess. The obsidian blade in Ellie's hand shook as she tried to push it home.

With a cry, Lottie thrust her own blade forward, sending Ellie's knife flying.

Vaguely aware of the king and queen calling her, and the crowd breaking into howls of confusion, all Lottie saw was the knife – it was a black mark gliding through the air that landed at Ellie's feet.

'Ellie, please listen to me,' Lottie begged, but Ellie immediately grabbed the knife again, ready to strike at whatever was in her way. And what was in her way right then was Lottie.

'You have to hear me,' Lottie pleaded, slashing the knife away again. The puppet Ellie was getting closer, her dead hollow eyes boring into her like two black holes. 'You have to fight this.'

But her princess was nowhere to be found. Everything that made her so wonderful had been entirely destroyed. Staring into her blank face, Lottie understood the true tragedy buried beneath it. Ellie had always felt she was not enough. That the real her was wrong and not worthy of love. How could she not understand that she was already perfect the way she was? This twisted dead-eyed version of Ellie was guided by that evil voice – the one that told you to be complacent, to behave, to be pretty and nice because that made you more palatable. Lottie's last remaining hope began to cloud over. How could she bring Ellie out of this poison when she'd been told her whole life that she had to hide who she truly was? She needed to wake the princess up.

Lottie gasped, the solution suddenly obvious. She choked out a laugh, and with tears on her cheeks she threw her sword down.

There was no way Ellie was completely gone. Lottie didn't doubt that for a second.

Dodging the black blade once more, Lottie ducked under it, throwing her arms round Ellie, like wings wrapped protectively round her, cradling her, even as she knew Ellie's hand was reaching up to stab down into her back.

'I love you, Ellie.'

Then she kissed her.

Something sweet landed on Ellie's mouth. Soft, like rose butter. She leaned into it, trying to make sense of the wonderful whispering touch. The world tilted and she felt out at sea, half drowned by violent waves where the sun couldn't reach.

Except now it did – a warmth like morning light landed on her face. She clung to it, desperately wrapping her arms round the sensation.

'I love you, Ellie.'

The words pierced something inside her, something painful. How could anyone possibly love her?

The voice came again, like a hand reaching deep into the waters of her mind. It hurt so much. 'Come back to me, Ellie. My perfect beautiful prince.' It was so sweet, so bright and clear, and said things Ellie had always wanted to hear.

In the murk of her mind, the words cracked like lightning, the darkness shattering with a sharp furious roar of thunder.

Ellie opened her eyes and saw an angel.

'You saved me.' There was nothing else to say. Tears spilled down her face, and Lottie smiled that perfect apple-cheeked smile. It promised safety. It felt like home.

'You're worth saving,' Lottie murmured against her cheek.

For the first time in her life Ellie believed the words. 'I love you,' she whispered back, and lightning flashed again deep within her, the storm alive and wild. What a precious wonderful thing – to love and be loved for who she was.

The joy blooming inside her was scented with roses and lavender, and Ellie laughed, finally seeing herself as Lottie did, as someone good and worth holding on to.

Ellie dipped Lottie low and kissed her. 'I love you, I love you, I love you!' she whispered between every delicious press of their lips. Sunshine and storm clouds spilled from their mouths until they were one, the strings of their souls tied together forever.

Growing murmurs from the ballroom slowly began to build, shock turning to confusion. Reluctantly coming back from their little heaven, Lottie brushed Ellie's cheek, blinking back the last of her tears. 'I'm sorry, Ellie,' Lottie mumbled, pulling away. 'There's one more thing I need to do.'

When Lottie turned to the crowd now, the angel of love and light transformed once again into something terrifying, righteous and monstrous.

Following her gaze, Ellie found their mutual target.

He looked so small from where they were standing. Claude Wolfson's face was contorted in disbelief, and then he fled.

Lottie snarled, throwing off her heels and picking up her sword. With one last look towards Ellie, the dark angel took off through the ballroom, determined to beat evil once and for all.

34

How could this have happened?

The palace was slipping through Claude's fingers, his plans crumbling to dust, and all because of some little brat. Running into the gardens, Claude retched, lamenting furiously that he hadn't killed that hideous girl when he had had the chance.

He stumbled, his feet catching on a vine, and when he tried to right himself he slipped on the ice and cut his hands where he landed, crimson dotting the white. The snow quickly swallowed up his blood, the palace feasting on his flesh.

That face! Claude thought, running as he clutched his injured hand. That face had reeked of retribution and was coming for him. He'd only known one other person to ever look at him like that – *Hirana* – and even the threat of murder hadn't stopped her planting the seeds to take him down.

Another vine whipped out seemingly from nowhere, wrapping round his ankle as he tried to pull free. He felt himself a mad man, imagining the palace grounds were attacking him.

'Get off me!' he screamed, desperately clawing at it. 'I'll give him back! I'll give your son back. Please – just let me

267

go.' He managed to pull himself free and bolted to the place they'd agreed to meet if anything should go wrong.

He heard ice cracking behind him and Lottie came barrelling up to him – sword raised, ready to strike.

Before her sword could reach him, a hand pulled him out of the way, but not before he got a look at her eyes again, where a blue flame promised to burn him to ash.

When Claude righted himself, he looked around and cackled. Leviathan were waiting for him – Sam, Stella, Haru, Phi, Julius and Ingrid, loyal Ingrid. He turned on Lottie, still laughing. 'You plan to take us all on, do you?'

Without even a second of hesitation, Lottie held up her blade again. Barefoot in the snow, she looked terrifying. Her gold hair whipped around her and her white dress rippled like a blizzard.

Something flashed through Claude's mind: a childhood fear that made his knees weak. It was the old story they used to tell in the palace of the lost princess Liliana, who hunted down wayward royals and swallowed their souls.

Her sword stayed trained on him, the edge glinting silver in the moonlight. 'I won't rest,' she announced, 'until we destroy you and everything you stand for.'

Claude took a cautious step backwards. 'We?' He laughed. 'I don't see anyone else on your side here. Do you?'

She let the sword drop, and Claude waited for her to retreat.

'You seem to have forgotten, Goat Man, that I'm not the only one you've annoyed.' Her eyes narrowed in a way that made him shudder.

Claude felt his eyebrows furrow. He turned just in time to see Ingrid lift her blade, and strike it down, hard and true, directly into his leg. He screamed and keeled over until he was on his knees. 'You ungrateful –'

No other words made it out of him, as Ingrid, his loyal little Ingrid, climbed over him to grab his hair and set her blade to his neck.

'I guess you were right,' she snarled, the rest of Leviathan coming to join her. 'I do ruin everything for you.'

From behind the wall the princess and his son walked side by side, two black-clad wolves who took their places either side of the terrifying Portman. They looked like a three-headed beast, a furious Cerberus who would rip him apart.

'You lose, Claude,' Jamie growled.

Claude felt a shift, as the ground beneath him moved. For the first time in hundreds of years the palace was alive.

Lottie had managed to persuade the guards to free the rest of Banshee from where they had been locked up. Those who were left of Leviathan consented to be detained – Sam, Stella, Ingrid, Julius and Phi agreeing to give as much information as needed on Claude. They'd truly turned their backs on him. Meanwhile all the guests were sent home, and an emergency medical bay was set up inside the throne room. Luckily, apart from Claude's leg, there were no serious injuries, and only a few minor cuts and scrapes to be tended to. Simien and Ellie's personal guard Samuel carried the worst wounds. They'd both been knocked out and shoved into a cupboard after the start of the ball. But even they were mostly unharmed, except for their pride.

King Alexander and the queen pounced on Lottie as soon as she had given her statement to the authorities, the two of them having stood patiently outside the door where she was being questioned.

The king stared down at her for a long moment, the lines on his face deeper than she remembered. Finally he bowed low and with a deep respect that made Lottie falter. 'How can we ever repay you?' he asked.

'That's really not necessary,' she said, leaning forward to assist him back up. 'I didn't do this out of any royal obligation. I did it to save the people I love.'

Arms crossed, Queen Matilde smiled, and the twitch of her lips reminded Lottie of Ellie.

'You should listen to her, darling.' She came up to Lottie's side, stroking her hair fondly. 'Besides, all these traditions and procedures – it's a bit silly, isn't it?'

The king and queen shared a look, and Lottie felt a shift. Something changing.

King Alexander nodded. 'We have a lot to think about.'

Leaving them, Lottie took off down the hall.

'Hey, little princess . . .'

Lottie turned at the sound of Ellie's voice. 'Will you come outside with us?'

Ellie and Jamie stood together, now changed out of their doom-stricken attire and wearing a set of matching fluffy white robes, looking new and clean like the sun on fresh snow.

'If it was up to me –' Lottie grinned, reaching out to the two of them – 'I'd never leave your side again.'

The palace was a crime scene. Rooms had been cordoned off to take statements and hazard tape blocked off sections of the grounds where evidence was being extracted. It made the estate seem even less real, like Lottie was a character in a detective novel.

Turning a corridor, they passed the room where Claude was being detained for questioning, and Lottie raised an eyebrow at the line of her friends leaning against the wall outside – Saskia, Anastacia and Emelia all entirely calm and nibbling on treats stolen from the ballroom.

Catching her eye, Anastacia waved. 'We're waiting until they walk him to the police car,' she explained.

Emelia looked Lottie dead in the eye. 'If I can't hit him with my fists, the least I should be allowed to do is nail him with one of these.' She held up a plate of fruit.

A smile pulling at his lips, Jamie shrugged. 'Who am I to judge your recovery process?' Then he added in an afterthought, 'Where's Sayuri?'

'She was giving her statement with the others and then she went off with Haru,' Emelia said. 'I think they have a lot to talk about.'

Jamie turned to Lottie and Ellie, and they each met his gaze in understanding. 'I think we all do.'

The snow had stopped falling. Now the sky was stained mauve, clinging to the last of the night before the sun broke through. Lottie leaned against the veranda railing, her hands leaving imprints in the frost. 'So,' she said, turning to her prince and princess, both of them lit by lanterns, 'have you two made up?'

They took a few moments to look at one another.

Ellie sighed, playfully punching Jamie on the arm, but Lottie could see the fatigue there, her body still recovering from the Hamelin Formula. 'We're getting there,' Ellie continued. 'I think we're better as cousins than we ever were as friends.'

Jamie nodded in agreement, and Lottie caught a glint in his eye – the stars were coming back to life. 'And you two,' he said, a smile playing across his lips, 'you're better like this than you were before.'

'Like what?' Ellie asked, crossing her arms.

'He means we're better in love,' Lottie answered.

'Oh . . . Oh, yes we are.' Embarrassed, Ellie shuffled forward and hid her head in the crook of Lottie's neck, nuzzling her like they were two wolves in a pack.

Lottie looked at Jamie over the black crown of Ellie's hair under her palm, imagining him there on the top of her hand, like a bird that had rested upon her for a moment, not hers to keep, only a support for a longer journey. 'And what about you, Jamie?'

'I've finally found what I was looking for,' he said.

He spoke with assurance, the prince shining through, a title he'd earned. Then he softened, his expression as sweet as a cherub. 'Are you proud of me?'

Lottie smiled. In her mind's eye, she released her hand and let him go. 'I'm so proud of you.'

Raising her head, Ellie looked between the two. She smiled. 'So we're good?'

'Yep,' Lottie replied and then raised an eyebrow. 'And with that out of the way I have to ask what was up with you trying to be me?'

A furious blush crept over Ellie's cheeks. 'I was not.'

Jamie chuckled. 'You really missed her that much, huh?'

272

'Shut up, you two,' Ellie said, but it only made them laugh.

'No, Ellie, I'm serious. It was very flattering; I could practically hear you reciting my mantra from across the ocean.'

Ellie immediately buried her face in her hands. 'Oh my God.'

'But –' Lottie pulled Ellie's hands away so she could look her in the eye – 'I was thinking you need a mantra of your own. One that works for you.'

Ellie stood up straight. 'I know what I want to be,' she said, excitement peppering her words. 'I'm going to be angry,' she declared. Lottie felt a deep resonance. 'I'm going to be rotten and wild and everything they told me not to be.'

'I like that,' Lottie replied, smiling. 'Maybe I'll use that too sometimes.'

Holding out her pinkie, Lottie waited for Ellie to wrap her own round it, both of them grinning as they shook them up and down with childish delight.

'Kind, brave and unstoppable!' Lottie chanted.

'Angry, rotten and wild!' Ellie roared back. She dipped her head into a kiss. 'Had to seal it,' she said with a wink.

'Hate to disturb this precious moment but look . . .' Jamie stepped against the veranda rail and pointed. 'The sun's coming up.'

It wasn't the bright orange sphere on the horizon nor the threads of pink woven into the sky that caught Lottie's attention. Instead she found herself marvelling at the garden. The snow had melted. 'What's that?' she asked, eyes narrowing.

Something hidden glistened like amber goldfish scales and rippled in the breeze, as if it were alive.

Descending the steps, Lottie moved closer. This strange gilded mass was eating up the threads of sunlight, its soft limbs outstretching into pointed glittering petals. She leaned down and cupped it gently in the palm of her hand, careful not to uproot this truly fragile thing.

'What is it?' the prince and princess of Maradova called down.

Lottie knew exactly what it was. It was the flower from the Wolfsons' fairy tale, a flower that hadn't bloomed in hundreds of years, which brought with it hope, truth and love.

She turned to them, holding out her hands, the dawn breaking behind her.

'It's Inessa's Gold.'

35

'Hello! This is MMBC news where the royal family of Maradova will be making an important announcement in just a moment. After the nearly catastrophic events at this year's Golden Flower Festival, we were given word that a new claim to the throne could possibly be on the horizon. The reports allege that the exiled Claude Wolfson had a son who was previously being raised as the princess's Partizan. According to the Maravish line-of-succession laws, the young prince would have a valid claim to the throne. The speech today is intended to give clarity on the situation and lay out the royal family's plan moving forward. We now go live to our correspondent Agatha Kemp at Wolfson Palace.'

'Thank you, Barbara. As you can see behind me, a huge crowd has come to witness the speech at the gates of the palace. The atmosphere here is confused but hopeful, and in an unlikely turn of events for our frigid country the sun is blazing out over the grounds and doesn't show any signs of going away. The princess and the prospective prince are stepping up to the podium now. We'll be back for interviews with the crowd after the speeches.'

'Good afternoon, citizens of Maradova and to the people of the world watching today. I have been your princess now for more *than a year and frankly I have not been a very good one. This is partly due to the defamation and brainwashing campaign orchestrated by my exiled uncle in an attempt to reclaim his place as king of this country, but also, and more simply, because I was never meant to rule Maradova.*

'Despite my uncle's unacceptable and treacherous behaviour, he has succeeded in bringing to light the unpardonable error made by my family in denying the rightful heir his place. This palace has been rotting from the inside out, and it is not only in the walls but in our lineage. We are an old and decaying idea that our country no longer needs. Something has to change, and it is with great hope for our future that I and your rightful prince intend to dismantle this archaic monarchy together and institute a fresh and fair democracy. I now hand the podium over to your prince, Jamie Wolfson.'

'Good afternoon, and thank you for your patience. I understand many of you will be shocked by our choice to bring an end to the Wolfson royal line, and we appreciate there is an attachment to traditions and the comfort they provide that can be hard to break away from. I urge you all to trust our decision in the same way that we are putting our trust in you to be able to choose your own leaders and representatives in the future. This country is yours, and you should get to choose what kind of place it is: a stubborn fortress of outdated ideals with a rotting monarchy or a bastion of change and innovation, pushing forward bravely with new politics to inspire the rest of the world.

'The move to democracy will be a long and thorough one, and we intend to approach these changes gradually over the next decade while we dissolve our powers and responsibilities; until

this time we will remain your prince and princess, but we intend to be the last this country ever sees.

'As for the palace, we will be selling parts of it to establish a new government fund to aid our future democracy, and we also feel it's important to let people know that we will use some of the funds for personal projects and charities that are important to us and close to our hearts.

'We understand this will be an unusual and unprecedented time and assure you all that the country will be stronger in the hands of the people. Thank you for your continued understanding. This concludes our speeches for today.'

36

Home was something Lottie had always dreamed of, a safe place to return to with people she loved and who loved her. Home was what she'd fought for her whole life, and it was now, staring at the gates of Rosewood, that she knew she'd found it.

They arrived in the late afternoon, the summer sun high and bright above them. With every step up the crunchy stone path, the wind blew at their ankles, the breeze carrying petals and the sweet scent of roses.

Once, the looming building with its thorn-sharp tower tops and streaks of golden ivy had felt overwhelming. But now Lottie felt every swaying rose, every buzzing bee and trickle of water fall in time with the rhythm of her own body. She smiled up at the stone walls like she was greeting an old friend.

This would be Lottie's last time entering Rosewood Hall. Ellie and Jamie were at her side just as they were supposed to be, just as it had been before. But now it was even better. The school had brought them together and that was a magic so powerful it would follow them forever.

'You ready to say goodbye?' Lottie asked, lips quivering as she turned to her prince and princess. After four years of misadventures Lottie was still a crybaby.

'Honestly?' Jamie spoke up first. His eyes revealed his emotions. 'No.'

Sniffing, Lottie let herself shed a tear, and was relieved when Ellie reached out, her hand wrapping round Lottie's as they stepped into the reception.

'Come on, little princess,' Ellie cooed, barely hiding her own overwhelming feelings. 'We'll be fine if we're together.'

Lottie had expected this to be an emotional day. It was a chance for the three of them to make peace with all that had happened by reuniting in the place that had brought them together. What she hadn't expected was the gaggle of people waiting for them in the courtyard.

In the summer light, dressed in uniforms, it was like staring at a picture of the past – except it was real. The whole Rosewood gang was there.

'What are you –'

But Lottie had no time to finish her sentence. Binah and the twins came rushing forward and pulled her into a tight hug. 'You're here, thank goodness,' Binah said as the twins squeezed their arms round her. In a hushed tone she added, 'Headmaster Croak was starting to look as if he might fall asleep standing up.'

Lottie looked to where Headmaster Croak stood waiting, dressed – of all things – in a Hawaiian shirt.

'This is such an exciting day!' Lola and Micky chirped in unison.

Anastacia, Saskia and Raphael approached next, sauntering over with all the casual confidence one would expect of Conch House graduates.

'We figured you'd want us here to celebrate,' Anastacia announced, flicking her hair behind her.

'You know how much we love a party,' Raphael hooted, only leaving Lottie more confused.

'Celebrate what exactly?' Lottie was starting to wonder if this was all some strange dream and she was actually still asleep in the car. Perhaps she'd never come to Rosewood at all and it was still four years ago on the train from Cornwall.

Percy stepped forward and he had something big in his arms.

'Vampy!' Jamie's voice cracked as he rushed forward, his affection for the grumpy black cat obvious. 'I missed you, you terrible little thing. Thank you again for taking care of him, Percy.'

The fluffy cat chirped happily as Jamie held him, nuzzling into his favourite human with so much force he looked as if he might knock them over.

'You're going to love the palace,' Jamie muttered to the cat. 'It's almost as grandiose as you.'

'Ahem!'

The sound of a throat clearing snagged their attention.

Lottie turned to the headmaster. She couldn't remember the last time she'd seen him in anything but fanciful capes and patchwork suits. In his colourful Hawaiian shirt and sneakers, he looked oddly like a dressed-up coconut – hairy and leathery yet somehow full of life.

'Good afternoon, Miss Pumpkin,' he rasped, his voice like a toad's.

'May I ask what's going on?' Lottie tried again, looking round at the grinning faces of her friends.

Finally Ellie came into view. She placed an arm round her, her roguish smile so dazzling it made Lottie's cheeks feel hot. 'We sort of have a surprise for you,' she explained.

'What have you done?' Lottie asked, narrowing her eyes, but Ellie only continued to grin back, not giving anything away.

As polite as ever, Jamie held the door open for Lottie and they followed Headmaster Croak into the main building.

Lottie peeped over her shoulder at their friends, who all offered gestures of encouragement as the door swung shut again.

The main building was one of the oldest structures at Rosewood, all rickety oak and squeaking floorboards. Every inch of it was indented with the familiar scent of roses.

After climbing the stairs to the headmaster's dusty round office, Lottie's eyes travelled up the peeling wallpaper to the painting behind the headmaster's desk. Years ago, Lottie had sneaked into this very room to discover this portrait for the first time. William Tufty, Rosewood's founder, peered out from behind half-moon glasses, which Lottie now knew to be part of his disguise. Or perhaps, she realized, this duality was part of them both. Both sweet William Tufty and his true identity as the wild and fierce lost princess Liliana Mayfutt contained multitudes, just like Lottie – all of them equally genuine.

'Now, Miss Pumpkin, if you would have a seat, we have some important matters to discuss with you.' The headmaster let out a pained sigh as he sat down, his joints popping like a burning log.

It was only then that Lottie noticed the man in a smart tweed suit standing on the other side of the desk with a pile of documents in front of him. When her eyes landed on his engraved pen she clocked who it was. *D. A.* Dominic Anderson, the solicitor who'd helped acquire her Portman money nearly a year ago. What on earth was he doing at Rosewood?

'Miss Pumpkin, it's wonderful to see you again,' Mr Anderson said cheerfully, genuine excitement flashing in his smile. 'I must say I've never had so much intriguing legal work from a single client before.'

Headmaster Croak reached under his desk and began pulling out an array of items – items Lottie knew very well. With methodical calm, the table began to fill: Liliana's diary, her sword, letters and paintings from her hidden office, each a puzzle piece slotting into place.

Hardly able to process that her secret was out, Lottie realized the headmaster had looked back up at her, his eyes glinting with that special spark that could only be found at Rosewood. 'The only piece missing, I believe, is your family tiara.'

Lottie turned to Ellie who gave her an encouraging nod, and with twitching fingers she reached into her bag for the velvet box in which she kept her tiara.

The atmosphere was electric as Lottie laid the box in the centre of the desk. With a gentle pop, she unfastened the lid to reveal her most sacred possession. It may have been her imagination, but in that split second, with all the pieces laid out together, Lottie was sure they glowed warm and bright.

'Wonderful, that should do it,' Mr Anderson said cryptically. The items made a map of Lottie's time at Rosewood. Every discovery, every secret unlocked, each one had brought her closer to her ancestry and to the school itself.

'Your friends here have collected enough evidence to prove the school rightfully belongs in your family,' Headmaster Croak explained. Lottie stared blankly back at him. 'That means, Miss Pumpkin, that you have the legal right to buy Rosewood Hall.'

'I-I'm sorry?' Lottie spluttered, her voice jumping two octaves as she tried to find the right words, or any words at all for that matter. She turned to Ellie and Jamie, her expression unable to settle on furious or thrilled.

They simply shrugged, with twin smirks on their faces that were characteristic of the Wolfson family.

'This is – I mean, I can't possibly –' Again the words dried up in Lottie's throat as she stepped towards the desk, but this time it wasn't because she was speechless. It was because she knew that she mustn't let this opportunity slip away.

Rosewood was in her blood and was meant to come back to the Mayfutts, back to their descendant, Lottie. She knew it like she'd know the scent of the school grounds blindfolded. All this time this had really been her dream, and she could finally allow herself to believe it could become a reality.

'If Rosewood is mine, what would change?' Lottie asked cautiously.

The headmaster looked thoughtful. 'Nothing if you so choose,' he said. 'Classes will continue as usual, run by the same teachers. It would simply be in your name.'

'I can't afford it,' she suddenly blurted out.

'Yes you can.' It was Ellie who spoke up. Both she and Jamie were standing by Lottie's side.

'Didn't you wonder what some of those *personal projects* were that we'd said we'd be using the palace money for?' Jamie asked devilishly.

'There's no way I could accept,' Lottie tried to reason. 'You can't –'

'Actually we can.' Ellie spoke with pure conviction, that storm igniting in her eyes. 'You saved us, Lottie. Every life you touch is better for it, and we can't put a price on that.'

'And I'm afraid we already filled out the paperwork,' Jamie added far too casually. 'So it would actually be more troublesome for us if you said no.'

The two of them grinned at her expectantly like wolves. As Lottie looked into their eyes, she saw that they would not be happy until she had everything she'd ever wished for. Her whole life Lottie had felt unworthy, always scared of troubling others and being a burden, but now when she searched herself for that feeling, she couldn't find it. With Ellie and Jamie, all she felt was love. She lit up, and the same glow she'd always felt when she wore her tiara spread through her. 'Where do I sign?'

Standing on the cusp of Rosewood Hall grounds, ten students stood in a line. Behind them, falling low on the horizon, the dwindling sun sent pinpricks of orange light across the sky, like a halo emerging from the school.

Swinging on their hinges, the gates sang their farewell.

There was no need to look back because this was not goodbye.

The students embraced one other. The school that had intertwined their lives was now with them forever.

'What shall we do now?' one of them asked.

The pumpkin princess smiled. She'd saved a prince and won the heart of a princess. Leaning up, she planted a kiss on her princess's lips. 'I think for now I'm going to have my happily ever after.'

Epilogue

Welcome to *Rosewood Hall Old Scholars 2046*. This has been an outstanding year for Rosewood alumni and a real testament to what our wonderful school can help people achieve. The following is a selection of news and successes from the past year from some of our notable alumni.

Stratus alumnus and previous head of year Binah Fae has appeared in our *Old Scholars* many times for her philanthropy and expeditions. This year Fae and her research partner Oliver Moreno have been awarded a Nobel Prize for successfully converting the controversial Hamelin Formula into a one hundred per cent safe and side-effect-free anaesthetic. The discovery is set to revolutionize the medical world.

Raphael Wilcox of Conch House, who is usually known for his acting roles, was nominated for another Academy Award, this time for his script *Endless Winter*, a biopic about writer, humanitarian and fellow Rosewood graduate Jamie Wolfson and the real-life story of the Maravish royal family. If he wins, it will be his third Oscar.

Michael and Dolores Tompkins of Stratus, along with Michael's husband Percival Butter of Ivy House, have been sharing the position of CEO at their confectionery company Butterkins for over a decade but have now announced an unexpected business venture. A Butterkins theme park will open in Florida next year, which early-access attendees have described as 'a whimsical candy land where the impossible is made possible'.

Conch graduates Saskia San Martin and Anastacia Alcroft LeBlanc will be celebrating their twenty-fifth wedding anniversary this year. Anastacia is currently editor-in-chief of *Toffee* magazine and Saskia is retired from boxing after the Olympics. This year both of them will be honoured with OBEs for their respective work in publishing and athletics.

Sayuri Chiba from Rosewood's sister school Takeshin has announced a new business partnership with Emelia Malouf of the Hubbub confectionery family. Malouf will not inherit the family business and the two have come together to build Machiba Engineering. The company's mission is to fast-track the world's automobile system to an entirely sustainable model. Their prototype solar-powered motorbike engine is currently in its last trialling stage and due to go to market next year.

After converting Maradova to a democracy with a presidential system, Ivy alumnus Jamie Wolfson, along with his partner Haru Hinamori, have dedicated the last fourteen years to transforming Wolfson Palace into a refuge and rehabilitation centre catering for misplaced children and ex-Partizans. This year Rosewood Hall will be paying tribute to Wolfson with a statue to be erected in his honour outside the theatre.

Jamie also holds the world record for owning the world's oldest cat, who according to Wolfson himself is 'simply too stubborn to pass away'.

After teaching English at Rosewood for over a decade, Ivy alumnus Professor Charlotte Pumpkin-Wolfson will be taking on the new role of headteacher following the passing of Arnold Croak. She lives on campus with her wife Eleanor Pumpkin-Wolfson, another Ivy graduate and lead guitarist of the Grammy-winning rock band Bad Wolf. They have two daughters, Marguerite and Liliana, who will soon be starting at Rosewood.

Acknowledgements

For the past five years, the Rosewood Chronicles have consumed most of my life, and, despite the turbulence of this half decade, Lottie, Ellie, Jamie and all the Rosewood gang have been a consistent home to return to for both myself and the readers. I'm extremely grateful to everyone who's been a part of this journey and want to take some time to thank you all.

To my absolutely amazing manager, Mark, who has been with me through every fashion phase and identity crisis, your ability to keep me in check is remarkable (really, I know how difficult I can be), and your enthusiasm and encouragement of every new step I take has been the backbone that kept me standing.

Richard, my agent, thank you for spurring the Rosewood fire and backing me all the way, and my accountant, Nick, who understands how VAT works so I don't have to.

My many wonderful editors, including Millie, my editor for the last two Rosewood books, it's been a joy to work with you. Even if our time was brief, your contribution to the series has been invaluable. You made these last books in the series such a delightful experience.

Wendy, my managing editor, who's been with me from day one, these books would not be the same without you. Reading through your edits and notes has always been one of my favourite parts of the writing process and I'm so thankful for every bit of magic you've sprinkled on the series.

To my band for letting me hack away at my edits during studio hours and providing me with a much-needed and purely Dionysian creative outlet between manuscripts.

To the snacks, Beckii, Becky, Hannah, Liam, Sparkles, Adele, Tom, Kelsey, Emily, Abi, Dodo: thank you for letting me borrow our one shared brain cell to write these books.

Charlie and Ellen, our friendship taught me what it means to find people who bring out the best in you, and without you Rosewood couldn't exist.

My amazing family, especially my mum and dad who were always happy to stack piles of food and tea around me while I whittled away at my manuscripts.

To Qinni, your enchanting artwork was vital in establishing the Rosewood series. You did so much for these books in both setting the tone and enticing an entire audience of readers. We miss you every day.

Carol, who did the cover art for the last two Rosewood books, you took up a great mantle and you did a remarkable job of keeping the torch burning and the magic alive.

My first publicist Simon, who made me laugh so much on the long train journeys between cities and would truly go the distance (even attempting to get me a real-life wolf for a book event before he realized I was been joking).

Katie Webber, whose support and enthusiasm when I first started out on my publishing journey made me feel welcomed and at home in a profession that can often feel alienating and lonely. I'm so lucky to have met you on that first book tour all those years ago.

To my entire Penguin team, both past and present, Holly and Ruth who took the series on at the start and taught me so much, Phoebe, Rowan, Sharon, Evelyn, Sonia, Sophia – thank you all for your hard work on the series.

And finally to the readers, reviewers and fans from all over the world, thank you so much for letting Rosewood become part of your life.

About the Author

Connie Glynn has always loved writing and wrote her first story when she was six, with her mum at a typewriter acting as her scribe. She had a love for performing stories from a young age and attended Guildhall drama classes as a teenager. This passion for stories has never left her, and Connie recently finished a degree in film theory.

It was at university that Connie started her hugely successful YouTube channel *Noodlerella* (named after her favourite food and favourite Disney princess). After five years of publicly documenting her life and hobbies to an audience of 900,000 subscribers on YouTube, Connie closed the book on the Noodlerella project in a bid for more privacy and to pursue her original passions in the performing arts. Connie now writes music and fiction full-time.

Follow Connie on YouTube, Twitter, Instagram and Tumblr
@ConnieGlynn
#RosewoodChronicles

The
ROSEWOOD
CHRONICLES

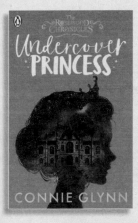

Also available as audiobooks